Paris
IS
ALWAYS A
Good Idea

ALSO BY NICOLAS BARREAU

One Evening in Paris

The Ingredients of Love

Paris
IS
ALWAYS A
Good Idea

....

Nicolas Barreau

St. Martin's Griffin
New York

PARIS IS ALWAYS A GOOD IDEA. Copyright © 2016 by Nicolas Barreau. All rights reserved. Printed in the United States of America. For information, address St. Martin's Press, 175 Fifth Avenue, New York, N.Y. 10010.

The Library of Congress Cataloging-in-Publication Data is available upon request.

ISBN 978-1-250-07277-1 (hardcover)
ISBN 978-1-4668-8463-2 (e-book)

Our books may be purchased in bulk for promotional, educational, or business use. Please contact your local bookseller or the Macmillan Corporate and Premium Sales Department at 1-800-221-7945, extension 5442, or by e-mail at MacmillanSpecialMarkets@macmillan.com.

First Edition: March 2016

10 9 8 7 6 5 4 3 2

*All journeys have secret destinations of which
the traveler is unaware.*

—Martin Buber

Paris
IS
ALWAYS A
Good Idea

One

....

Rosalie loved the color blue. It had been like that for as long as she could think. And by now it had been twenty-eight years.

That morning, as she did every morning when she opened her little postcard shop at eleven o'clock, she raised her eyes, hoping to discover a streak of blue in the gray Parisian sky. She found it, and smiled.

One of Rosalie Laurent's earliest and pleasantest childhood memories was an unbelievably blue August sky over a turquoise sea bathed in light that seemed to extend to the end of the world. That was when she was four years old, and her parents had left the heat of Paris with its stony houses and streets to take their little daughter to the Côte d'Azur. That same year, after they had returned home from that light-drenched summer in Les Issambres that seemed never to want to end, Aunt Paulette had given her a box of watercolors. Rosalie could remember that equally clearly.

"Watercolors? Isn't that a bit excessive, Paulette?" Cathérine had asked, an unmistakably disapproving note in her thin, high voice. "Such an expensive box of paints for such a small child? She'll have no idea what to do with them. We'd better put them aside for a while, don't you think, Rosalie?"

But Rosalie had not been prepared to give up her aunt's precious present. She threw a tantrum and clung to the paint box like grim death. Finally her mother, with a sigh of annoyance, gave in to the defiant little girl with the long brown braids.

That afternoon Rosalie was utterly absorbed for hours filling page after page with brush and watercolors until the watercolor pad was full and the three little pots of blue paint in the box were nearly empty.

Whether it was because that first view of the sea had burnt itself into the little girl's retina like a metaphor for happiness, or because she had developed early on a desire to do things differently from other people, the color blue enchanted Rosalie more than any other. With amazement she discovered the whole gamut of the color, and her childish thirst for knowledge was almost unrestrainable. "And what's this called, Papa?" she would ask again and again, pulling at her good-natured and indulgent father's sleeve (which was, of course, blue), pointing at everything blue that she could find. She would stand in front of the mirror for hours, her brow wrinkled in concentration, studying the color of her own eyes, which at first glance seemed to be brown, though if you looked at them carefully and for long enough you would realize that they were actually deep, dark blue. At least that was what Émile, her father, had told her, and Rosalie had nodded with relief.

Even before she could read and write properly she knew the names of the finest distinctions and shades of blue. From the lightest and most delicate silken blue, sky blue, gray blue, ice blue, powder blue, or glassy aquamarine, which gives wings to the spirit, to that powerful, radiant azure that almost takes your breath away. Then there was also invincible ultramarine, cheery cornflower blue, cool cobalt blue, greenish petrol blue, which conceals the colors of the sea within it, or mysterious indigo, which almost shades over into violet, on to deep sapphire blue, midnight blue, or almost black midnight blue where blue finally reaches the end of its spectrum—for Rosalie there was no other color that was so rich, so wonderful, and so multifaceted as this. And yet she had never expected that she would one day encounter a story in which a blue tiger played an important role. Even less did she expect that this story—and the mystery that lay behind it—would change her life completely.

Chance? Fate? They say that childhood is the ground we march on our whole lives long.

Later, Rosalie often wondered if everything might not have turned out differently if she hadn't loved the color blue so much. At the thought of how easily she might have missed the happiest moment in her life she almost panicked. Life was frequently so impenetrable and complicated, and yet surprisingly everything always made sense in the end.

When, at the age of eighteen, Rosalie—her father had died a few months before of a protracted bout of pneumonia—announced that she intended to study art and be a painter, her mother nearly dropped the Quiche Lorraine she was carrying into the dining room in shock.

"For heaven's sake, child, please—do something sensible!" she shrieked, inwardly cursing her sister Paulette, who had obviously put these foolish ideas in the girl's head. She would never have cursed out loud, of course. Cathérine Laurent, née de Vallois (which gave her a somewhat exaggerated idea of herself), was a lady through and through. Unfortunately the wealth of this once noble family had been seriously reduced over the last couple of centuries, and Cathérine's marriage to Émile Laurent, a clever and lovable, but unfortunately not very assertive, physicist, who ended up stranded at a scientific institute rather than producing the hoped-for success in the world of business, did little to improve matters. In the end they didn't even have money for proper servants anymore, apart from the Filipina cleaning lady who was hardly able to speak French and came twice a week to the old Parisian house with its high, ornate plaster ceilings and herringbone parquet flooring to dust and clean. Nevertheless, for Cathérine it was out of the question to give up on her principles. If you didn't stick to your principles, everything would go to the dogs, she thought.

"A de Vallois doesn't do that sort of thing" was one of her favorite phrases, and of course she also sent her only daughter, who was regrettably developing in a totally different direction from the one her mother had marked out for her, on her way that day with this phrase ringing in her ears.

With a sigh, Cathérine put the white porcelain dish with its steaming quiche down on the grand oval table that was set for just two and thought once again that there was hardly anyone she knew for whom the name Rosalie was less fitting.

Back when she was pregnant, she had in her mind's eye a delicate girl, blond like herself, polite, gentle, and somehow . . . delightful. But Rosalie turned out to be anything but that. Admittedly, she was clever, but she was also very strong willed. She knew her own mind, and sometimes she said nothing for hours on end, which her mother found peculiar. When Rosalie laughed, she laughed too loudly, and that was hardly elegant, even if other people assured her that Rosalie had something so refreshing about her.

"Let her be, her heart is in the right place," was what Émile always said as he gave in to yet another of his daughter's whims. Like the time when, as a child, she had dragged her new mattress and the expensive bedclothes onto the damp balcony to sleep out in the open air. Because she "wanted to see how the world spins!" Or the time she baked her father a disgusting blue birthday cake colored with food dye that looked as if the very first bite would cause fatal poisoning. Just because she had this thing about blue. That was really taking things too far, thought Cathérine, but Émile naturally thought it was great and insisted that it was the best cake he had ever eaten. "You all have to taste it!" he shouted and served up the spongy blue mess on the guests' plates. Oh, good old Émile! He simply couldn't refuse his daughter anything.

And now this latest idea!

Cathérine wrinkled her brow and looked at the tall, slim girl with her pale face and dark eyebrows as, lost in thought, she played with her long, brown, carelessly braided pigtail.

"Get that idea right out of your head, Rosalie. Painting will never pay your way. I cannot and will not support anything of the sort. What do you think you'll live on? Do you think people are just waiting to snap up your pictures?"

Rosalie carried on twisting her pigtail and gave no answer.

If Rosalie had been an enchanting Rosalie, Cathérine Laurent, née de Vallois, would certainly have had no worries about her daughter's livelihood. After all, there were enough well-heeled men in Paris—and then it would not matter if their wives did a little painting on the side, or had any number of passing enthusiasms. But she had an uneasy feeling that her daughter didn't think in those categories. God knew whom she'd finally end up with!

"I'd really like you to do something sensible," she repeated emphatically. "That's what Papa would have wanted, too." She put a slice of the steaming quiche on her daughter's plate. "Rosalie? Are you even listening to me?"

Rosalie looked up, her dark eyes unfathomable.

"Yes, Maman. I should do something sensible."

And that is what she did do. More or less. The most sensible thing that Rosalie could imagine, after a couple of semesters studying graphic design, was to open a postcard store. It was a tiny establishment on the rue du Dragon, a pretty little street of medieval houses in the heart of Saint-Germain, a stone's throw from the churches of Saint-Germain-des-Prés and Saint-Sulpice. There were a few boutiques, restaurants, cafés, a hotel, a *boulangerie,* and Rosalie's favorite shoe store; Victor Hugo had even lived here at one time, as a plaque on house number thirty showed. If you were in a hurry, it didn't take many strides to pass through the rue du Dragon, to reach either the very lively Boulevard Saint-Germain or—in the other direction—the somewhat quieter rue de Grenelle, which led to the elegant houses and palaces of the government quarter and then ended on the Champ de Mars beneath the Eiffel Tower. But you could also, of course, just stroll aimlessly along the little street and stop again and again because you'd seen something nice in one of the displays—something that cried out to be tasted, picked up, or tried on. On those occasions it could take quite a while to reach the end of the street. That was how Rosalie had discovered the FOR RENT sign in the empty antique shop whose owner, feeling herself too old to continue, had given up her business a short while before.

As a rule, the more slowly you walked, the more you actually saw.

Rosalie had fallen in love with the little store straight away. There was a sky-blue frame surrounding the single display window and the entrance to its right, with the old-fashioned silver bell the previous owner had left behind hanging over the door. The light fell on the old black-and-white tiles of the floor in little circles. There was a cloudless sky over Paris that day in May, and it seemed to Rosalie as if the little shop had just been waiting for her.

Admittedly, the rent was anything but cheap, but it was probably still reasonable for the good location, as Monsieur Picard, a tubby, elderly man with receding hair and crafty brown button eyes, assured her. There was also another room above the store, reached by a narrow wooden spiral staircase, with a little bathroom and a tiny kitchen beside it.

"So you have an apartment as well, right on the spot, ha ha ha," joked Monsieur Picard, and his little belly quivered with satisfaction. "What sort of business are you thinking of, mademoiselle? I hope it's nothing that makes a noise or smells—after all, I live in this building, too."

"A stationery store," said Rosalie. "Gift wrap, writing paper, pens and pencils and beautiful cards for very special occasions."

"Aha. Well, well. Good luck, then!" Monsieur Picard seemed a bit nonplussed. "Tourists always like buying cards with the Eiffel Tower on them, don't they?"

"A *postcard store*?" her mother shouted down the phone in disbelief. "*Mon Dieu!* My poor child, who still writes cards these days?"

"I do, to name but a few," Rosalie answered and then just hung up.

Four weeks later she was up on a ladder outside her store, fixing a painted wooden sign over the entrance.

It said LUNA LUNA in large, curving letters and beneath, slightly smaller: ROSALIE'S WISHING CARDS.

Two

....

As far as Rosalie was concerned, it would have been fine if a lot more people wrote letters and cards. The minor—and sometimes major—pleasure still provided even nowadays to the receiver and also the writer of a handwritten letter could simply not be compared with an e-mail or a text, which would be quickly forgotten and lost in the abyss of meaninglessness. That brief moment of wonderment when you suddenly found a personal letter in the mail, the joyful anticipation as you turned over a postcard, carefully unstuck an envelope or ripped it open impatiently. The possibility of holding in your hands a piece of the person who had thought of you, studying their handwriting, sensing their mood, maybe even catching a trace of tobacco or perfume. That was so very vivid. And even if people nowadays wrote letters ever more infrequently, because apparently they had no time for them, Rosalie didn't know anyone who wouldn't like to receive a personal letter or a handwritten card. The present with all its social networks and digital gadgets had very little charm, she thought. It might all be effective or practical or fast—but it definitely lacked charm.

In the past, opening the mailbox must have been a bit more exciting, she thought as she stood in the lobby of the building before the row of mailboxes. The only thing you regularly found there these days was bills, tax demands, and junk mail.

Or notices of a rent increase.

Rosalie looked at her landlord's letter with annoyance. This was now the third increase in five years. She had seen it coming. In recent weeks Monsieur Picard had been so exceptionally friendly every time she met him in the hall. And every time as they parted he had sighed deeply and said that life in Paris was getting dearer all the time.

"Do you know what a baguette costs these days, Mademoiselle Laurent? Or a croissant? Do you know what they charge for a croissant in the boulangerie? It's unbelievable! I ask you, what is there in a croissant—water and flour, and nothing more, is there?" He had shrugged his shoulders and made an accusatory gesture, looking at Rosalie with a mixture of indignation and despair, before shuffling off without waiting for an answer.

Rolling her eyes, Rosalie went into her shop. Of course she knew what a croissant cost. After all, she ate one every morning—much to René's annoyance.

René Joubert was tall, dark haired, and extremely sporty. He'd been her boyfriend for three years and was a personal trainer. Perhaps, Rosalie sometimes thought with a sigh, in the reverse order. René Joubert took his profession very seriously. He preferred working with well-heeled women from the upper ranks of Parisian society who were very happy to have their figure, their fitness, and their health looked after by this good-looking young man with his sports diploma, his gentle brown eyes, and his well-honed body. René's appointment book was always full, but, as it seemed, the top layer of Parisian society was not enough of a challenge to his abilities. At least, he never failed to take every opportunity to try to convert Rosalie to a healthy, exercise-filled life (*mens sana in corpore sano!*) and to point out the dangers that lurked everywhere in food. On his death list—at the very top!—were the croissants Rosalie loved so much. ("White flour is poison for the bowels!" "Have you never heard of wheat belly?" "Do you actually know how much fat there is in those things?")

Rosalie, who had her own idea of what makes for a happy life (which did not necessarily include power training, muesli, or soy milkshakes), was not at all impressed, and all her boyfriend's missionary efforts had so far failed miserably. Rosalie just couldn't see why she should eat "grain." "Grain is cow fodder and I'm not a cow," she used to say and then spread thick layers of butter and jelly on a piece of croissant and stick it in her mouth.

René watched her with a pained expression.

"And anyway, nothing tastes better with a *café crème* than a croissant or a baguette," she went on, brushing a few crumbs off the bedclothes. "You have to admit that."

"Then just leave out the café crème, a kiwi and spinach smoothie is healthier in the morning anyway," retorted René, and Rosalie nearly choked on her croissant with laughter. That was really the most absurd thing she'd ever heard. A morning without coffee was like—Rosalie tried to find a suitable comparison—was . . . just unimaginable, she concluded to herself.

At the very beginning, when she'd only just met René, she had allowed herself to be persuaded to join him on his early-morning run through the Jardin du Luxembourg. "It'll be great—you'll see," he had said. "At six in the morning Paris is a totally different city!"

He might well have been right, but the old, pleasantly familiar Paris, where you stayed up late at night and drew, wrote, read, debated, and drank red wine, then began the next day comfortably in bed—best of all with a large cup of milky coffee—was much more to Rosalie's taste. And while René ran beside her under the old chestnut trees with great gazellelike strides, trying to involve her in relaxed conversation ("you should only run at a pace that allows you to chat properly"), she started to puff after the first hundred meters and finally stopped with a stitch.

"The beginning is always the hardest," said her coach. "Don't give up now!"

Like everyone who's in love and tries very hard at the outset to merge symbiotically with their partner and adopt their preferences, Rosalie had even given in to René's entreaties and tried it one more time—but alone, and not at six o'clock in the morning—but after a centenarian with a tottering gait, his body bent terrifyingly forward, his arms swinging wildly, had overtaken her, she finally said goodbye to the idea of becoming sporty.

"I think my walks with William Morris are enough for me," she explained with a laugh.

"Who's William Morris? Should I be jealous?" René was concerned. (At that point he had not yet been in her shop, and he had no clue about William Morris the artist. But that was forgivable—after all, she didn't know the name of all the bones and ligaments in her body, either.)

She'd given René a kiss and explained that William Morris was her little dog, whom she—as the owner of a stationery store—had named after the legendary Victorian painter and architect, among other reasons because he had produced the most wonderful designs for fabrics and wallpaper.

William Morris—the dog—was an extremely agreeable Lhasa Apso, and he was now almost as old as the postcard store. During the day he lay peacefully in his basket near the entrance; at night he slept behind the kitchen door on a blanket, and sometimes, when he was dreaming, his paws would jerk in his sleep and bang against the door frame. As the man from the animal shelter had explained to her when she got him, this small breed of dog was so particularly peaceful because they had in the past accompanied wandering Tibetan monks who had taken a vow of silence.

René liked the Tibetan connection, and William Morris himself greeted the young man with the broad shoulders and big feet with a friendly wag of the tail when, after four weeks, Rosalie invited him into her apartment for the first time. Well . . . perhaps *apartment* wasn't exactly the right word for that one poky little room over the store with only enough space for a bed, an armchair and wardrobe, and a big drawing table under the window. However, the room was extremely cozy, and Rosalie had only discovered its best feature after she moved in: through a second little window at the back of the building you could get out onto an area of flat roof that Rosalie used as a terrace in the summer. It was sheltered and secluded by old stone tubs with plants and a couple of weather-worn trellises, which were covered with glowing blue clematis in the summer, so that it was almost completely hidden from view.

This was where Rosalie had set the table in the open air when René visited her for the first time. She was no great shakes as a cook—she was much more skilled with her pencil and brush than she was with a ladle—but on the rickety wooden table with its white cloth there were flickering tea lights in a variety of sizes, and there was red wine, pâté de foie gras, ham, grapes, a little chocolate cake, artichoke hearts drenched in lots of oil, salted butter, Camembert, goat cheese, and—a baguette.

"Oh, my God!" René had sighed in comic despair. "Nothing but unhealthy stuff! Total overkill! You'll come to a bad end. Someday your metabolism will collapse and then you'll become as fat as my aunt Hortense."

Rosalie took a great gulp of red wine from her glass, wiped her mouth, and pointed her finger at him. "Wrong, my dear," she said. "Nothing but *delicious* stuff." Then she stood up and with a quick movement stepped out of her dress. "Am I fat, then?" she asked, dancing half-naked over the roof with graceful steps and flowing hair.

René couldn't put his glass down quickly enough.

"Hey, wait!" He'd run after her, laughing, and eventually caught her. "No, you're just right," he'd murmured, his hands running sensuously over her back, and then they'd stayed on the roof, lying on a woolen blanket until the damp of the morning crept up on them.

Now, as she stood in the gloomy hall, which always smelt of orange-scented cleaning fluid, and closed the mailbox, Rosalie thought back to that night on the roof with a degree of melancholy.

In the past three years the differences between her and René had become more and more obvious. And where she had earlier sought and found common factors to unite them, she now saw everything that divided her from her boyfriend with all too much clarity.

Rosalie loved breakfasting in bed; René had no time at all for "crumbs all over the bed." She was a night owl; he was an early riser. She enjoyed her moderate walks with her little dog; he had bought himself a racing bike on which he sped like the wind through the streets and parks of Paris. When traveling was in question, nowhere was too far away for him, while Rosalie could not imagine anything more pleasant than to sit in one of the little old squares in the cities and towns of southern Europe and just watch the time go by.

But what she most regretted was that René never wrote her letters or cards, not even on her birthday. "But I'm here," he would say when she looked in vain for a card on the breakfast table on her birthday. Or, "But we can always phone," when he was at one of his seminars.

At the beginning Rosalie had still written him notes and cards she drew herself—for his birthday, or when he broke his foot and had to spend a week in hospital, or just when she was leaving the house on some errand or other, or when she'd gone to bed late at night and he was already asleep. "Hi, Early Riser: please be quiet and let your little night owl sleep in—I worked very late tonight," she would write, and put a note with a little owl perching on a paintbrush beside his bed.

She'd left her little messages all over the place: tucked in behind the mirror, on his pillow, on the table, in his sneakers, or in a side pocket of his carryall—but one day, she couldn't really remember exactly when, she'd given up.

Fortunately they each had their own apartment and a certain degree of tolerance, and René was a positive, life-affirming guy without any hidden depths to speak of. He seemed to her as calm as her little Lhasa Apso. And when they did occasionally quarrel (about little things), they always ended up in bed where their conflicts and frictions faded away in the soothing darkness of the night.

When Rosalie spent the night at René's place, which happened relatively seldom, because she liked to be close to her store and he lived in the Bastille Quarter, she would, just to please him, eat a couple of spoonfuls of the mush with the dried fruits and nuts that he kept on preparing for her with such enthusiasm—he never ceased to assure her that she would one day develop a taste for it.

She would then smile half-heartedly and say "I'm sure I will, someday," and as soon as he'd gone she'd scrape what was left in the muesli bowl down the toilet; then on her way to the store she'd buy a croissant, still warm from the oven, from a boulangerie.

Still on the street, she'd tear off a hunk and stick it in her mouth, happy that such heavenly things existed. But of course she didn't say a word about that to René, and since her boyfriend didn't exactly have a lively imagination he would certainly have been astounded to catch his girlfriend in this little affair with a croissant.

The croissant led Rosalie back to Monsieur Picard and his

annoying rent increase. She frowned as she stared anxiously at the figures in the letter, which seemed quite threatening to her. Even if Luna Luna did by now enjoy a regular clientele, and there were always new customers and tourists who stopped outside the little stationer's with its lovingly decorated display window, and then went in and, with exclamations of delight, picked up gift cards, pretty notebooks, or paperweights and never left the shop without buying something, Rosalie was still not in a position to live it up. There was no way of making big money with postcards and beautiful stationery these days, not even in the former literary quarter of Saint-Germain.

Nevertheless, Rosalie had never regretted her decision. Her mother, who had eventually provided her with a little start-up capital out of her father's estate, had in the end breathed a resigned sigh and said that of course she would do what she wanted anyway, and that it was at least better to run a store, no matter what kind, than to be a painter in free fall. But still, only a little better.

Cathérine Laurent would probably never accept the fact that her daughter had not studied for a sensible profession. Or at least married an ambitious young (or, as far as she was concerned, older) man. (Oh please not that good-natured fitness trainer with the gigantic feet, so boring he almost brought her to tears!) Cathérine almost never visited her daughter's store, and she told her friends from the genteel 7th arrondissement that Rosalie was now running an office supplies store—that at least sounded a *bit* more serious.

Well, "office supplies" wasn't exactly right—in fact, it was totally wrong. You would search in vain for ring binders, staplers, hole punches, plastic folders, glue, in-boxes, and paperclips in the magical paper store that was Luna Luna. But Rosalie considered it superfluous to throw light on this confusion. She smiled and said nothing and felt happy every morning when she went down into her little store and pulled up the steel blinds to let in the sun.

The walls glowed a gentle hydrangea blue. In the middle of the room stood an old, dark, wooden table on which many treasures were spread out: flower-patterned boxes containing all kinds of cards and envelopes; glazed ceramic mugs in delicate colors, produced by a local artist, in which there were pens decorated with patterned paper. Beside them, writing cases with old rose prints. Pretty scribbling pads and notebooks were piled beside writing paper and little boxes containing sealing wax and wooden stamps.

In the bright shelves on the side wall there were rolls of luxury gift wrap and writing paper and envelopes shelved according to color and size; big rolls of gossamer gift ribbon hung down beside the little softwood table where the till stood, and on the blue painted back wall hung tiles with white doves, dark grapes, and pale pink hydrangeas—old motifs whose brightness had been restored by a thick layer of lacquer—and a large oil painting that Rosalie herself had painted, showing a little girl in a purple dress with streaming blond hair running through a fairytale wood. In the corner next to the till there was a tall, locked glass display case containing expensive fountain pens and silver letter openers.

The display window was decorated with filigree card holders, which from a distance were reminiscent of bright patchwork quilts. Behind a rectangular pattern of silver wire twisted into heart shapes, a medley of all kinds of cards created an artwork of its own. Right behind them hung lengths of dark blue, turquoise, and reseda green gift wrap printed with William Morris's exquisite patterns, and below all this there were cards laid out in fans and pretty card boxes with flower motifs or pictures of women at the seaside or reading books. Between them heavy glass paperweights rested on tissue paper in boxes: they had pressed roses in them, or etchings of old sailing ships, painted hamsa hands, or words and sayings that you could read every day without ever getting tired of them. There was the word PARIS painted in delicate brown brushstrokes on a background of chamois color. *L'Amour ou La beauté est partout*—"Love, or Beauty, is everywhere."

At least that was what the sculptor and painter Auguste Rodin had said, and when Rosalie looked around in her shop, she was happy to make her contribution to the abundance and beauty that life had to offer.

What was really special about Luna Luna, however, were the handmade cards in the two revolving postcard stands, which stood just to the right of the door and only just fitted into the little stationer's, although they were probably the most important things there.

That the little store in the rue du Dragon had actually survived all these years was mainly due to Rosalie's idea of the wishing cards. They were her specialty, and very soon word had gotten around that you could get handmade cards for every occasion—even the most unusual—in the Luna Luna stationer's store.

In the evening after closing time and late into the night Rosalie sat at her big table in the room above the store and drew and painted watercolor cards for everyone who still believed in the magic of the written word. They were enchanting miniature works of art on laid paper with deckle edges, with a sentence or a saying for which Rosalie thought up a picture. For example, "Do not forget me" was written in blue India ink, beneath which there was a drawing of a little woman with two suitcases offering the viewer an oversize bouquet of delicately stippled forget-me-nots. Or "Behind the clouds the sun is shining"—here you saw a sad-looking girl with a red umbrella on a rainy street, while on the upper edge of the picture little angels played ball with the sun. "When I woke up, I wished you were here" announced another card showing a stick figure looking longingly into the distance while sitting on a bed in the middle of a meadow blowing at a dandelion clock whose individual parachutes transformed into little spinning letters that formed the word *yearning*.

Rosalie's wishing cards, faintly reminiscent of Raymond Peynet's drawings, sold like hot cakes, and after a while her first customers began returning with their own suggestions and ideas.

Of course it was mostly the usual events (birthdays, get-well wishes, gift certificates, invitations, Valentine's Days, weddings, and Christmas or Easter greetings), but again and again there were very special requests.

Daughters wanted something for their mothers, mothers wanted something for their sons, nieces wanted something for their aunts, grandmothers something for the grandchildren, and women something for their female friends. But the most inventive wishes came from people who had fallen in love.

Just recently a gentleman—no longer in the bloom of youth—with silver glasses and a very correct suit had come in to the store and handed in his order. He laboriously removed a piece of paper from his leather briefcase and laid it on the counter with some embarrassment.

"Do you think you can do something with this?"

Rosalie read the words on the paper and smiled.

"Oh yes," she said.

"By the day after tomorrow?"

"No problem."

"But it must be especially beautiful."

"Don't worry."

That evening she had sat down upstairs at her drawing table, where, in the light of an old black metal lamp, pens, pencils, and brushes of all sizes stood in orderly rows in thick glass preserving jars, and had drawn a man in a gray suit and a woman in a lime-green dress holding hands and—borne aloft by four fluttering doves with blue ribbons in their bills—floating in the sky over Paris.

Finally she had taken her drawing pen and written in elaborately curving script: "For the woman I long to fly with."

Rosalie couldn't have said how many of these unique works she had produced over the years. So far all her customers had walked out of the wishing-card store satisfied, and she hoped that all their wishes had hit their target as surely as Cupid's darts pierced the hearts of people in love. But as far as her own wishes were concerned, the lovely stationer had had much less luck.

Every year on her birthday Rosalie went to the Eiffel Tower with a card she had painted herself. Then she climbed the 704 steps that led to the second platform and, with pumping heart (she was, as we have already mentioned, by no means an ambitious mountaineer), sent the card with her wish on it sailing through the air.

It was an innocent little ritual that not even René knew about. Rosalie was generally a great believer in little rituals. Rituals gave some shape to life and helped to put the confusion inherent in existence in some kind of order and helped one stay in control of things. The first coffee in the morning. A croissant from the boulangerie. Her daily walk with William Morris. A little *tarte au citron* on every uneven day of the week. The glass of red wine when she closed up the store. The wreath of forget-me-nots when she visited her father's grave in April.

In the evening, as she drew, she always liked to listen to the same CDs. Sometimes it was Georges Moustaki's smoky chansons, other times the lighter touch of Coralie Clément. Recently her favorite CD had been by the Russian musician Vladimir Vysotsky. She followed the sound of the songs—sometimes lyrical, sometimes virile—whose words she didn't understand, while the music created pictures in her head and her pens flew over the paper.

When she was a girl, Rosalie had kept a diary to record the things that she thought important. She hadn't done that for ages, but since she'd opened the store, Rosalie had made a habit of writing down the worst and the nicest moment of the day in a little blue notebook. Only then did her day come to an end, and she could sleep peacefully.

Yes, it was rituals that gave you stability and something to reliably look forward to. And so every year Rosalie looked forward to the twelfth of December, when she stood on the top of the Eiffel Tower with the whole city spread out at her feet. She had no fear at all of heights—quite the contrary, she loved the feeling of distance, the free, open vista that allowed her thoughts to soar, and as her card fluttered away, Rosalie would close her eyes for a moment and imagine her wish coming true.

Yet so far not one of her wishes had ever been fulfilled.

The first time she'd climbed up there with a card, she'd wished for her favorite aunt, Paulette, to regain her health—at the time there was still a glimmer of hope that a complicated operation would be able to save Paulette's eyesight. But although the operation went well, her aunt ended up blind.

Another time she'd wished that she would win a competition for up-and-coming young illustrators. But the coveted prize, the book contract, and the prize money of over ten thousand euros went to a gawky young man who only painted palm trees and hares and was the son of a rich Parisian newspaper publisher.

Before she'd met René and was living alone after a few rather disappointing relationships, she'd wished to meet the man of her dreams who would one evening take her up to Le Jules Verne— the restaurant at the top of the Eiffel Tower, which had probably the most spectacular view over the whole of Paris—and then, when they were there, high up over the sparkling city, ask her the question of questions.

This wish also remained unfulfilled. Instead, she met René, who literally ran into her one day on the rue du Vieux-Colombier, apologized a thousand times, and then dragged her into the nearest bistro to declare over a *salade du pays* that he'd never seen anything as beautiful as her. But René would rather have taken her on a trekking tour to Kilimanjaro than to an expensive— and in his view totally superfluous—restaurant on the Eiffel Tower. ("The Eiffel tower? Pur-lease, Rosalie!")

Another time she'd wished for peace with her mother—a pious hope! She'd also wished for a little house by the sea—well, that was a little extravagant, but there was nothing to stop her wishing.

On her last birthday—it was her thirty-third and unpleasant; icy rain was pouring down on Paris and its Christmas decorations—Rosalie had marched off in her thick, blue winter coat and climbed up the Eiffel Tower once again. There was nothing much going on that day—some skaters were gliding over the ice rink that was always put up on the first level in the winter and a few Japanese tourists in rain slickers seemed never to tire of photographing each other with thumbs raised and broad grins.

This year Rosalie had a very modest wish.

On the card in her hand was a drawing of a bridge, its honeycomb rail hung with hundreds of little padlocks. A little man and a little woman were standing beside it, kissing.

The bridge was unmistakably the Pont des Arts, a pedestrian bridge across the Seine from which there was a wonderful view of the Eiffel Tower or the Île de la Cité. On summer evenings it was always a very lively place.

Rosalie loved the simple, narrow iron bridge with its wooden walkway. She sometimes went there, sat on a bench, and looked at the large number of padlocks attached to the railing, each of which proclaimed a love that was meant to last forever.

As long as love lasts, it's eternal. Who had said that?

Rosalie didn't know why, but every time she sat there she was moved by the sight of all these hopeful little padlocks, guarding love as staunchly as tin soldiers.

It may have been silly, but her secret heart's desire was a padlock like that.

Whoever gives me a padlock like that is Mr. Right, she thought as she leaned over the damp steel framework of the Eiffel Tower and threw her card into the air in a high arc.

As she did so, of course, she was thinking of René.

One bright winter's day at the beginning of December she had walked over the Pont des Arts hand in hand with her lover, and the railing with its padlocks had sparkled in the sun like Priam's Treasure. "Look, how lovely!" she had cried.

"A wall of gold," René had said in an unusual fit of poetry and had stopped for a moment to inspect the inscriptions on the padlocks. "Unfortunately, not all that glitters is gold," he added with a grin. "I'd like to know how many of the people who have eternalized themselves here are still together."

Rosalie wouldn't have liked to know.

"But still, isn't it wonderful that people still fall in love and want to show it? I mean, I'm kind of moved by these little padlocks."

She didn't say anything else, because it was the same with birthday wishes as with the wishes you make when you see a shooting star: you weren't allowed to reveal them.

René had taken her in his arms with a laugh. "Oh lord, don't tell me you're seriously keen on a stupid padlock? They're pure kitsch."

Rosalie had laughed with embarrassment and thought to herself that even pure kitsch could have an attractive side some of the time.

Two weeks later she was standing on the Eiffel Tower, calmly watching the card fluttering downward like a wounded dove. She was startled when a heavy hand was suddenly placed on her shoulder from behind.

"Hé, mademoiselle, qu'est-ce que vous faites là?" thundered in her ear.

Rosalie started and nearly lost her balance with the fright. A man in a blue uniform and a kepi gazed piercingly into her eyes.

"Hey! What do you think you're doing, giving me such a shock?" Rosalie replied furiously. She felt both caught out and disturbed in her sacred ritual. Ever since the government had placed all the tourist attractions under surveillance for fear of pickpockets, you couldn't be safe from interference even on a rainy December day. It made her crazy.

"So? What are you doing here?" repeated the policeman harshly. "You can't just throw your trash away up here."

"That was no trash, that was a wish," Rosalie replied irritably, noticing that her ears were burning.

"Now don't try and get smart with me, mademoiselle." The officer folded his arms and pulled himself up to his full height in front of her. "Whatever it was, you're going down right now to pick it up, is that clear? And this empty chips bag here"—he pointed to a crumpled plastic bag at her feet with raindrops dripping from it—"you can take that with you as well."

He watched the young woman in the blue coat as she tramped grumpily down the steel framework step by step.

When she reached the bottom, Rosalie, overcome by an attack of curiosity, walked round the base of the tower, actually looking for her wishing card. But it had vanished into thin air.

AFTER THE SOMEWHAT BIZARRE event on the Eiffel Tower, which Rosalie obviously had not told anyone about, more than three months had passed. The cold damp of the winter rain had given way to a stormy January and then a surprisingly sunny February. Her birthday was long past, Valentine's Day came and went, but this time, too, her wish remained unfulfilled.

René proudly offered her a box containing running shoes ("breathable, superlight, the Porsche among running shoes, for my love on Valentine's Day!").

In March, too, nobody had the idea of giving Rosalie a little golden padlock. And by now it was April.

So many wishes, so many disappointments. The results of the last few years led Rosalie to the view that it might well be high time to give up her childish birthday ritual and grow up. If nothing happened this year, she wouldn't climb up the Eiffel Tower again.

The air was mild and spring was gradually taking hold. And spring sometimes fulfills the promise that winter has failed to.

At least, that was what Rosalie was writing on one of her cards when there was an energetic knock at the door below.

Three

....

Le Vésinet was an enchanting little town lying about twenty kilometers west of Paris in a loop of the Seine. Even today you could sense that this little place in the Île-de-France region had previously been a forest where the king had enjoyed hunting. The impressionists had also visited it and conjured up the untouched natural beauty of the dreamy green banks of the Seine: many of the paths still look today as they did in the paintings of Manet or Monet.

Old upper-class villas were protected behind hedges and stone walls; green meadows, parks, and calm lakes delighted the eye; and when you drove along the old allées and the light fell through the lofty trees, many of which were over a hundred years old, you were automatically embraced by a sense of great peace. In other words, Le Vésinet was the perfect place if you wanted a quiet life.

Unless, thought Max Marchais grimly, you had a publisher on your back who wouldn't leave you in peace.

The famous children's book author was sitting at his desk looking out at the spring morning, at his idyllic garden with the broad lawn, the old chestnut tree and the blooming cherry tree, the little, dark-green garden pavilion, and the hydrangea bushes when the phone rang yet again.

It had been going on like that all morning, and Max Marchais knew exactly why. Whenever that guy Montsignac set his mind on something, he was like a terrier with his teeth fastened in his victim's ankle—almost impossible to shake off. For the last week he had been bombarding his author with letters, e-mails, and calls.

Max Marchais grinned. His case had obviously become a matter for the boss to deal with. He had to admit that he found this quite flattering.

He had first been contacted by a Mademoiselle Mirabeau, evidently editor in chief at Opale Jeunesse—the children's literature imprint of Éditions Opale—who looked after the reprints of his children's books, which were still very successful.

Mademoiselle Mirabeau, with her delicate birdlike voice, had been polite but very determined. She had returned to the attack again and again, attempting to convince him to think up one more concept for a children's book.

Finally, Max had cut her off with a definite no. What was so difficult to understand about the word "no"?

No, he had no desire to write another book. No, he had no more fantastic new ideas. No, it wasn't a matter of the advance. And no, he fortunately no longer needed to earn money. He hadn't written a children's book in a long time, and since his wife had died four years previously, Max Marchais had withdrawn once and for all from Paris and social life.

Marguerite's death had been as tragic as it was pointless. And it had come without warning.

She had been cycling along the street to the market without a care in the world when the door of a parked car flew open and Marguerite took such an unfortunate fall that her neck was broken. The arbitrary nature of Fate left Max a shattered and embittered man. Then life simply went on. But it was emptier.

Max took his daily walk through the friendly streets and parks of Le Vésinet; when the weather was fine he sat out in his wicker chair in the shade of the chestnut tree, looking out at the garden his wife had so lovingly created. Now a gardener took care of it.

The rest of the time Max's favorite activity was sitting at his desk writing short contributions to learned journals or commemorative volumes. Or he made himself comfortable with a book on one of the two sofas in the adjoining library with its big fireplace, where thousands of books in the ceiling-high shelving contributed to the homey atmosphere.

As he grew older, his interest in contemporary literature had declined. He preferred reading the classics that had captured his imagination as a young man and, if you looked closely, were beyond comparison with what were hyped up as "literary sensations" by today's publishing houses. Who nowadays could write like a Hemingway, a Victor Hugo, a García Márquez, Sartre, Camus, or Elsa Morante? Who nowadays had anything really important to say? Something of lasting value? Life was becoming ever more space consuming, faster and shallower—and books seemed to be doing the same. It was worst of all in the case of novels. For his taste there were too many of them anyway. The market was congested with banalities. Nowadays anyone who had any kind of knowledge of the French language felt they had to write, he thought grumpily. It was too much and at the same time not enough. The eternal return of the same old thing.

Max stared tetchily at the phone on his desk, which was still ringing shrilly. "Oh, shut up, Montsignac," he said with a growl.

Perhaps it was also something about him. Perhaps he had simply gotten tired of continually experiencing the new, and therefore he returned to what was tried and trusted. Perhaps he really was on the way to becoming a grumpy old man, as his housekeeper, Marie-Hélène Bonnier, had accused him of being the previous week after he first complained about the weather, then about a neighbor's garrulousness, and then about the food.

So what!

His back had been causing him trouble again recently. That didn't help his mood much, either. Max sighed as he tried to find as comfortable a position as possible in his writing chair. He shouldn't have tried to move that heavy beech-wood tub in the garden—a fatal error! It was enough to make you sick. You had to watch out all the time that you didn't get a chill or pull some muscle or other. Your old friends and acquaintances all had their little quirks, which got ever more difficult to put up with. Or they simply died, and the loneliness and the feeling that someday you'd be the last to survive grew ever greater.

It was really boring. Whoever invented the idea of a golden old age must have been a complete idiot or a cynic. It just wasn't easy to get old and remain likeable. Especially on bad days.

The telephone went quiet, and Max twisted his face into a triumphant grin. I've won!

He looked out, his gaze resting for a moment on the hydrangea bushes that stood in front of an old stone wall in the rear part of the garden. A squirrel emerged from hiding, scuttled over the lawn and disappeared between the rosebushes. Hydrangeas and roses had been his wife's favorite flowers; she herself had the name of a flower. Marguerite had been a passionate gardener.

He examined the photograph on his desk: it showed a woman with bright, friendly eyes and a delicate smile.

He missed her. Still. They had met quite late in life, and the calm, level-headed cheerfulness with which Marguerite dealt with things in life—and that had lasted until the very end—had been good for him, restless spirit that he was.

He bent over his handwritten notes once more and then banged out a few sentences on the keyboard of his computer. Now that was a fabulous invention. Not everything that was new was bad, not at all. How simple writing had become these days. How easily you could alter things without leaving any trace. In the newspaper office in the old days they had all written on rattling typewriters whose letters kept getting hooked up on each other. With carbon paper. It hadn't been possible to print things out as often as you wanted and there was no simple way of copying them. And if you'd made a mistake, correcting it was a really tedious business every time.

He tried to concentrate on his work again—an essay on the theme of "abstraction as a philosophical phenomenon," which he was supposed to write for a small academic publisher. Max Marchais had not always been a children's author. After finishing university he had worked as a journalist and occasionally written articles for academic journals. But it was only through his children's books that he had become known—no, famous. And he didn't even have children! The irony of Fate! The tales of Plum-Nose the Hare, the adventures of the little Ice Fairy, and the seven books about the little knight Donogood had made him richer than he would ever have thought possible. But soon after their marriage Marguerite had only just survived an ectopic pregnancy—and that was the end of it. At the time Max had just been eternally grateful not to have lost his wife. Their life together had been good even without children, and the years had just flown by.

This year he would be seventy. As a young man he'd never have thought it possible that it would happen to him. Seventy! He didn't like thinking about it.

"You should go out more, Monsieur Marchais. Find something to do, go back to Paris occasionally, go to the café, meet your friends, go to your holiday house in Trouville or invite your sister from Montpellier for a visit. It's not good for you to bury yourself in the house the whole time. You'll end up completely alone. Every human being needs to talk to someone sometimes—that's what I think."

Marie-Hélène and her long-winded reproaches sometimes drove him mad.

"But I've got you," he said.

"No, no, Monsieur Marchais, you know exactly what I mean. You're withdrawing into yourself more and more. And your moods are getting worse all the time." Marie-Hélène had been in the library, energetically dusting the shelves. "I'm starting to feel like the housekeeper of that, now, what was his name, that grumpy man who also did nothing but stay at home and found out everything through his housekeeper. . . ."

"Marcel Proust." Max completed her sentence drily. "Now don't get carried away, Marie-Hélène, and stop talking such nonsense. I'm just fine. And I like my life exactly as it is."

"Oh yes," Marie-Hélène had said, holding up her feather duster like a lance. "I don't believe a word of it, Monsieur Marchais. Do you know what you are? A lonely old man in a big, empty house."

Those were powerful words. He'd have liked them if he'd read them in a novel, thought Max with amusement.

The silly thing was that his housekeeper had hit the nail right on the head.

When the telephone began ringing again two hours later, Max clapped his computer shut crossly and put his notes on the theme of abstraction to one side. Then he reached firmly for the phone.

"Yes, hello, who's there?" he said irritably.

"Aaaah, Marchais, it's great that I've gotten through to you at last. The bird had flown the coop, huh, ha ha. I've been trying all day."

"I know." Max rolled his eyes. Of course—Montsignac, he should have guessed. The publisher's voice oozed friendliness.

"My dear Marchais, how are you? Everything in the garden blooming? Has our enchanting Mademoiselle Mirabeau told you about the little proposition we have for you?"

"Yes, she has," he growled. "But I'm afraid we're not going to agree on that."

"But, but Marchais, don't be so pessimistic, there's always a way. Why don't we meet in Les Editeurs next week and discuss everything at leisure, just you and I?"

"You can save yourself the bother, Montsignac. My answer is still no. I'm almost seventy—things have to come to an end sometime."

"Poppycock. I beg you, Marchais, don't be childish. Seventy?

What sort of argument is that? You're not old. Seventy is the new fifty. I know a lot of authors who only start writing at your age."

"Good for them. Why don't you ask them?"

Montsignac obviously felt there was no need to respond to this and simply carried on talking.

"It's precisely *because* you're turning seventy that you should write another book, my dear Marchais. Think of all your fans; think of all the children you've made happy with your books. Do you know how many copies of *Plum-Nose the Hare* are still sold over the counter every month? You're still the greatest children's writer in this country: France's Roald Dahl, so to speak." Max heard him laughing. "Except that you have the unbeatable advantage of being only just seventy and can still write books." He began to wax lyrical.

"A new children's book that we can bring out on your round-numbered birthday. *Et voilà*: that should hit the spot. I tell you, it'll be a sensation. I can see it now: all the papers will be in a feeding frenzy. I can see thirty foreign licenses. And then we'll promote your entire backlist. It'll be a real celebration."

Max Marchais could almost hear old Montsignac rubbing his hands. "Old Montsignac"—he had to laugh, almost against his will, as the euphoric publisher's prophesies whizzed past him.

In reality Montsignac wasn't actually that old. Only in his midsixties, younger than he was himself, but the tall, well-built man with his early-graying hair and the shirts—always so pristine white—that stretched so perilously over his belly when he was seized by one of his terrifying fits of rage had always seemed older to him.

He'd known the publisher of Éditions Opale for almost thirty years now. And although they had had serious arguments, he appreciated this lively, impatient, bubbling, obstinate, often unjust but ultimately always good-hearted man who had been his publisher for so many years. Montsignac had given Max Marchais the contract for his first book when the author himself was still an unwritten page. He had even engaged one of the best children's book illustrators for the work of an author who, completely unknown at the time, had already been turned down by several publishing houses.

His courage as a publisher, for which Max had always admired him, had more than been repaid. The adventures of the hare with the plum-nose were a great success and were sold in many countries. All his other books had also appeared under the Opale Jeunesse imprint, and some of them were by now regarded as children's classics.

When Marguerite died, Montsignac had canceled all his appointments at the book fair and driven out to Le Vésinet to shake his hand at the graveside. "Life will go on, Marchais, believe me, life will go on," he had whispered in his ear, laying a friendly arm around his heaving shoulders.

Max Marchais had never forgotten that.

"Tell me, Marchais . . ." All of a sudden the publisher's voice took on a suspicious tone. "You're not going to leave us, are you? Is there another publisher in question? Is that it? You wouldn't do that after all that we've done for you, would you?"

He gasped in amazement. "Please, Montsignac, what do you take me for?"

"Well, then I can't see any reason why we can't embark on this great project together," said Montsignac with relief.

"What project?" countered Max. "I can't remember any project."

"Oh, come on now, Marchais, don't play so hard to get. There's still something there, I can sense it. A little story that's just a piece of cake for you."

"Listen, Montsignac. Just leave me in peace, will you? I'm a bad-tempered old man who no longer has any desire to eat cake."

"That was very well expressed. Bravo! Do you know what, Marchais? I really like you, but your self-pity is unbearable. It's high time you came out of your lair. Get out and about, my friend. Write. Allow something new to happen. Allow a little bit of light to enter your life. You've buried yourself behind your boxwood hedges for far too long."

"Stone walls," objected Max, staring at the hydrangea bushes that nestled against the stone walls at the back of the garden. It was the second scolding he'd had in a single week. The publisher was obviously in cahoots with his housekeeper.

"But I haven't written a children's book for ages," objected Max after a pause.

"Believe me, it's just like riding a bike: it's not something you forget. Is there any other reason?" As always, Montsignac wouldn't take no for an answer. Max sighed.

"I just don't have any ideas anymore, that's the reason."

The publisher burst out laughing. "That was good," he said when he'd calmed down.

"Honestly, Montsignac, I just don't have any good stories left."

"Go on, just look, Marchais, just look! I'm absolutely certain that you'll find a really good story in the end." He said that as if you simply had to go to the closet to rummage for a story like a pair of old socks. "So, next Friday at one o'clock in Les Editeurs, no argument!"

TOURISTS SELDOM WANDERED INTO Les Editeurs. It was a little restaurant off the beaten track behind the Odéon Métro station. It was where publishers met their authors and license people negotiated with foreign editors who were visiting the Salon du Livre. You sat in comfortable red leather armchairs under a gigantic station clock, surrounded by books, and ate a tasty little snack from the menu or just drank a coffee or a *jus d'orange pressé*.

Monsieur Montsignac, who usually was uncomfortable on the hard wooden chairs in other cafés, really appreciated the comfort of these soft armchairs. And this was one of the main reasons why he always returned to the little restaurant when he had a business meeting.

He stirred his *café express,* his eyes resting benevolently on his author who, two hours before, had walked into the restaurant in a blue suit, his silver-gray hair carefully combed back. He had recently adopted a walking stick (an elegant one, of course, with a silver lion's head as the knob, which he claimed to need because of his bad back), but Montsignac couldn't help feeling that good old Marchais sometimes used his age as an excuse, which meant that he needed to be cajoled into action.

At the same time he was—still—a man who was pleasing to the eye, thought Montsignac. His lively bright blue eyes revealed an alert mind, even though he had become somewhat uncommunicative after the death of his wife.

Anyway, Montsignac had realized immediately that there was good news when Marchais dropped into the armchair with a strangely embarrassed smile. "Well then, you old tormentor," he'd said without beating around the bush. "I do have one story left."

"Now why doesn't that surprise me?" Montsignac gave a satisfied laugh.

The publisher had not been surprised—not even when Marchais sent him the new story a week later, almost before the ink had dried on the contract. Some authors just needed a little push, and then they would run by themselves.

"A wonderful story. Very good!" he had shouted down the line after reading the manuscript and calling his author straight away—he had picked up so quickly this time that he must have been sitting beside the telephone. "You've surpassed yourself this time, my old friend."

But then Montsignac had had to apply all his powers of persuasion to convince Marchais that they should change the illustrator for the new book.

"Why on earth do you want to do that?" Max objected stubbornly. "Why can't we use Éduard again? I really appreciate his work, and I've always enjoyed collaborating with him."

Montsignac had groaned inwardly. Éduard Griseau's labored drawings—the man was approaching eighty and was now devoting himself to his woodcuts—just weren't what people expected in children's books these days. They had to move with the times. That's the way it was.

"No, no, Marchais, it must be livelier. I have a particular illustrator in mind—she has a very personal style that I really like.

She's not very well known yet, but she's full of ideas. Unspoiled. Hungry. Original. She'd be exactly right for your story about the blue tiger. She paints postcards."

"*Postcards?*" repeated Marchais suspiciously. "Griseau is an *artist*—and you want to involve a dilettante in the work?"

"Don't be so judgmental, Marchais. Always keep an open mind—her name is Rosalie Laurent and she has a little postcard store in the rue du Dragon. Why don't you just call in and then tell me what you think of her?"

And that is how it came about that Max Marchais was standing outside Rosalie's postcard store a few days later, impatiently banging his walking stick on the locked door with the blue frame.

Four

....

At first Rosalie hadn't heard the knocking at all. With tousled hair, she was sitting drawing at her table in jeans and a pullover, and in the background Vladimir Vysotsky was singing the song about Odessa—the only words she understood were *Odessa* and *Princessa*. Her foot was tapping to the lively beat of the music.

Monday was the only day that Luna Luna, like so many other small businesses in Paris, was closed.

Unfortunately the day hadn't begun well. Her attempt to amicably dissuade Monsieur Picard from the planned rent raise had ended in a loud argument. She'd been unable to just keep her mouth shut and had finally called her landlord a capitalist cutthroat.

"I don't have to take that, Mademoiselle Laurent, I don't have to take that," Monsieur Picard had shouted, his little button eyes flashing angrily. "Those are the prices in Saint-Germain nowadays. If you don't like it, you can move out. I can rent the store to Orange in a flash, for your information they'll be ready to pay double what you do."

"Orange? What on earth is that? Oh, you mean that cell phone provider? I just don't get it. You want to turn my lovely store into a *cell phone outlet*? Is there nothing you won't sink to?" Rosalie had shouted, and her heart had begun to beat alarmingly quickly as she ran down the worn stone stairs in a rage (Monsieur Picard lived on the third floor) and slammed her door behind her with a bang that resounded through the whole building. Then for the first time in ages she lit a cigarette with trembling hands. She stood at the window and blew the smoke out into the Paris morning sky. It was more serious than she'd thought. It looked as if there was no way she could avoid pouring her hard-earned money into Monsieur Picard's capacious maw. She only hoped she would always have enough money to do it. A pity the shop didn't belong to her. She'd have to think about it. Something was sure to occur to her.

She'd made herself a coffee and returned to her drawing table. The music and the work on the drawing helped her to calm down. *We'll see about that, Monsieur Picard,* she thought as she wrote the message on the new card with an energetic flourish. *You won't get rid of me that quickly.* There was a knock at the door, but she didn't hear it. She regarded her work with satisfaction.

"The spring sometimes fulfills the promise that winter has failed to."

"Let's hope so," she said, more to herself. Downstairs there was more knocking—loud, and this time audible—at the door of the store. Rosalie finally heard it. She stopped in surprise and put her pen down. She wasn't expecting anyone. The store was closed, the mail had already arrived, and René had appointments with his clients all day.

"Okay, I'm coming," she called, twisting her hair up and fastening it with a barrette as she hastily climbed down the narrow wooden steps of the spiral staircase that led to the store.

William Morris, who was lying down there in his basket, raised his head briefly, and then let it sink back on to his white paws.

Outside the door there was an elderly gentleman in a dark-blue raincoat and a matching Paisley scarf knocking impatiently on the glass pane of the door with his stick.

She turned the key, which she'd left in the door, and opened it. "Hey, hey, monsieur, what's all this about? You don't have to break my door down," she said crossly. "Can't you read? We're closed today." She pointed to the sign that was hanging on the door. The old gentleman didn't think it necessary to apologize. He raised his bushy white eyebrows and examined her critically.

"Are you Rosalie Laurent?" he then asked.

"Not today," she replied sharply, pushing a lock of hair behind her ear. What was going on here? Some kind of interrogation?

"What?"

"Oh, nothing. Just forget it."

The gentleman with the Paisley scarf seemed confused. Perhaps he was hard of hearing.

"The best thing would be to come back tomorrow, monsieur," she said, louder this time. "We're closed here today."

"You don't have to shout," the gentleman replied with annoyance. "I can still hear very well."

"I'm glad to hear it," she replied. "Well then, *au revoir.*" She shut the door and was turning to go when the knocking on the glass resumed. She took a deep breath and turned round again.

"Yes?" she said, after opening the door once more.

He looked at her searchingly. "Well, is it you or not?" he asked.

"It is," she said. This was beginning to get interesting.

"Oh, that's good," he said. "At least it's the right store. May I come in?" He took a step into the store.

Puzzled, Rosalie stepped backward. "We're actually closed today," she repeated.

"Yes, yes. You've already said that, but, you know"—he began to walk about and look around the store—"I've come to Paris specially, in order to see if your drawings really are suitable." He moved on, and banged into the corner of the big wooden table in the middle of the store; one of the ceramic mugs of pens began to wobble perilously.

"There's not much room here," he remarked reproachfully.

Rosalie straightened the mug as he reached for a flowery card that lay on the table with his big hand.

"Did you paint this?" he asked sternly.

"No." She shook her head in wonderment.

He narrowed his eyes. "Just as well." He put the card back. "That wouldn't do at all."

"Aha." Rosalie had no idea what he meant. This well-dressed elderly gentleman was obviously not quite right in the head.

"My cards are in the stand by the door. Did you want to order a wishing card?" she tried once again.

He looked at her once more in amusement with his gleaming blue eyes.

"A wishing card? What on earth is that? Something to do with Santa Claus?"

Rosalie was offended and said nothing. She folded her arms and watched as he approached the postcard stand and took one card after another from the stand, holding each of them close to his eyes with wrinkled brow and then carefully putting them back.

"Not bad at all," she heard him murmur absently. "Hm . . . yes . . . that might do . . . it really might."

She coughed impatiently. "Monsieur," she said, "I don't have all day. If you want to buy a card, then do it now. Or come back another day."

"But, mademoiselle, I don't want to buy a card." He looked at her in surprise, pushed his brown leather shoulder bag behind him, and retreated a step. "Actually, I wanted to ask you—"

He got no further. As he stepped back, he had, without noticing, thrust his stick into William Morris's basket. To be more precise, he hadn't noticed William Morris either. The dog, who a second before had been lying there as peaceful and motionless as a ball of wool, yelped with pain and began to bark like mad—which set a fatal chain reaction in motion.

William Morris barked, the old gentleman was shocked, tumbled against the postcard stand, which entangled the strap of his bag, lost his stick—and then everything moved so fast that Rosalie had no chance to prevent the work of destruction that flooded over her with an earsplitting racket like a domino effect and ended with the gentleman in the Paisley scarf stretched out his full length on the stone floor as he grabbed at the—by now empty—postcard stand, which brought the second stand down, so that the cards exploded through the air and then fluttered gently down to earth.

There was a moment of deathly silence. The shock had even stopped William Morris from barking.

"Oh, my God!" Rosalie clapped her hands to her mouth. A second later she was kneeling beside the man—a sky-blue card had landed on his forehead. "Every kiss is like an earthquake," it said.

"Are you hurt?" Rosalie carefully picked up the card and gazed into the stranger's pain-racked face. He opened his eyes and groaned.

"Oooh . . . dammit . . . my back," he said, trying to get up. "What happened?" Confused, he looked at the twisted wire rack that lay on his chest and all the cards that were scattered on the floor around him.

Rosalie looked at him with concern and freed him from the empty stand. "Don't you know?" Good grief, hopefully the old guy didn't have a concussion. "My dog barked and you knocked over the postcard stands."

"Yes . . . that's right." He seemed to be thinking it out. "The dog. Where did he suddenly spring from? The stupid mutt really gave me a fright!"

"And you gave him a fright—because you put your stick down on his paw."

"Did I?" He sat up with a groan, rubbing the back of his head.

Rosalie nodded. "Come along, I'll help you. Do you think you can stand up?"

She took his arm and he struggled up with her help.

"Ouch! Dammit!" He reached for the small of his back. "Give me my stick. Goddamn back!"

"Here!"

He took a couple of wary steps, and Rosalie took him over to the old leather armchair that stood in the corner next to the counter. "Sit down for a moment. Would you like a glass of water?"

The man sat down gingerly, stretched out his long legs, and attempted a wry smile as she handed him the glass.

"Such bad luck," he said, shaking his head. "But at least— Montsignac was right. You're just right for *The Blue Tiger*."

"Eh . . . what?" Rosalie opened her eyes wide and chewed her lower lip. It was obviously worse than she'd thought. The man seemed to have been seriously injured. That was all she needed. She felt panic rising within her. She had no indemnity insurance for her dog. What if the man was permanently damaged?

Rosalie was a grand master of the art of anticipation. In any situation she was able to think through every terrible thing that could possibly happen to the bitter end in a matter of seconds. It was just like a movie, only quicker.

In her mind's eye she could already see a horde of enraged relatives arriving in the shop, pointing accusatory fingers at the basket where little William Morris was sitting with a guilty look. She heard the nasal voice of Monsieur Picard, who "had always said that the dog shouldn't be in the store." But William Morris was as gentle as a lamb. And he hadn't done anything bad. He sat quivering under the table in the store, staring at her wide-eyed.

"It's strange, but you remind me of someone," said the stranger with the Paisley scarf. "Do you like children's books at all?" He leaned forward a little and groaned.

Rosalie swallowed. The man was completely out of it, that much was clear.

"Listen, monsieur, you just sit quiet for a while, okay? Don't move. I think it would be better if we called a doctor."

"No, no, it's all right." He waved her away. "I don't need a doctor." He loosened his Paisley scarf and breathed deeply.

She looked at him more closely. At the moment he seemed to be perfectly normal again. But appearances could be deceptive.

"Should I . . . should I call someone to come and pick you up?"

He shook his head again. "Not necessary. I'll just take one of my dumb tablets, and then everything will be all right."

She thought for a moment. *One of his dumb tablets?* What did he mean by that? Psychotropic drugs? Perhaps it would be better to let someone know.

"Do you live near here?"

"No, no. I used to live in Paris . . . but that was a long time ago. I came by train."

Rosalie began to feel even more uneasy. This man had been strange from the very first second. She looked at him dubiously. You were always hearing about people with dementia who escaped and then wandered around the streets looking for their former homes.

"Tell me, monsieur—what's your name? I mean . . . can you remember your name?" she asked cautiously.

He looked at her, somewhat surprised. And then he began to laugh.

"Listen, mademoiselle, it's not my head that's giving me problems, but my back," he explained with a grin, and Rosalie could feel herself blushing.

"Forgive me for not introducing myself to you before." He

stretched out a hand, which she took with some hesitation. "Max Marchais."

Rosalie stared at him in amazement, becoming—if that were possible—even redder. "I don't believe it," she stammered. "*You're* Max Marchais? I mean, *the* Max Marchais? The children's writer? Who wrote *Plum-Nose the Hare* and *The Little Ice Fairy*?"

"That's exactly the one," he said, smiling. "Would you by any chance like to illustrate my new children's book, Mademoiselle Laurent?"

Max Marchais had been the hero of her childhood. As a little girl Rosalie had read all his books avidly. She had loved the story of the little Ice Fairy and she knew the adventures of Plum-Nose the Hare almost by heart. The books, which she had so happily taken on holiday and taken to bed in the evenings, showed serious evidence of use: dog-ears, creases, and, yes, even some chocolate stains—and they were still there in the bookshelf in Rosalie's old bedroom. But that she would one day meet Max Marchais in the flesh—that was beyond Rosalie's wildest dream. And that she would one day be asked to illustrate one of his books—that, well, that bordered on the miraculous.

Even if her first encounter with the famous children's author had gone rather turbulently—not to say stormily—the rest of the day went very pleasantly.

Max Marchais had told her about his publisher, a certain Montsignac, who moreover had become aware of Rosalie because his wife, Gabrielle, on an extensive shopping trip through Saint-Germain, had acquired not only a pretty purse from Sequoia in the rue du Vieux-Colombier and three pairs of shoes from Scarpa in the rue du Dragon but also some of Rosalie's wishing cards.

Without causing havoc in the store, however!

After the initial shock had been forgotten and all misunderstandings cleared up, Rosalie had picked up the cards with a laugh and put them in their proper places in the store.

Unfortunately her unexpected guest was unable to give her a hand in doing this, much as he would have liked to. Max Marchais had been unable to get up from his chair. In the end, Rosalie didn't actually call the doctor, but she did telephone René.

"Lumbago" had been René's expert opinion, and he'd contacted Vincent Morat, a chiropractor whose practice was a few streets away. And that was where the groaning children's author was sitting a short while later—or rather, he was lying. On a leather couch. Under the ministrations of Vincent Morat, which were as knowledgeable as they were hearty, the bones of his sacroiliac joint gave several audible cracks—and then Marchais left the practice both amazed and completely free of pain.

He felt ten years younger and stepped out briskly with his stick as he returned to the rue du Dragon to invite the owner of the little postcard store and her boyfriend out for a meal. After all that had happened, that was the least he could do. And he noticed to his surprise that he was genuinely looking forward to it.

He had a good feeling about Rosalie Laurent. And he was free of the pain in his back.

That was what you called killing two birds with one stone.

That night Rosalie could hardly sleep for excitement. Beside her, René was sleeping sweetly—after a jolly liquid evening with two bottles of red wine, an excellent coq au vin and one of the most calorie-rich crème brûlées he'd eaten in a long time, he'd fallen into bed like a stone and begun snoring softly. And behind the kitchen door, William Morris, exhausted by the excitement—he had not come out from under the store table for the rest of the day, eyeing the postcard stand suspiciously—lay asleep, his paws jerking.

Rosalie stared at the ceiling and smiled. Before weariness finally conquered her, she took her blue notebook out from under the bed and made an entry.

The worst moment of the day:

An unfriendly old man comes to the store on my day off and knocks over the postcard stand.

The best moment of the day:

The unfriendly old man is MAX MARCHAIS! And I, Rosalie Laurent, am going to illustrate his new children's book.

Five

A few days later, on a springlike day in April, the story of the blue tiger entered Rosalie Laurent's life and changed it forever. Ultimately there is a story in every life that becomes the fulcrum about which it revolves—even if very few people recognize it at first.

In the morning, when Rosalie opened the door of her store and, as usual, looked up, a porcelain sky arched over the rue du Dragon, as delicate and fresh as it can only be after an April shower in Paris. The cobbles in the street were still wet, two little birds were squabbling over a chunk of bread on the sidewalk, blinds were going up on the other side of the street, the odors of the morning wafted over Rosalie's nose, and all at once she had the feeling that today was one of those days when something new was about to begin.

Ever since Max Marchais's extraordinary visit, she had been waiting for the promised mail. She still found it hard to believe that she was the one who was going to illustrate Marchais's new book. She hoped she was not going to disappoint the illustrious author and his publisher. No matter what, she would give it her all. This was her big chance. "Illustrated by Rosalie Laurent." She felt a boundless surge of pride. This would show her mother. Not to mention Aunt Paulette—oh, poor Aunt Paulette! What a pity she could no longer see anything.

Nobody knew yet that she'd gotten the job. Apart from René, of course. "Cool," he'd said. "Now you're going to be really famous." That was something she liked about René. He was happy when she achieved success and had never envied her anything. He wasn't the kind of guy to compare himself to other people and that was—as well as all his sporting activity—the real reason he was so laid-back, even if he definitely never thought about it himself.

When she went into the hallway, her heart gave a little leap of joy. Even from a distance she could see the big white envelope that was sticking halfway out of her mailbox and knew at once that it was Marchais's manuscript.

There were days that were so perfect that even the mailbox had only good things to offer! With thundering heart Rosalie pressed the envelope to her chest. She was burning with desire to read the story and hurried back to the store. But the fine weather this Saturday had tempted people out onto the streets quite early, and before Rosalie could even open the envelope a young woman came into the store. She wanted to buy a pen for her godchild and required a great deal of advice before she finally left with a dark-green marbled Waterman fountain pen.

All day long the little stationery store was well patronized. Customers came and went, bought postcards and gift wrap, bookmarks and little music boxes or chocolates with quotations from famous writers. Some of them left orders for wishing cards. The little silver bell that hung over the door tinkled continuously and Rosalie had to curb her impatience until, toward evening, the last and youngest customer had left: a ten-year-old boy with red hair and freckles who wanted to buy his mother a paperweight for her birthday and simply could not make up his mind.

"Should I take the rose heart? The cloverleaf? Or the sailing ship?" he kept asking, his eyes lingering covetously on the paperweight with the old three-master. "What do you think— would Maman like a sailing ship? That's really something, isn't it?"

Rosalie had to smile when, at the last moment, he decided on the heart made of roses.

"A good choice," she said. "With hearts and roses you can't go wrong where women are concerned."

At last everything was quiet in the store. Rosalie locked the door, lowered the grille, and emptied the till. Then she took the white envelope that had been lying on the softwood table the whole day and mounted the stairs to her own little kingdom. She went into the tiny kitchen, put on the kettle, and took her favorite cup from the shelf over the sink—it was from the *l'oiseau bleu* series by the Gien porcelain factory, and she'd snapped it up at a flea market.

She sat down on her three-quarter bed, which was transformed into a sofa during the day by a blue-and-white-patterned throw with matching large and small cushions, switched on the floor lamp, and took a sip of *thé au citron*.

Beside her, the white envelope gleamed, full of promise. Rosalie opened it carefully and took out the manuscript. There was a business card with a few handwritten lines stapled to it.

Dear Mademoiselle Rosalie, I was delighted to make your acquaintance. Now here's The Blue Tiger *for you. I'm curious to see what you make of it, and eagerly await your suggestions.*

Best wishes, Max Marchais

P.S. Give my regards to William Morris. I hope he's recovered from the shock.

Rosalie smiled. Nice of him to mention the dog. And then his mode of address: *Mademoiselle Rosalie.* So old-fashioned. Respectful and personal at the same time, she thought.

She plumped up a couple of cushions and leaned back, the pages of the manuscript in her lap.

And then she finally began to read.

Max Marchais
THE BLUE TIGER

On Héloïse's eighth birthday something extremely strange happened. Something that was hardly believable, and yet it happened just like that.

Héloïse was a lively girl with blond hair and green eyes, a funny freckled nose, and a mouth that was slightly too large; like most little girls she had a vivid imagination and often thought up adventurous stories.

She firmly believed that her stuffed animals secretly talked to each other at night and that there were little elves in the bluebells in the garden that were so tiny that the human eye could not see them. She was almost sure that you could fly on carpets if you only knew the magic word, and that when you had a bath you must be sure to get out of the bath before pulling out the plug so that the water spirits couldn't pull you down the drain.

Héloïse lived with her parents and their little dog Babu in a pretty white villa on the edge of Paris, very close to the bois de Boulogne, which is a massive, massive park—more of a forest, really. Héloïse often went there with her parents on Sundays for a picnic or a boat ride, but her favorite place was the parc de Bagatelle, an enchanting little park with a wonderful rose garden. How lovely it smelled there! Héloïse always breathed in very deeply when she went for a walk there.

In the parc de Bagatelle there was also a little castle. It was painted the most delicate pink you could imagine, and Héloïse's daddy had told her that long, long ago a young count had built it for a queen in only sixty-four days.

Héloïse, who would also have very much liked to be a princess, found that very impressive. "When I grow up, I'll only marry a man who can build a castle in sixty-four days for me, too," she said, and her father laughed and said that it would probably be best to marry an architect.

Now Héloïse didn't know any architects, but she did know Maurice, a boy who lived with his mother at the end of the street in a little house surrounded by an overgrown garden with lots of apple trees.

One day, as Héloïse was skipping along the street, Maurice was standing by the fence. "Would you like an apple?" he asked, and, with a shy smile, handed her a big red apple over the fence. Héloïse took the apple and took a bite out of it, then handed it back to the boy with the tousled blond hair, so that he could have a bite, too.

From that day onward they were friends, and more than that: Maurice had promised Héloïse faithfully that he would later build her a little castle just like the one in the parc de Bagatelle, no problem! He'd even already secretly gotten hold of some bricks and hidden them in a corner of the garden, because Maurice, as you can well imagine, was deeply in love with the golden-haired girl who could tell such wonderful stories and loved laughing. If Héloïse had wanted the moon as a lamp for her room, Maurice would surely have become an astronaut so that he could get it down from the sky for her.

On the morning of her eighth birthday Héloïse took a trip to the bois de Boulogne with her class. The birthday girl was allowed to choose exactly where the trip should go, and of course she picked the parc de Bagatelle. The sun was shining warmly and the teacher, Madame Bélanger, had said that the children should take their paint boxes and sketch pads, because they were going to paint in the open air that day. And while Madame Bélanger sat down in the shade of a tree with her biology book, the children sat on rugs or on the grass, enthusiastically painting birds, rosebushes, the little pink castle, or one of the magnificent peacocks that strode proudly over the lawns with nodding heads as if they owned the whole park.

At first Héloïse couldn't decide what she wanted to paint. And while the other children painted busily away on their pads, she lay on her rug and looked up at the blue sky where a thick cloud was drifting lazily past. It looked as if a friendly tiger were going for a walk up there, thought Héloïse. She sat up, got her paint box out of her bag, and dipped her brush in the water jar.

Two hours later Madame Bélanger clapped her hands and asked all the children to show their pictures. When it was Héloïse's turn, she proudly showed them a magnificent indigo-blue tiger with silver stripes and sky-blue eyes. She'd taken a lot of trouble over it and thought that it was one of the best pictures she'd ever painted.

Some of the children nudged each other and began to laugh.

"Ha ha ha, Héloïse, what on earth have you painted?" they shouted.

"Tigers aren't blue!"

Héloïse went as red as a tomato. "Well mine is!" she said.

"But a tiger is yellow and has black stripes—everybody knows that," said Mathilde who was the best in the class and knew everything.

"But my tiger is . . . a cloud tiger, and they are always blue with silver stripes, and that's how it is," replied Héloïse, and her lower lip began to tremble a little. How could she have forgotten that tigers were yellow?!

Madame Bélanger smiled and raised her eyebrows very high.

"Well," she said. "There are polar bears and brown bears, green woodpeckers and blue foxes and snow leopards. But I've never heard of a blue cloud-tiger."

"But," said Héloïse in embarrassment, "I'm sure there must be blue tigers somewhere. . . ."

The other children rolled around in the grass in delight.

"Yes, and pink elephants! And green zebras! Just go to the zoo, Héloïse!" they shouted.

"That's enough now, children," said the teacher, raising her hand. "Even if there aren't really any blue tigers, I think your picture is very pretty, Héloïse."

In the afternoon the guests arrived for the birthday party. There was a big chocolate cake, raspberry ice cream, and lemonade, and Héloïse played sack races, hide-and-seek and catch-the-ball in the garden with her friends. It was only after supper, when she'd already said good night to her parents and gone up to her room, that she noticed she'd left her bag with her painting things and the picture of the blue tiger in the park. That was just too bad! Mommy would really scold her, because the watercolor paint box with the twenty-four colors was brand-new.

Héloïse thought for a moment, and then climbed out of window and crept off through the garden while her parents watched television in the living room.

The sun was already low in the sky when she arrived a little later—out of breath—at the entrance to the parc de Bagatelle. She pushed firmly against the old iron gate, which fortunately was not locked, but just creaked a little. She ran past the pink castle, the rose beds, and the little waterfalls that gurgled over the rocks and soon came to the grassy glade where the whole class had sat painting that morning. She looked around, searching—and there, under the old tree where her teacher had been sitting earlier on, was her red cloth bag, and someone had propped her drawing block against the trunk of the tree.

But the picture of the blue tiger had vanished. Had someone taken it?

Or had the wind blown it away?

Héloïse narrowed her eyes to be able to see better, and took a few steps in the direction of the white pavilion which perched like an aviary on the top of a little hill.

Suddenly she heard a sighing sound, which seemed to be coming from the old grotto beneath the pavilion. It was called the Grotto of the Four Winds. Why it was called that, nobody could say, but Héloïse, who had hidden there before, was convinced that it was an enchanted place.

If you stood in the middle of the stone vault, facing the waterfall that flowed into a lily pond behind the grotto, and whispered a wish, the wind would carry that wish to all four points of the compass and it would someday come true—Héloïse was convinced of it. Very carefully, she approached the entrance to the grotto, which was bathed in golden light by the last rays of the setting sun.

She heard the sighing noise again—it now sounded more like a sorrowful growling. Very carefully, she approached the entrance to the grotto.

"Hello?" she called. "Is anybody there?"

Rustling, scrabbling, the patter of paws—and there he was in front of her.

A blue tiger with silver stripes. He looked just like the tiger in her picture.

Héloïse opened her eyes wide. "Goodness gracious!" she murmured, now a bit surprised herself.

"Why are you staring at me like that?" growled the blue tiger, and at first Héloïse was so frightened that it never crossed her mind to be surprised that this tiger could talk.

"Do you happen to be the blue tiger?" she finally asked—very carefully.

"Can't you see?" the tiger replied. "I'm a cloud-tiger." He threw Héloïse a bold glance from his shining blue eyes.

"Oh," said Héloïse. "I should have realized that straight away." She looked at him doubtfully. "Are cloud-tigers dangerous?" she asked.

"Not a bit," answered the blue tiger, twisting his muzzle into a grin. "At least, not to children."

Héloïse nodded with relief. "May I stroke you?" she asked. "It's my birthday today, you know."

"If that's the case, then you can even ride on me," said the blue tiger. "But first you must help me. I've stupidly managed to get a thorn in my paw from that rose bed over there."

He came a bit closer, and Héloïse saw that he was limping on his right paw.

"Oh dear," said Héloïse, who had also once had a splinter in her foot. "That hurts, I know. Let me look, Tiger."

In the dying rays of the sun, the tiger stretched out his paw to her, and Héloïse, who had very sharp eyes, saw the thorn and pulled it out with a determined tug.

The blue tiger roared with pain, and Héloïse jumped back in fright.

"Sorry," said the tiger, licking his wound.

"We ought to bandage it," said Héloïse. "Wait a moment, we'll use this!" She reached into her painting bag and took out a white rag, which did admittedly have a few spots of paint on it, but was otherwise all right, and bound it round the blue tiger's paw.

"I'm sorry about the spots of paint," she said. "But it's better than nothing."

"I especially like the paint spots," purred the blue tiger. "Where I come from, they say that paint spots are the most beautiful things in the world." He looked at the spotted cloth that was now wound around his paw with some satisfaction. "And sky-blue pebbles, of course—the kind that you only find in the Blue Lake beyond the Blue Mountains. They are also very precious, because they only fall from the sky every couple of years. Sky pebbles bring luck, they say where I come from. Do you have one?"

Héloïse shook her head in wonderment. She'd never seen a sky-blue pebble, and certainly not one that had fallen from the sky.

"And where do you come from?" she wanted to know.

"From the Blue Land."

"Is that far from here?"

"Oh yes, very far. So far that you have to fly."

"In an airplane?" Héloïse had never flown in her life.

The tiger rolled his eyes. "For heaven's sake, not in an airplane! They're far too noisy and far too slow. And anyway we don't have any airfields. No, no, the only way to reach the Blue Land is by longing."

"Aha," said Héloïse, puzzled.

The sun had gone down, and in the sky that was now

quickly getting darker and darker they could see the moon rising, fat and round.

"How about it?" asked the blue tiger. "Shall we take a little trip?" He bowed his head a little and pointed to his silver-and-blue-striped back. "Climb on, Héloïse."

Héloïse was not at all surprised that the tiger knew her name. Nor was she surprised that he could fly. After all, he was a cloud-tiger. She climbed on his back, wrapped her arms around his neck, and nestled her face in his soft fur that was now gleaming silver in the moonlight.

And then off they flew.

Soon they had left the Grotto of the Four Winds, the white pavilion, the little pink castle, the babbling waterfalls, and the sweetly scented rose beds far behind them. They crossed the dark forest of the bois de Boulogne and saw in the distance the city with its thousands and thousands of lights, the Arc de Triomphe rising majestically out of the star-shaped crossroads, and the Eiffel Tower soaring slim and shiny into the night sky, watching over the city.

Héloïse had never seen Paris from above before. She hadn't known that her city was so beautiful.

"This is so amazing!" she cried. "Everything is so different when you see it from above, don't you think, Tiger?"

"It's always good to look at things as a whole from time to time," said the blue tiger. "And that is best done from above. Or from a distance. Only when you see the whole picture do you realize how well everything fits together in reality."

Héloïse snuggled in close to his soft fur as they flew back toward the Bois de Boulogne in a broad curve. The air was summery and warm and her golden hair fluttered in the wind. Below them on the Seine, which wound through the city like a dark satin ribbon, the tourist boats glided on with their bright lamps, and if anyone had looked up from below he would have seen a long streaming indigo-blue cloud with a shimmering fringe of gold and probably been more than a little surprised. But perhaps this person would also have believed that it was the tail of a shooting star and wished for something.

"I'm so happy that you really exist!" cried Héloïse in the tiger's ear as they swooped down on the parc de Bagatelle and the scent of the roses wafted in her freckled nose. "At school they all laughed at me."

"And I am glad that you exist, Héloïse," said the blue tiger. "Because you are a very special girl."

"No one's going to believe this," said Héloïse, after the blue tiger had landed softly on all four paws in her garden.

"So what?" he replied. "Wasn't it great anyway?"

"Absolutely wonderful," said Héloïse, shaking her head a little sadly. "But they won't believe me. No one will believe me when I tell them I've met a blue cloud-tiger."

"That doesn't matter a bit," said the blue tiger. "The most important thing is that you believe it yourself—and, by the way, that's the most important thing in every case."

He sprang lithely to a spot under the open window Héloïse had climbed out of to collect her forgotten painting things and the picture of the tiger.

It seemed to her as if an eternity had passed since then, but it couldn't have been that long, because through the lighted window she could see her parents still watching their TV program. No one had noticed that she'd been away. Apart perhaps from Babu, who was standing in the big living-room window wagging his tail and barking excitedly.

"You can climb on my back if you like—then it will be easier to climb into your room," said the blue tiger.

Héloïse hesitated. "Will I see you again?"

"Probably not," said the blue tiger. "Because you only meet a cloud-tiger once in a lifetime."

"Oh," said Héloïse.

"But you mustn't let that make you sad. Whenever you want to see me, just lie down in the grass and wait until a cloud-tiger cloud flies past. That will be me. And now go."

Héloïse put her arms around the tiger for one last time.

"Just don't forget me," she said.

The tiger raised his bandaged paw. "How could I forget you? I've got your cloth with the paint spots."

Héloïse stood at her window a little longer, watching the blue tiger as he bounded across the garden in a couple of great leaps. He jumped over the hedge, flew away over the treetops, making their leaves rustle softly, and then rose above the bright disc of the moon for a brief moment before he was finally lost against the dark night sky.

"I won't forget you either, Tiger," she said softly. "Never!"

When Héloïse woke up the next morning, the sun was

shining brightly into the room, the window was wide open, and her clothes and her red painting bag were lying on the floor.

"Good morning, Héloïse," said her mother, who had almost tripped over the satchel. "You shouldn't just drop things on the floor all the time."

"Yes, Maman, but this time it's different," said Héloïse, sitting up in bed excitedly. "Yesterday evening I went back to the park because I'd forgotten my painting things, and my bag was still there but my picture had vanished, and then in the Grotto of the Four Winds I met a blue tiger who looked just like my picture, blue with silver stripes, and he could even talk, Maman, because he was a cloud-tiger, but he'd hurt himself on the rosebushes and I bandaged his paw, and then he let me ride on his back and we flew all over Paris together and—" Unfortunately, Héloïse had to stop for breath at this point.

"My goodness," said her mother with a laugh, stroking her daughter's hair. "You've had a really adventurous dream. That's probably because of all the chocolate cake you ate yesterday."

"But no, Maman, it wasn't a dream," said Héloïse, leaping out of bed. "The blue tiger was in our garden. He was standing here, outside my window, before he flew away again."

She went over to the window and leaned out to look into the garden, which was calm and peaceful—actually just like every other morning. "It was a cloud-tiger!" she insisted.

"A cloud-tiger . . . well, well," repeated her mother,

amused. "I'm really glad that he didn't gobble you up. And now get dressed and Papa will take you to school."

Héloïse was going to explain that cloud-tigers are no danger at all to children, but her mother had already left the room. "That child really has a lively imagination, Bernard," Héloïse heard her say as she went downstairs.

Héloïse wrinkled her forehead and thought as hard as she could. Could it really be true that she had just dreamed the whole thing? Thoughtfully she put on her dress and stared at the red bag with her painting things, which was still lying beside her bed. She lifted it and looked inside.

There was a box of watercolors, a couple of brushes, a sketch book with empty pages. An opened pack of cookies. The white rag with the paint spots was missing. And then Héloïse noticed something shiny right at the bottom of the bag.

It was a round, flat, sky-blue pebble!

"Héloïse, are you coming?" she heard her mother call.

"Coming, Maman!"

Héloïse clenched her fingers tight around the smooth blue stone and smiled. What did grown-ups know about anything?

After school she'd go to her friend Maurice and tell him the story of the blue tiger. And she was absolutely sure he'd believe her.

Long after she'd read the last sentence, Rosalie lay on her bed, allowing the story to work its magic on her. While reading, she had seen everything so clearly in front of her that she was almost surprised to see that she was in her own bedroom. Little

Héloïse with her golden hair. An apple being handed over a hedge, the park with the ancient trees and the castle in the parc de Bagatelle, which was colored the most delicate pink you could imagine. The cloud-tiger in the Grotto of the Four Winds. The Blue Land which could only be reached by longing. The flight over Paris by night. The little girl's fluttering hair. The promise never to forget. The blue pebble. The rag with the paint spots.

Pictures began to form in her head, colors merged with one another, gold and indigo blue, silver and pink—what she really most wanted to do was to take her pens and brushes out and start painting.

Outside the window overlooking the street a night-blue sky had spread imperceptibly. Rosalie sat there unmoving for a long time, sensing the deep truth that lay in the story and that, for all the amusing elements in it, there was also a gentle melancholy that touched her in an inexplicable way. Suddenly, she couldn't help thinking of her father, and all that he'd given her along the way.

"Yes," she said softly. "The paint spots are the most important thing. The longing you should never lose. And belief in your own wishes."

Six

....

Paris had welcomed him with a cloudburst.

Almost like the first time he'd arrived there. He'd just turned twelve, a gawky adolescent with long blond hair who had suddenly gone through a growth spurt, wearing the inevitable jeans. His mother had given him the trip as a birthday present.

"What do you think, Robert—a week in Paris, just you and me? Won't that be great? Paris is a wonderful city. You'll see, you'll love it."

It was six months after the death of his father, Paul Sherman, an attorney in the well-known New York practice of Sherman & Sons, and in reality nothing was great anymore. Even so, Robert had felt quite excited as their flight approached Paris. At that time his whole family lived in the sleepy little town of Mount Kisco, a good hour's journey north of New York City. But his mother, whose own mother originally came from France, had often talked to him about Paris, where she, urged by her parents, had once spent a summer as a young woman. For that reason she spoke very good French and had insisted that her son learn the language as well.

As they then drove through the night in Paris with the raindrops pattering on the taxi roof, he had become infected with his mother's enthusiasm, and almost twisted his neck trying to see the lights of the Eiffel Tower through the cab's rain-smeared windows; and then the Louvre, the spherical street lamps on a magnificent bridge, whose name he had immediately forgotten, and the wide boulevards, lined with dark trees whose gnarled branches, reaching up for the sky, were hung with little lamps.

The wet streets reflected the city lights, blurring the contours of the tall stone buildings with their curved iron balconies and the lighted windows of the host of cafés and restaurants, so that for a moment Robert felt as if he were gliding through a city of gold.

Then the street became increasingly bumpy and narrow until the taxi stopped outside a little hotel and he stepped straight out into an ankle-deep puddle, soaking his sneakers immediately.

It was strange what kind of details you occasionally remembered. Things that actually were of no importance at all. Nevertheless, they remained hidden in a corner of your mind only to creep out again years or decades later.

It must have been the beginning of November when they arrived in Paris that time; a cold wind swept through the streets and parks, and what he remembered most of all was that it had rained a lot. They had gotten soaked more than once and had frequently had to retreat into one of the many small cafés with the jolly awnings for a hot, milky coffee.

It was the first time he'd drunk a real coffee, and he suddenly felt big and grown-up, almost a man.

He also remembered the dark-skinned woman with the broad

smile and colorful parrot-print headscarf who had brought breakfast up to their room every morning, because it was quite normal in Parisian hotels to have breakfast in bed. And the *assiette de fromage* he had ordered in the Café de Flore ("the writers' café," his mother had explained to him). It was a plate of cheeses that were totally unknown to him, with the individual pieces cut into circles and arranged in order of taste, from mild to strong, which had greatly impressed him. One evening they had gone to a dimly lit jazz bar in Saint-Germain: they had dinner there, and he'd tasted crème brûlée for the first time in his life. It had a sugary crust, which splintered in his mouth with a soft crackle. He remembered the Mona Lisa, crowded round by people whose raincoats smelled of rain; a boat trip on the Seine that took them to Notre-Dame (it had rained there, too); and the Zippo lighter with the name PARIS on it, which he'd bought at the top of the Eiffel Tower after they had climbed the steps together.

"We should come back sometime when the weather is better," his mother had said as they stood up there on the platform with the wind gusting in their faces. "When you've finished college we'll come back and drink a champagne toast." She laughed. "By then I'm afraid I probably won't be able to get up here on foot. But fortunately there's an elevator."

For some reason they had later lost sight of the Eiffel Tower project, as you do, with time, forget so many projects thought up on the spur of the moment, and then one day it was too late.

One afternoon they had walked through one of the big city parks—he no longer knew if it was the Jardin du Luxembourg or the Tuileries, but he still clearly remembered the big white monument he had climbed up on. À PAUL CÉZANNE was written

on it in golden letters. That had suddenly reminded him of his
father and the inscription on his grave in the graveyard in Mount
Kisco, and it was a little bit like having Dad there with them.
The photo his mother had taken then, showing a laughing blond
boy in a cap and scarf holding a Zippo lighter on a big block of
white stone, had hung in the kitchen until she died. When he
sold the house, he took it down from the wall and cried.

He also had a clear memory of the time they went into a
boulangerie and bought some gigantic pink meringues tasting
of sugar, air, and almonds, and how their coats had then been
covered in pink dust—and how his mother had burst out laughing. Her eyes were shining again for the first time in ages. But
then, and he couldn't tell why, her moment of happiness had
given way to sudden sadness, which she tried to conceal, though
he still sensed it.

On the last day they had gone to the Orangerie and stood
hand in hand in front of Monet's great water lily paintings, and
when he had worriedly asked her if everything was all right, she
had simply nodded and smiled, but her hand had involuntarily
grasped his hand tighter.

All this came back to Robert when he arrived in Paris that
morning. Since his last visit, twenty-six years had passed. He still
had the Zippo lighter. But this time he was here alone. And because he was looking for an answer.

His mother had died a couple of months before. His girlfriend
had presented him with an ultimatum. He needed to rethink the
future course of his life, and he was not sure which path to take.
He had to make a decision. And all at once he'd felt that it could
be helpful to put as many miles as possible between himself and
New York, and to come to Paris to think things out in peace.

Rachel had been beside herself. She had shaken her dark-red curls and folded her arms over her chest, and her quivering body was a living reproach.

"I just don't understand you, Robert," she had said and her little pointed nose seemed, if possible, to grow a little more pointed. "I *really* don't understand you. You get the incredible chance of a top position at Sherman and Sons, and instead you want to take up this measly little underpaid, short-term job at the university—for *literature*?!" She had spat the word out as if it were a cockroach.

Well, the "measly" job was at least a guest professorship, but he could still understand her disappointment to some extent.

As the son of Paul Sherman, a man who had been a lawyer with heart and soul (and, by the way, so had his father and grandfather), a legal career seemed to be just what he was cut out for. But if he were to be honest, he had had a sneaking feeling even while he was studying that he was the wrong man in the wrong train as he traveled to Manhattan in the mornings. And so—to the astonishment of the entire family—he had insisted on starting a second course of study, this time for a bachelor of arts.

"If you think it'll be good for your soul," his mother had said. Although she didn't share his passion for books to such a great extent, she nevertheless had enough imagination to understand what it was like for someone to be enthusiastic about something. Her own passion was museums. Even when Robert was little, his mother had gone to museums as naturally as other people went for walks—and for the same reasons. When she was in a good mood, she would say to her son: "It's such a lovely day. Why don't we go to a museum?" And if she was sad or pensive, or something nasty had happened, she would take him by the hand, get on the train for New York, and drag the child through the Guggenheim, the Metropolitan Museum of Art, or the Frick Collection.

After his father's death, Robert remembered, sorrow had driven his mother to spend hour after hour in the MoMA, the Museum of Modern Art.

As a young man Robert had often felt that Faust's famous two souls were actually living in his breast. On the one hand, he didn't wish to disappoint his father, who, had he lived, would certainly have wished his only son to continue the tradition of Sherman & Sons and become a good lawyer. On the other hand he increasingly felt that his heart beat for something different.

When he finally decided to leave Sherman & Sons and work at the university as a lecturer in English literature, everyone thought that it was just a phase.

His uncle Jonathan (also a lawyer, of course!) had run the practice on his own after his brother's death, and he clapped him on the shoulder with a disappointed expression:

"It's a damn shame, my boy, a damn shame! The law is in your blood. The Shermans have *always* been lawyers. Well, I just hope that after taking this time out in the ivory tower you'll find your way back to the family business."

But his uncle's hopes were not to be fulfilled. Robert had quickly found his feet in the university world and felt very much at home there, even if he earned considerably less. He specialized in Elizabethan theater and wrote essays on *A Midsummer Night's Dream* and articles on Shakespeare's sonnets, as well as giving lectures that attracted a certain amount of attention even beyond the confines of New York.

On a bench in Central Park, under the bronze memorial to Hans Christian Andersen, he one day encountered Rachel, an ambitious management consultant with exciting green eyes who was very impressed when she heard that the likeable young man who was so good at telling stories and reciting poetry was a Sherman of Sherman & Sons. They quickly became a couple and moved into a tiny and far too expensive apartment in SoHo. "You'd have been better off if you'd stayed in the practice," said Rachel. In those days that was still a joke.

And then, a couple of years later—it was a sunny day at the beginning of March and the world was showing a deceptively beautiful face—catastrophe struck the literature lecturer with the sky-blue eyes. He was just browsing in McNally's bookstore— one of his favorite Saturday-morning activities—and was about to sit down at one of the little tables in the store with the books he'd just bought and a cappuccino (McNally's cappuccino was as excellent as their selection of books) when his cell phone rang.

It was his mother. Her voice sounded nervous.

"Darling, I'm at the MoMA," she said in a quavering voice, and Robert sensed that something was wrong.

"What's happened, Mom?" he asked.

She took a deep breath and sighed heavily into her phone before answering. "I've got something to tell you, darling. But you must promise me you won't be upset."

"I'M GOING TO DIE. Soon." She had summed up the whole terrible truth in five words, and each of them had hit him like a wrecking ball.

It was cancer of the pancreas in an advanced stage. Out of the blue. Nothing could be done. Perhaps it was better that way, his mother had thought. No surgery. No chemotherapy. None of that absurd torture that did not prevent the inevitable end, but only prolonged it.

Sensible morphine dosage and a very understanding doctor had made dying easier. It had all gone very quickly. Unbelievably quickly.

His mother had died three months later. She, who had always been terribly afraid of death, had been very composed at the end—with an almost cheerful serenity that had put Robert to shame.

"My dear boy," she had said. She'd taken his hand and pressed it firmly once again. "Everything is all right. You mustn't be so unhappy. I'm going to a country that is so far away that you can't even reach it by airplane." She smiled at him, and he had to swallow. "But you know I'll always be with you. I love you very much, my son."

"And I love you, Mom," he'd said softly, as he had done in the old days after a bedtime story, when she'd leaned over his bed and given him a good night kiss, and the tears had run down his face.

"But we didn't make it to the Eiffel Tower," she suddenly murmured, and her smile had stroked him like the wing beat of a dove. "Don't you remember—we still had a date to keep in Paris."

"Oh, Mom," he'd said—and he'd actually smiled, too, even though the lump in his throat was growing bigger.

"To hell with Paris!"

She had shaken her head almost imperceptibly. "No, no, my son, believe me: Paris is always a good idea."

ON THE DAY OF the funeral the sun was shining. Lots of people had come. His mother was a likeable and much-loved woman. Her most delightful quality was probably the fact that she had always maintained an almost childlike capacity for joy and enthusiasm. He'd said as much in his eulogy. And in truth—Robert knew no one else who could enjoy life as much as his mother.

She was sixty-three when she died. Far too early, said the mourners who sadly shook his hand and put an arm round his shoulder. But if you loved someone, death always came too early, thought Robert.

After the notary had given him a thick envelope containing his mother's will, some important papers, a few personal letters—everything his mother had thought important—Robert had once more gone through the empty rooms of the white wooden house with the big veranda that had been his whole childhood.

He'd stood for a long time in front of the watercolor of sunflowers that his mother had liked so much. He'd gone into the garden and put his hand on the rough trunk of the old maple tree where the nesting box his father had made so long ago still hung. This year the leaves would turn such wonderful colors, as they did every year. That was both curious and comforting. That was something that would always be there.

Robert looked up into the top of the tree, where the blue spring sky was shimmering. As he looked up, he thought about his parents.

And then he finally said goodbye. To Mount Kisco. And to his childhood.

THE SUDDEN DEATH OF his mother had brought Uncle Jonathan on the scene: he was beginning to be concerned about the future of Sherman & Sons. At seventy-three he himself was no longer exactly young; he could see how quickly things could change—the ice he was moving on was very thin.

He let a couple of weeks pass, giving Robert space to mourn, to sort out what was necessary and to return to normality, but then—by now it was August—he invited his nephew to his house for dinner so that he could prick his conscience. Foolishly, Rachel was there at the meal as well.

"You should come back to the practice now, Robert," Uncle Jonathan had said. "You're a good lawyer and you ought to think in dynastic terms. I don't know how much longer I can run the practice, and I'd be glad to hand it over to you. We need you at Sherman and Sons. More than ever."

Rachel had nodded in agreement. You could see that she found his uncle's words very reasonable.

Robert had squirmed uncomfortably in his chair and then hesitantly taken an envelope out of his jacket pocket. "Do you know what this is?" he had asked.

The letter had, because life is so interwoven that everything happens at once, been in his mailbox that morning. And it contained an offer from the Sorbonne in Paris.

"Admittedly it's only a guest professorship and the contract is only for a year, but it's what I've always wanted to do. I could start my lectures in January." He smiled with embarrassment, because nobody spoke as a very unpleasant silence spread through the room. "After all, I'm not a committed lawyer like dad, Uncle Jonathan, even if that's what you'd like me to be. I'm a man of books—"

"But nobody wants to take away your precious books, my boy. It's a fine hobby, of course, but you can still read a good book in the evening. Your father did that, too. After work," Uncle Jonathan had said, shaking his head in bafflement.

But that was nothing in comparison with the bitter reproaches Rachel later flung at him when they got home. "You only think of yourself!" she shouted angrily. "What about me? Us? When are you ever going to grow up, Robert? Why do you have to spoil everything just because of a couple of poems, really, I ask you!"

"But . . . it's my job," he objected.

"Oh, job—job! What kind of job is it? Everyone knows that university teachers never make a success of themselves. The next thing will probably be writing novels!"

As she talked herself into a rage, he caught himself thinking that perhaps writing a book wasn't actually such a bad idea. Anyone who works with literature or comes under its spell has the idea at least once. But not everyone gives in to the temptation— which is probably a good thing. In a calmer moment he'd think it over properly.

"Really, Robert, I'm beginning to doubt if you have any sense at all. You can't be serious about Paris, can you? What can you do in a country where people still eat frog legs even today?" She pulled a face as if a cannibal had just crossed her path.

"They're frog thighs, Rachel, not legs!"

"That doesn't make it any better. I assume that no one in that totally politically incorrect country has ever heard of animal protection."

"Rachel, it's only a year," he said, without rising to her preposterous argument.

"No." She shook her head. "It's more than that, you know that very well."

She went over to the window and looked out. "Robert," she tried again, this time more calmly. "Just look out here. Look at this city. You are in New York, my dear, the center of the world. What can you do in Paris? You don't know Paris at all."

He thought of that week in Paris with his mother.

"And you know it even less," he retorted.

"The things I've heard are quite enough for me."

"And what might they be?"

Rachel made a little grimace. "Well, everyone knows: French men think they're the greatest seducers of all time. And the women are total drama queens who live on lettuce leaves and are madly complicated. They use plastic bags for everything and torture geese and songbirds. And they all lie around in bed until noon and call it *savoir-vivre*."

He had to laugh. "Aren't those a few prejudices too many, darling?"

"Don't call me darling," she spat. "You're making a big mistake if you reject your uncle's offer. He presented you with your future on a silver tray today. He wants you to take over the practice. Do you actually realize what that means? You'd be a made man. We would never have to worry about money."

"So it's all about money," he interrupted. Perhaps it wasn't particularly fair, but she snapped at the bait like a starving fish.

"Yes, it's about money, *too*. Money's important in life, you idiot! Not everyone had as carefree an upbringing as you!"

Rachel, who had had to pay her own way through university, ran excitedly back and forth in the apartment and began to sob, while he sat on the sofa and buried his head in his hands with a sigh.

Finally she came to a halt in front of the sofa.

"Now listen," she said. "If you go to Paris it's all over between us." Her green eyes shone with determination.

He raised his head and looked at her in consternation. "Okay, Rachel," he said. "I need to think about this calmly. Four weeks. Give me four weeks."

A few days later he was sitting in the plane to Paris. In his carry-on he had a Paris guide and his old Zippo. Their parting had been frosty, but Rachel had at least accepted that he needed some time out. Then they'd see.

As the taxi stopped outside the little hotel in the rue Jacob it was raining just like the time he arrived in Paris with his mother. Except that this time it was the beginning of September and early in the morning.

A sudden torrential downpour caused the water in the gutters to rise in seconds. As Robert got out of the taxi, he stepped right in the middle of a puddle. Cursing, and with wet shoes (this time they were suede moccasins and not sneakers), he dragged his case across the uneven cobbles and went into the little hotel that he'd found on the Internet under the heading "small is beautiful." It was called the Hôtel des Marronniers, which as far as he knew meant "Chestnut Trees," which was a strange name for a hotel, but he had immediately fallen for the pictures and the description:

In the heart of Saint-Germain, a charming oasis of calm with a rose garden in the inner courtyard and very pleasant rooms. Antique furniture.

Tip: A room overlooking the courtyard is an absolute must!

Seven

....

Paris is always a good idea, his mother had said. It doesn't matter if you're in love or not. If you're unhappy or not in love, Paris can even be a *very* good idea, his mother had said. That's what sprang to Robert Sherman's mind as, with a sigh, he wiped the remains of a pile of dog poop from his shoe with a rolled-up newspaper. He was standing in the rue de Dragon, a few steps away from a little postcard shop, and he cursed the sentimental impulse that had brought him to Paris.

The room overlooking the courtyard had turned out to be a disappointment. When he eagerly opened the shutters in the claustrophobically tiny room on the fourth floor, his gaze was met by a gray stone wall. If you twisted your head to the left and leaned so far out of the window that you were risking your life, there was a slight chance of glimpsing a small section of the enchanting inner courtyard, where among the statues and roses a few old-fashioned white cast-iron chairs and tables with curved legs invited you to breakfast.

As he rattled down in the tiny elevator to complain, it made an alarming racket. The young brunette at reception looked at him in amazement when he gave his key back and demanded another room.

"But monsieur, I do not understand: that room *does* overlook the courtyard," she said in a friendly tone.

"That may well be, but I can't *see* it," Robert responded in a rather less friendly way.

The girl leafed through a large ledger for a couple of seconds, probably to placate him.

"Je suis desolée," she said regretfully. "We're fully booked."

After a discussion that was as short as it was pointless, Robert grabbed his case, which he had at first left at reception, expecting some kind person to bring it to his room (which, of course, had not happened). He pressed the button impatiently, but the tiny elevator had obviously decided in the meantime to give up the ghost completely. The girl from reception shrugged her shoulders regretfully once more and hung a sign on the door of the elevator. HORS SERVICE, it said. "Out of order."

So Robert had carried his own case up the narrow stairs to the fourth floor—they were obviously not designed to allow the passage of larger items of baggage. Then he sat for a while on the bed with its old-fashioned coverlet, staring out of the window at the stone wall, and finally decided to take a bath.

The bathroom was a dream in marble—the old-fashioned water-blue tiles on the walls were utterly charming—but its dimensions had obviously been conceived for dwarves. Robert sat in the bathtub with his knees around his neck, allowing the water to splash over his head, and began to wonder if it had really been such a good idea to come to Paris.

Perhaps his ideas had been a bit too romantic. And his memories of that first trip suffused with the golden glow of nostalgia.

He was a stranger in a foreign city, an American in Paris; but so far it wasn't turning out to be as wonderful and funny as in those old films with Gene Kelly and Audrey Hepburn that his mother had so loved watching.

The rain had stopped when he set out on a short walk to reconnoiter Saint-Germain. A bad-tempered waiter in a café near the hotel resolutely failed to notice him until he finally condescended to bring him a coffee and a ham baguette. Robert Sherman thought sadly of the friendly service in New York coffee shops. He missed the automatic, "Hi, how are you today?" or, "I like your sweater, looks cool!"

As he afterward walked lost in thought along the rue Bonaparte, a cyclist had almost run him over and not even apologized. Then he'd bought himself a newspaper on the boulevard Saint-Germain and a short time later on the rue du Dragon, a few steps away from a little postcard store, he'd trodden in a pile of dog poop. He couldn't believe that this day would bring anything good.

But in that respect Robert Sherman was completely wrong. Only a few steps stood between him and the greatest adventure of his life. And since the greatest adventures in life are those of the heart, you might also say that this American professor of literature was only a few steps away from love.

But Robert Sherman was totally unaware of this when he glanced appreciatively at the attractive display in the stationer's window as he walked past. And then suddenly came to a halt in bewilderment.

Eight

....

For two weeks Rosalie had been living on cloud nine.

As she filled the postcard stand with fresh cards that morning, humming as she did so, she couldn't help admiring the big poster that was hanging on the wall behind the till.

It showed a big, blue tiger—the illustration from the title page of *The Blue Tiger,* the book that had appeared two weeks previously—and at the bottom of the poster you could see two faces, and, written beneath them, two names: MAX MARCHAIS and ROSALIE LAURENT.

She smiled proudly and thought back to the reading that had taken place in Luna Luna three days before. Every seat in the little store had been occupied as Max Marchais presented his new book.

And since the author didn't like reading in public and Rosalie really did, he had gladly left that part to her and simply signed books and answered questions afterward.

The audience had been enthusiastic. Even her mother had sat

there, completely satisfied, and had come up to her daughter after the reading and hugged her with a happy sigh.

"I'm so proud of you, my child," she had said. "If only your father could have been here to see it."

The reading in the store had been set up by Montsignac, the jolly fat publisher. Montsignac thought it would be a nice idea if the book, after the extremely glamorous launch in the publishing house itself and some other events in major bookstores, could also be presented in the place where the illustrations had been produced.

In his humorous introductory speech he had naturally not failed to mention that it had been he—Jean-Paul Montsignac, with his infallible nose for people and talent ("A good publisher immediately recognizes talent")—who had brought these two lovable freelances together (those were his exact words, and Rosalie and Max had looked at one another in astonishment and then grinned conspiratorially).

The publisher from Opale Jeunesse had every reason to be in a good mood. Since *The Blue Tiger* had appeared at the end of August on the very day of Max Marchais's seventieth birthday, the book with its imaginative illustrations had already sold forty thousand copies, and anyone who believed that Max Marchais, the children's author who had been living in seclusion for many years, had been forgotten by his readers had been proved wrong. Praised by reviewers, loved by readers great and small, the book had even been shortlisted for the *Prix littérature de jeunesse*.

"Well, what a birthday present that is, *mon vieil ami*," the beaming Montsignac had said, clapping his old companion on the shoulder. "There are some people who have to be forced to be lucky, eh?" And then he had burst into laughter.

The *vieil ami* had not caught the reference, and so had smiled back, but the person who had beamed the most was Rosalie, who still couldn't believe her luck. Since the launch of the book other publishers had also shown an interest in the young illustrator, and there was already a contract for a postcard book with ten different motifs. The demand for wishing cards had also mushroomed: many people came to Luna Luna because they'd read about it in the papers. If things carried on this way there would be no need to worry about rent raises, thought Rosalie with satisfaction. The only worry was how to cope with all the extra work.

"You should consider hiring someone to help you in the store," René had said to her a few days before as she was sitting at her drawing table until late in the night. "You're working round the clock these days. But everyone knows that the sleep you get before midnight is the most healthy." And then, with a reproachful and concerned expression, he'd given her one of his lectures on the human body and what was good and bad for it.

Good old René! In the last few weeks and months he really hadn't seen much of her. She'd thrown herself into creating the pictures for the tiger book with fiery enthusiasm. The sketches and trial drawings that she made initially had—with the exception of one picture—found favor both with the publisher and the author. She'd traveled to Le Vésinet three times to visit Max Marchais and discuss the selection of the illustrations with him. She appreciated his directness and humor, even if they had not always agreed about the choice of scenes that she wanted to illustrate. Finally they had sat in the delightful garden with its blue hydrangea bushes and eaten a delicious *charlotte aux framboises* that Madame Bonnier, the housekeeper, had baked. Without noticing it, they had begun to tell each other things that had nothing to do with the illustrations and the book. Like a loving couple they couldn't stop recalling the circumstances surrounding their first meeting, and Rosalie had finally confessed to Max that she had at first taken the unfriendly customer who had stumbled into her store on her day off for a crazy old man who talked nonsense and had gotten lost.

Max had then revealed to her that he had at first not been at all enthusiastic about trying out a "dilettante" and that he'd really only visited the rue du Dragon to be able to tell Montsignac with a clear conscience that he found the scribblings of this postcard store owner execrable.

They had both had a good laugh and eventually Rosalie had revealed to Max that blue had always been her favorite color, that—to use her mother's words—she had a real thing about blue, and then she'd looked directly in to his bright eyes and asked: "Do you believe in coincidences, Monsieur Max?" (Although they were becoming increasingly close they had still remained on formal terms.)

Max Marchais had leaned back in his wicker chair with a smile and fished a raspberry from his plate with his fork.

"There's no such thing as coincidence," he had said, adding with a grin, "it's not something I said." He shoved the raspberry into his mouth and swallowed it. "That was said by a far more important man than I am. But anyway it was the first time in my life that I had to knock a postcard stand over to get to know a pretty woman."

"Monsieur Max!" Rosalie had exclaimed in amusement. "Are you flirting with me?"

"Could be," he'd replied. "But I'm afraid I'm years too late.

Tragic!" He shook his head with a deep sigh. "And anyway, you already have a boyfriend. That . . . René Joubert. Hmm. A nice young man . . ."

The way he said that confused her.

"But?" she had asked.

"Well, yes, my dear Rosalie. A nice young man, but he's not the one for you."

"How can you be so sure?"

"My experience of human nature?" he suggested with a laugh. "Perhaps I'm just envious. I'm an old man with a walking stick, Mademoiselle Rosalie, and that sometimes gets on my nerves. But I wasn't always like this, you know. If I were younger I'd risk anything to steal René's pretty girlfriend from him. And I'd bet a bottle of Bollinger that I'd succeed."

"What a shame you can't lose the bet," Rosalie replied cheekily. "I'd like to drink Bollinger someday."

"It's a very fine wine, Mademoiselle Rosalie, you don't just drink it any old how. They say that anyone who hasn't had a sip of that champagne hasn't lived."

"You're making me curious."

"Well, perhaps the occasion will arise," Marchais replied.

And then—it was weeks later, on a hot August day and Rosalie had completely forgotten about the Bollinger question—Max Marchais had called her one morning and asked if she was free that evening, because the occasion had arrived.

"What occasion?" she asked in some confusion.

"Bollinger," he answered drily. "There is something to celebrate!"

"But it's not your birthday yet!" Rosalie had said in surprise, quickly glancing at the calendar to make sure. Marchais's birthday was the last day in August, and that was two weeks away.

"What . . . my birthday?" he'd said in the indignant way she had come to know so well. "Childish nonsense! Now . . . are you free?"

"But why—"

"It's a surprise," he said in a voice that allowed no contradiction. "And wear something pretty: we're going somewhere really high class. I'll pick you up in a taxi."

HE'D INVITED HER TO Le Jules Verne. Le Jules Verne of all places! Rosalie had been too awestruck to react appropriately.

"I hope you don't find this hopelessly old-fashioned," Max Marchais had said somewhat apologetically, as she entered the restaurant at his side, dressed in a plum-blue wild-silk dress. "I don't know what's in in Paris these days."

"Old-fashioned? Are you crazy? Did you know I've always wanted to eat up here?" Her eyes shining, Rosalie had walked over to the table with its white cloth that had been reserved for them in the window and looked out over the lights of the city. The view was breathtaking. She hadn't known that it was so beautiful.

Behind her a soft tinkling sound rang out. A black-coated waiter was carrying a silver champagne bucket over to their table; it contained a dark-green bottle of Bollinger with its gold label, in a bed of thousands of fragments of crushed ice. The waiter dealt skillfully with the bottle, releasing the cork from its neck with a gentle *plop*. After they had sat down and the waiter had poured the champagne into their cut-glass flutes, Max pulled something out of his briefcase: it was wrapped in a paper bag and looked suspiciously like a book.

He put the package down on the table, and Rosalie felt her heart begin to pound. "No!" she exclaimed. "Could that be . . . already? Could it be?"

Max nodded. "The book," he said. "I was sent a prepublication copy yesterday, and thought this would be the perfect occasion to drink a toast with you, my dear Rosalie. In Bollinger, as you wished. Excuse all the cloak-and-dagger stuff. But I thought it would only be right to celebrate this occasion alone with you."

They raised their glasses and clinked them. The clear ringing tone resounded for a moment above the murmured conversations of the guests at the other tables. Max Marchais smiled at her. "To *The Blue Tiger*! And to the wonderful way that he brought us together!"

Then Rosalie had carefully unwrapped the book, stroked the shining cover, which showed an indigo-blue tiger with silver stripes and a friendly catlike grin, and leafed through the pages with appropriate reverence. It had turned out exceptionally beautifully, she thought. Her first book! So that's what it felt like. Rosalie could have sung for joy.

"Are you satisfied?"

"Yes, very," she replied happily. "Very, very satisfied." She leafed back to the title page once more.

"I'd like you to write something in it for me," she said—and that was when she first saw the dedication: FOR R.

"Oh, my goodness!" she said, turning pink with joy. "That's incredibly nice of you. Thank you. Gosh—I just don't know what to say. . . ."

"Don't say anything."

Rosalie was so overjoyed at this proof that she was appreciated that she almost didn't notice the old man's embarrassment as he looked at her with a peculiar smile.

THE EVENING WAS A long one, with delicious food, and when the bottle of Bollinger was empty, Rosalie heard herself saying—to her own astonishment—"Did you know that I actually come here on my birthday every year?"

Max had raised his eyebrows. "What, here? To Le Jules Verne?"

"No, of course not here. I mean to the top of the Eiffel Tower. I had already decided to give it up, and then you walked—or rather fell—into my life." She giggled, already a little tipsy, pushed her hair, which she was wearing loose that evening, from her forehead, and lowered her voice. "I'd like to tell you a secret, Max, but you must promise not to tell anyone. And you mustn't laugh at me even if it sounds a bit childish."

"I'll be as silent as the grave," he assured her. "And I'd never laugh at you. I write children's books, as you are well aware."

And so it came about that Max Marchais, the creator of a blue cloud-tiger that could fly through the night sky and believed in the magic of wishing, became the first person with whom Rosalie shared her Eiffel Tower secret. And of course all the secret wishes that had fluttered down with the postcards—unexpectedly, three of them had been fulfilled in recent months: She had been discovered as an illustrator. Her mother was satisfied for the first time in her life. And she'd been invited to dine in Le Jules Verne—even if not by the man of her dreams.

"But, well . . . ," she ended gaily. "I hope you won't get me wrong, dear Max. I should really be sitting here with my boyfriend, but even so this is lovely as it is."

"I'll take that as a compliment," said Max with a chuckle.

And when they parted on the avenue Gustave-Eiffel later that evening, he said, "So, if I've counted right, the only things still missing are the house by the seaside and a man with a sense of poetry who will give you a silly little padlock for the railing on the bridge." He had twinkled at her. "I'm afraid that will be a real challenge. But don't give up hope."

ROSALIE LOOKED OVER AT the store window, where several copies of *The Blue Tiger* formed part of the display, and had to smile as she thought back to the evening with Max Marchais—now more than three weeks ago. Of course she would never in her life be given a silly little padlock, but that didn't matter. This was one of those days when everything seemed to be going right with the world.

On the street outside she noticed a man who was cursing and wiping something off his shoe—his view of the world at that moment was clearly somewhat more critical. He was tall with dark-blond hair, and he was wearing a light, medium-blue summer pullover under a sand-colored suede jacket as he sauntered past her store. As he did so he cast a fleeting glance at the display, then stopped, and stood in front of the window for a while, staring at it with fascination.

He had the loveliest blue eyes that Rosalie had ever seen—they shone a pure azure blue—and Rosalie stared at the stranger with at least as much fascination as he was staring at the books she had used in her display.

"Not bad," was the thought that shot through her mind, and she caught herself feeling an extremely pleasant buzz as a result.

The man outside the window then frowned and a vertical crease appeared on his forehead. He looked at the display with indignation—possibly even with shock, and Rosalie wondered if there was something there that was not suitable for the display in a stationery-store window: a big tarantula, for example, or maybe a dead mouse.

At that moment William Morris gave a little snort and she looked over toward the basket where her little dog was lying asleep.

When she looked up again, the good-looking stranger had vanished. Rosalie gazed at the empty street, feeling a stab of disappointment that seemed completely uncalled for.

If anyone had told her that only a quarter of an hour later she'd be quarreling bitterly with that apparently likeable man, she would not have believed them.

Nine

....

For years the little silver bell over the door at Luna Luna had done its job perfectly well. Was it coincidence that made it fall off at precisely the moment when the man with the azure-blue eyes whom Rosalie had seen looking at the window display seconds before entered the store?

The door was pushed open, and the little bell produced a clear tinkle and then hurtled to the ground, but not without an intermediate landing on the back of the stranger's head. He started in shock, raising his hands instinctively and stepping aside—straight into the dog basket beside the door. William Morris howled furiously, and the stranger gave a cry of surprise and tumbled backward, straight for the postcard stand.

Stunned, Rosalie watched it rocking wildly, feeling that she was going through a déjà vu experience, but this time she was quicker: with two strides she reached the stand and held it up firmly, while the man, his arms rowing frantically, managed to regain his balance.

"Are you okay?" asked Rosalie.

"For heaven's sake, what was that?!" said the man, rubbing the back of his head. He had an unmistakable American accent, and he looked at her reproachfully. "Something attacked me."

Rosalie bit her lower lip to stop herself laughing. The way he was standing there as if he'd just survived an alien attack was just too funny. She coughed and regained her composure.

"That was the doorbell, monsieur. I'm very sorry—it must have fallen off somehow."

She bent down and picked up the heavy silver bell that had rolled under the table. "Here, you see. That was the fatal missile. The cord has snapped."

"Aha," he said. Her barely concealed amusement had obviously not escaped his notice. "And what's so funny about it?"

"Um . . . nothing," she said. "I'm so sorry. I hope you haven't been hurt."

"It's all right." He drew himself up to his full height, looking at her suspiciously. "And what was that infernal row?"

"That was my dog," she explained, feeling a laugh about to burst out again. She turned away and pointed to the dog basket, where William Morris was now lying asleep like Snow White. "He's normally very peaceful. You scared him."

"I'd say it was he who scared me," retorted the American. Nevertheless he allowed himself a brief smile before saying with a frown: "Are you actually allowed to keep a dog in a store? I mean, isn't it dangerous?"

That morning Rosalie had decided that it was a particularly lovely day, and that she was feeling particularly lovely herself. She was wearing her favorite dress—a bright millefiori dress with tiny blue flowers, a round neckline, and a little row of cloth-covered buttons. She was wearing sky-blue ballerina slippers and her only adornment was a pair of turquoise earrings that swung jauntily back and forth. She had no intention of letting her mood be spoiled by anyone—certainly not by a tourist with a dog phobia. She stood in front of the man in the suede jacket, crossed her arms behind her back, and gave him a sweet smile—but one to be enjoyed at his peril. Her eyes sparkled as she asked, "You're not from here, are you, monsieur?"

"No, I'm from New York," he explained.

"Aaaah," she said, raising her eyebrows. "An American! Well, monsieur, perhaps you should know that in Paris it's quite normal to have your dog in your store. *C'est tout à fait normal.* We have a more relaxed view of things here. Come to think of it, all the shops I know have dogs in them," she lied.

"Oh, really?" said the man from New York. "I suppose that explains the lamentable state of your streets. I hope it wasn't your sweet little dog who produced the sweet little mess that I just trod in."

Rosalie looked at his brown suede shoes and suddenly became aware of the acrid smell of dog poop.

"You're right, it's still a bit smelly," she said, smiling even more broadly. "But I can assure you that my dog had nothing to do with it. He's already done his business in the park."

"That's reassuring. Then I'd better not go for a walk in the park today."

"As you wish. But here we say that it's lucky to step in dog mess."

"Nobody needs that much luck," he retorted, the corners of

his mouth twisting sardonically. "Anyway . . ." He looked around the shop as if searching for something, and Rosalie decided to change the subject.

"How can I help you, monsieur?"

"You have a book there in your window display," he said, taking a random paperweight from the table and weighing it in his hand. "*The Blue Tiger.* I'd like to take a look at it."

"Of course, monsieur," fluted Rosalie, and then she went to the counter and took one of the books from the pile. "Here you are." She handed him the book and pointed to the only chair in the store—in the corner near the counter. "You can sit down if you like."

He took the book, flopped into the chair, and crossed his legs. Rosalie saw that his eye was momentarily caught by the big poster behind the counter.

He looked over at her and raised his eyebrows in some surprise.

"Is that *your* book?"

She nodded proudly. "You could say so. I made it together with Max Marchais. He's a very well-known children's author in France; I'm the illustrator." All at once she felt it would be right and proper to introduce herself. "Rosalie Laurent," she said.

He nodded briefly in her direction, and then obviously felt obliged to give her his name.

"Robert Sherman," he replied curtly and opened the book.

"We had a reading here in the store two days ago. Do you know Max Marchais?" asked Rosalie with interest.

The American shook his head and immersed himself in the pages.

Rosalie leaned on the counter, observing him unobtrusively. Robert Sherman seemed both nonplussed and keyed up at the same time, as he ran his fingers through his curly, dark-blond hair. He had shapely, sinewy hands with long fingers. She saw his eyes flickering back and forth, she noticed the vertical crease between his eyebrows, his straight, somewhat fleshy nose, the mouth that was pursed in concentration as he read, and the little dimple in his chin. The way he read and leafed through the pages led her to believe that he often had a book in his hands. Perhaps he worked at the university. Or in publishing, she suddenly thought. Perhaps he was a publisher like Montsignac, on the lookout for a good children's book? She thought for a moment and then rejected the idea. Too unlikely. He was probably just an American tourist spending his summer vacation in Paris who was looking for a present for his child.

"Are you looking for a present for your child?" she blurted out, hurriedly adding: "The book is admirably suited for children from five upwards. And you also learn a bit about Paris"— she tried to see it from a tourist's point of view—"the Eiffel Tower, the bois de Boulogne—"

"No, no, I don't have any children," he interrupted irritably. He shook his head again, and she could see his expression darkening.

Didn't he like the story? But if so, why was he reading every page almost compulsively? Peculiar. That was what her gut feeling told her. Peculiar. This Monsieur Sherman from New York was a little strange, she decided as the door opened again and a new customer came in. It was Madame de Rougemont, an elderly lady from the 7th arrondissement who never left her house without gloves and always wore her chin-length, ash-blond, dyed hair in carefully arranged waves. If Grace Kelly hadn't been killed so early on she would definitely have looked like Madame de Rougemont when she got older. Almost every week the old lady came to the rue du Dragon and bought something in Luna Luna; Rosalie wished her a friendly good day.

"Oh," said Madame de Rougemont. "Your doorbell's not working." She looked up with interest to where the remains of the broken cord were hanging.

"No." Rosalie looked a little embarrassedly toward the man in the chair. "The bell . . . well the bell unfortunately gave up the ghost and made a break for it, you might say." No reaction from the chair. "What can I do for you, Madame de Rougemont?"

The old lady smiled and spread her delicate hands in their openwork, cream leather gloves. "Oh, my dear, I'm just browsing. I need a present for a friend and some pretty cards. You always have such lovely things it's really difficult to decide." She swept the table with the writing materials, postcard boxes, and accessories with a glance, and looked curiously at the frowning gentleman in the suede jacket who was still reading *The Blue Tiger* and had paid not the slightest attention to her arrival.

"The reading on Wednesday was really charming," she said, a little louder than necessary. "A wonderful book. So . . . magical, isn't it? I bought it straight away for my little niece. She has a lively imagination, just like little Héloïse in your story."

While Madame de Rougemont tripped over to the card stands and absent-mindedly pulled out a couple of cards, Rosalie sat down on her revolving chair behind the counter and looked over expectantly at her other customer, who was still reading. Suddenly the man in the chair clapped the book shut with a bang and stood up abruptly.

"And . . . do you like the story?" asked Rosalie. For some reason she would have found it nice if the taciturn American had been enthusiastic about the story—and above all the illustrations, of course.

Robert Sherman fixed his eyes on her, and Rosalie was almost a little scared when she saw the restrained anger flashing in them.

"Well, Mademoiselle . . . Laurent," he replied slowly. "I like the story very much. I might even say *extraordinarily* much. You know, I *love* the story of the blue tiger. For reasons I do not have the slightest inclination to explain here, it is a very important story for me. The funny thing is that I already know it."

"What . . . what do you mean?" asked Rosalie, who didn't have the first idea what he was getting at.

"Just what I say. I've known this story for many years. Since I was five, to be exact. It is, if you will, my story." He slammed the book down on the counter making Rosalie start with shock. "And I wonder how shameless someone has to be to copy a story word for word and then publish it as their own?!"

"But . . . Monsieur Sherman! That cannot be. What are you talking about?" Rosalie responded in disbelief. "Max Marchais wrote that story and the book has only just appeared. So there's no way you can already know it. I'm sure you're making some kind of a mistake."

"*I'm* making a mistake?" he repeated furiously, turning pale with anger. "Don't try that with me. Do you know what this is called? Theft of intellectual property, Mademoiselle Laurent!"

Rosalie slipped down from her revolving chair and supported herself on the counter with both hands. "*Attends!* Just stop right there, monsieur. You just waltz in here and claim that Max Marchais is a thief? Who are you, anyway? Are you trying to claim that one of the best-known children's authors in France needs to steal anyone's ideas? Why should he?"

"Well, it probably wouldn't be the first time something like that has happened. Perhaps the good Monsieur Marchais has just run out of ideas."

Rosalie felt herself going red. She was not going to allow this jumped-up American to insult the author she admired so much.

"Monsieur Sherman, that will do! I know Max Marchais personally, and I can assure you that he's an absolutely honest and honorable person. Your accusations are totally fanciful."

"Oh yes? Is that so? Well, you're probably both in this together."

"You cannot be serious!" Rosalie gasped for air. "Do you know what, Monsieur Sherman? You're probably suffering from paranoia," she spat crossly. "Americans are well known for their tendency to believe the most far-fetched conspiracy theories."

"A little less prejudice if you please, mademoiselle! Why don't you ask your honorable Monsieur Marchais where he got his story?" His tone was poisonous.

Rosalie stared at Robert Sherman with as much distaste as if he had just transformed himself from Dr. Jekyll into Mr. Hyde. How could she have imagined even for a second that this obnoxious jerk was attractive?

"I'll do that, monsieur, don't you worry. And I already know the answer." Rosalie angrily swished her long braid over her shoulder.

"Well, I hope you don't have a nasty experience. Because I can *prove* that the story belongs to me."

Rosalie rolled her eyes and put a hand to her forehead. She was clearly dealing with one of those people who was always right.

"Okay. I see," she said ironically. "That's fine. You can prove it. Is that all, or is there anything else I can do for you?"

"No, I'm afraid that's not all, not by a long shot. You can't fob me off like that. I'll take you to court. I'm an attorney with Sherman and Sons, and you'll be hearing from me!"

"I can hardly wait!" Goodness, he was a crazy lawyer. She might have realized. She watched him with a cold smile as he took his wallet out of his jacket pocket, pulled out a fifty-euro bill, threw it on the counter, and snatched up the book.

"Keep the change," he snarled.

"Hello?! Who do you think you are? Don't they teach you any manners where you come from? You're not in a burger bar here, monsieur. Keep your stupid money and stop your imperialistic posturing. You can have the book for free!" shouted Rosalie and threw the bill at him. It sailed unnoticed to the tiled floor.

At that moment something clattered. Madame de Rougemont had just dropped a box of postcards in shock.

"It's nothing," said the old lady, frozen like a pillar of salt as two pairs of enraged eyes turned toward her. "Nothing. Please don't let me interrupt."

Robert Sherman turned back to the counter.

"Imperialistic? Well, well. I don't know your views on the matter, Mademoiselle Laurent, but I at least pay for things that don't belong to me," he responded bitingly. "Have you ever heard of copyright? Or are you a bit more relaxed about that as well in France?"

"Now you've gone too far! Get out, this minute!" cried Rosalie, her voice beginning to crack.

William Morris was no longer feeling comfortable in his basket. Things had definitely gotten too loud. He gave a jerk and began to bark excitedly as he heard the shrill tones of his mistress.

It could be that Robert Sherman was taking "this minute" too literally. Could be that the little dog got in his way, yapping and circling round him like the Indians did round the cowboys' covered wagons in the Old West. Whatever it was, the American, in trying to storm out of the store and at the same time avoid the little yelping beast, managed to pull over one of the postcard stands, which fell to the ground behind him with a thunderous crash.

"Damned mutt!" cursed Sherman as he, without even turning round, flung open the door and stormed out into the street.

"Oh great!" said Rosalie. "What a performance!" With a few strides she reached the door. "Idiot!" she screamed after the man in the suede jacket as his long strides took him away into the distance.

Ten

....

Robert Sherman couldn't remember when he'd last been so angry. The buildup of adrenaline in his body was phenomenal.

With great strides he stamped down along the rue du Dragon toward the boulevard Saint-Germain, his eyes fixed on the ground—and not just on the lookout for possible dog piles. Perhaps Rachel had not been so unfair in her opinion of Frenchwomen. How uppity and insolent that little salesgirl had been! "We're not in a burger bar!" "Don't they teach you manners where you come from?" As if he were some kind of uncouth klutz from the Midwest!

He shook his head. She had looked at him with her big, dark eyes and made a total mockery of him. "'We're a bit more *relaxed* about things like that here, monsieur!'" he muttered indignantly to himself. Such arrogance! As if he were nothing but an uptight petit bourgeois and she, as a Frenchwoman, had a monopoly on the free spirit. *Liberté toujours,* was that it? Dog poop and plagiarism—he could well do without that sort of freedom of spirit!

"Stupid French cow!" he burst out furiously, almost bumping into a woman who was coming toward him along the narrow sidewalk with her shopping, trailing a little boy behind her.

The woman looked at him disapprovingly and he heard the boy asking, "What's wrong with the man, Maman?"

Yes, what was wrong with the man? Robert clutched the book to himself and tramped on. That Rosalie Laurent hadn't even felt it necessary to apologize. Not when the bell fell on his head, not when that little yappy beast attacked him. Attacked him *twice*! Just think of that! He could be glad that he hadn't been bitten, as he had that time as a child when the Millers' fox terrier from next door had jumped up at him and bitten his lip, and he'd fainted for the first time in his life. Ever since then he'd been wary of those little yapping creatures: they were particularly devious. A good thing he'd been quick enough, otherwise he'd have had to see about a tetanus injection! He could already see the nurse—who looked strikingly like the owner of the postcard store—tapping on a syringe of dubious quality, her eyebrows raised ironically. "We're more relaxed about these things here, monsieur."

Why did these words get to him so much? Perhaps because it was evidence of a laxity that made a mockery of any kind of discernment and responsibility. The business with the book was really beyond belief!

He'd seen it in the window display totally by chance, and a strange mixture of curiosity and confusion had made his heart beat faster. When he entered the little store, he had nearly fallen over. And when he left in a hurry as well. He could have seriously injured himself. Not to mention all the rest.

But that didn't bother the stationery store's owner—who

obviously had no problem adorning herself with borrowed plumes—in the slightest. Instead, she'd shouted "idiot" after him—he'd heard it quite clearly.

The safety regulations in this city left a lot to be desired, in Robert's opinion. And the politeness!

He turned onto the boulevard Saint-Germain and marched automatically in the direction of the Sorbonne. He'd actually originally intended to take a look around the university campus. In the next few days he wanted to arrange a meeting with the dean. But for some reason he wasn't particularly interested in the Sorbonne at this moment. The unexpected discovery of the book had stirred him up at least as much as the store owner's reaction had enraged him.

The exercise did him good. Gradually his strides slowed down and his heartbeat became calmer. He left the noisy boulevard and turned into the bustle of the little streets of the Latin Quarter.

When he came to Paris, he'd been expecting anything and everything. It was going to be a time out. He wanted to think about all the things that were worrying him, at leisure and without any outside influence. He'd wanted to look around this city that was no more to him than a childhood memory. He wanted to climb the Eiffel Tower once more in memory of his mother. He wanted—of course!—to go to Shakespeare and Company, to browse among the books and imbibe the atmosphere of that almost vanished time when literature still moved worlds.

After his difficult departure from Mount Kisco and all the hassle at home he'd hoped for a few summery, untroubled days far away from everything, maybe even an innocent little flirtation—yes, that too! In the city on the Seine he'd hoped to rediscover all the lightheartedness that had somehow gotten lost from his life. He'd hoped to find answers to his questions, clarity, a positive decision. And behind everything, like a promise, shimmered his mother's words: "Paris is always a good idea."

He'd reckoned on just about everything as he took the taxi from Orly Airport into Paris early in the morning, thought Robert Sherman meditatively, as he sat a little while later outside a small café, with rickety wooden chairs, that would certainly not find a mention in any guidebook.

But not on finding *The Blue Tiger* in the window display of a stationer's in Saint-Germain.

Since his childhood the story of the blue tiger had been as familiar to him as his old teddy bear, Willie. When he was a little boy his mother had told him the story at bedtime evening after evening. He loved the story and never tired of hearing it, even though he knew in advance what each of the characters was going to say. If his mother occasionally tried to shorten the story a little because she and Dad had been invited out to dinner, Robert immediately noticed. "Mommy, you've forgotten to say that they met in the Grotto of the Four Winds," he would say. Or: "But Mommy, the painting bag was red and not green." No detail could be left out; he insisted on every little thing. For many years the story of the blue tiger was a fixed part of his bedtime ritual, and even when other books lined his shelves it remained his favorite story. When they came to the part where Héloïse flies over Paris on the tiger and her fluttering golden hair glistens like a falling star, his mother always paused and looked at him meaningfully. "When you see a shooting star, you can make a wish," she would say. "Come on, let's make a wish!" And then they would hold hands and each of them would make a silent wish.

Remarkable how the things you experience as a child influence you even many years later, thought Robert. Even today, as a man in his late thirties he still automatically looked out for shooting stars on clear summer nights. However, in Manhattan they were very hard to find—or rather you never found them, because the city lights and the exhaust fumes so polluted the sky that there were hardly ever any clear, starry nights.

Robert took a sip from the thick white cup that the graceful girl with the ponytail who served him had put on the little round table with a friendly smile and a glass of water, and he had automatically smiled back.

Not all Frenchwomen were bitches, he corrected himself, as he leaned back in his chair, raising his face to the sun.

He looked at the book, suddenly remembering how, as a young boy, he had asked one evening if the story of the blue tiger was a book as well. But his mother had shaken her head and said that this story belonged just to the two of them, and that she would give it to him. And that was what she had done, many years later.

Robert had a lump in his throat as he remembered how, in the thick brown envelope the lawyer had handed over to him after her death, he had found the manuscript, in a blue binding, among all kinds of papers, documents, and old photographs.

On the flyleaf were the words *The Blue Tiger*. And beneath them, *For R.* His mother had attached a note to the manuscript. In her familiar round handwriting with the oversize up and down strokes she had written:

For my dear Robert in memory of the many evenings we spent with our friend the tiger. They were infinitely precious to me.

He was no longer a little boy when he found the story in the envelope, but at the sight of the manuscript, which was like a final farewell from his mother, his eyes filled with tears.

The time had come when he was too old for bedtime stories. That was when she had probably written it all down for him, every detail. Moved, he'd leafed through the pages, which had been written on an old-fashioned typewriter, and read the story once again after such a long time. It had been pleasant and sad, just as it is always pleasant and sad when you return to a place that you once loved very much and discover that nothing stays the way it once was.

It reminded him of what his mother had said in her last moments. "I'm going to a country that is so far away that you can't get there by plane," she had said. But it was only when he had the manuscript in his hand that it became clear to him that the words referred to part of the story.

And then he'd stood in front of a stationer's window a few hours ago, in a foreign city, on a foreign continent, and suddenly seen this book. This book that couldn't actually exist, because only two people knew the story and the only manuscript was in a brown envelope almost four thousand miles away.

It had left him speechless.

Confused, he'd first carried on for a few paces, then turned around to make sure.

When he asked to see the book, written by the famous children's author, an elderly man with a beard and gray, neatly combed hair, as he could see from the big poster for the reading in the stationery store, he'd still thought that it must be a totally different story that just happened to have the same title. But then he'd begun to read, and after just a few sentences he knew it was the story his mother had left him.

He felt he'd been robbed—yes, robbed was the right word! Like someone who comes home to find that his apartment has been burgled. Powerless and furious at the same time.

Someone had taken possession of his precious memory and thrown it on the marketplace to make a profit out of it. Robert could not as yet explain how that could have come about, but he'd find out. He would defend his rights. You didn't have to be an expert in copyright law to recognize immediately that the whole affair stank to high heaven.

He picked the book up again and leafed through it. He actually found the brightly colored illustrations painted by the young woman with the braid who had abused him so insolently pleasing, but that didn't make it any better. However this supposedly so-honest French author had gotten hold of the story of the blue tiger, he had brazenly copied it. Unfortunately that was how it was these days. People had no respect for intellectual property. At least you learned in college that you should always identify your sources. All the rest was copy and paste, and most people seemed to find that perfectly normal. But in this case they were definitely taking it too far. "You don't have to put up with everything," his father had often said. And he had been right.

For the first time in his life Robert Sherman was glad that he came from a family of lawyers. He knew his way around. He sat in the sun for a while longer, feeling his body giving in to exhaustion and getting heavier and heavier. All at once he was seized by such weariness that he almost fell asleep there on the wooden chair. Jet lag and the aggravations of the day were taking their toll.

He finished his café crème, which had already gone cold, took a few coins out of his pocket, put them on the table, and decided to return to his hotel. On the way he'd have a meal somewhere.

It was five thirty when he set off, actually too early to dine in Paris, but all the hassle had made him hungry. What he needed now was a good steak and a glass of red wine. He'd go to bed early and let Rachel know that he'd arrived safely. And the next day he'd check that Marchais guy out much more thoroughly. He wouldn't expect much help from Mademoiselle Laurent in that respect.

As he strolled along the rue Saint-Benoît, a little street leading to the rue Jacob where his hotel was, he noticed some people standing chatting outside a restaurant—from inside came the tempting smell of well-grilled meat. Without much thought, he joined the line.

LE RELAIS DE L'ENTRECÔTE was a classic *steak-frites* restaurant. To be more precise, they only had steak and fries, but they were excellent. Robert found that the lemony sauce they served with the meat took a little getting used to at first, but then it grew on him; the *pommes frites* were crisp and fried a golden brown and the meat was well seasoned and tender. The first part of the evening—if you ignored the fact that an overzealous waiter whipped his plate away from under his nose as soon as Robert intimated that he didn't want any dessert—could be regarded as a success. He'd drunk two glasses of red wine that had rolled strong and smooth over his tongue, he'd eaten well, and he was now looking forward to his bed. But that was when the second part of the evening began. With a check that was quite affordable—and yet not affordable, at least not for someone whose wallet had vanished.

With increasing nervousness Robert had felt in all the pockets in his pants and jacket while the waiter stood beside the table demonstrating an exquisite combination of impatience and arrogance and the next guests were already waiting to be seated.

"I don't believe it!" Robert flushed at the thought that it wasn't just his money that was in his wallet, but also all his cards. After all the problems with his room that morning, followed by the problems with the elevator—had it only been that same morning?!—he'd completely forgotten to put some of his valuables and some cash in the safe in his room as he usually did. Where was his bloody wallet?

It was normally in the inside pocket of his jacket, but there was nothing there. All of a sudden he was completely awake and alert. This was the day for adrenaline rushes, that much was clear. He tried to explain to the irritated waiter that he was not a con-man who was trying to eat out for nothing, but an American tourist who'd had quite a lot of hassle on his first day in Paris.

"My wallet's gone!" he explained with a look of panic.

The waiter showed little sympathy. He simply responded, *"Alors, monsieur!"* shrugged his shoulders and seemed still to be expecting monsieur to conjure his wallet out of thin air.

With some effort he managed to scrape together a ten-euro bill and a few coins that he had loose in his pockets. The total came to nineteen euros and fifty cents.

"C'est tout!" he declared. "I don't have any more."

The waiter remained stony faced. Robert was just about to offer him his watch—it was, after all, his father's old TAG

Heuer—when it suddenly came to him where he had lost his wallet.

He jumped up, grabbed his jacket from the back of the chair, and shouted to the nonplussed waiter:

"Wait! I'll be right back. *Je reviens!*"

When he arrived, totally breathless, outside the little post-card store in the rue du Dragon, it was a quarter past seven. The wide-mesh steel shutters had been let down in front of the display window and the entrance, but there was still a light burning in the store.

Robert saw a slim form in a flowery summer dress with a long braid leaning over the cash register, and he leaned his forehead against the shutter for a moment in relief. Thank God, she was still there. He hammered at the door like a madman.

"Mademoiselle Laurent! Mademoiselle Laurent! Open up! I forgot something!"

She looked up, started, and came to the door. He felt something almost like a wave of happiness as she swept toward him and looked at him through the glass with her big eyes.

When she saw that it was him, she narrowed her eyes like a cat and shook her head energetically.

"Hey, mademoiselle, you have to let me in, it's important!"

She raised her eyebrows. Then, with a triumphant smile, she turned the sign that was hanging inside the door.

It said FERMÉ. Closed. She shrugged her shoulders like a mime and pointed to the sign.

Adrenaline rush!

"Dammit, I can see that you're closed, I'm not stupid," he shouted, rattling the shutter. With a cold smile, the silly cow then actually left him standing outside the door. He watched as she went back to the counter in perfect calm.

"Hey! Open up! Dammit, my wallet is still in the store. I want my wallet—now, do you hear?"

It was quite obvious that Rosalie Laurent didn't have the slightest desire to hear him. She turned round briefly and showed Robert Sherman her middle finger with a malicious smile, then turned out the light and disappeared up the little spiral staircase.

THAT NIGHT ROBERT SHERMAN slept like a dead man. After going straight back to the Hôtel des Marronniers and dragging himself with heavy tread up the stairs to his little room on the fourth floor (the elevator was still out of order; they'd offered him a free breakfast the next morning as compensation), he'd only had enough energy for a text to Rachel.

Hi, Rachel, I've arrived safely. Paris is full of surprises, puzzles, and arrogant people. I lost my wallet and made the acquaintance of a real French bitch. More tomorrow. Dead tired, love Robert

It was stifling in the room. Robert opened the window wide and turned out the light. In the darkness the stone wall, looming pale gray a couple of yards from his window, looked like an outsize cinema screen.

Eleven

....

That evening Rosalie sat for a long time beneath her window on the roof, with her legs folded under her and a glass of red wine, and thought over her strange day. The night was mild and a pale moon was hiding behind a delicate dark-gray cloud.

René had already gone to bed.

"Don't worry about it, that crazy American will soon come to his senses. He's completely off his head. But if it gets to you, then just call Marchais and ask him." He'd ruffled her hair with his hand. "Come to bed soon, *chérie,* okay?"

Rosalie had nodded, slid a little farther down the wall, and leaned her head against it. It would have been the perfect moment for a cigarette, but under René's good influence she'd given up smoking. Or at least tried, which meant that she rarely had cigarettes in the house.

She sighed and gazed up at the night sky. It was astonishing, the turn the day had taken, a day that had begun so well. Her elation of the morning had given way to utter confusion.

That dreadful American had actually returned shortly after seven and raged and shouted up and down outside her store. She'd hardly understood a word, but she realized that he wanted to get into the store at all costs. And clearly not to apologize to her. Perhaps he already had his statement of claim with him!

She giggled with satisfaction as she recalled how dumbfounded Robert Sherman had looked when he realized that she didn't intend to open the store again for him.

After Sherman had given the shutters a final shake and then retreated in a shower of wild imprecations, which had fortunately only reached her in muffled form upstairs in her little apartment, it had become clear to her that the man was a choleric and obviously right out of control. Well, that wasn't going to be her problem.

"A pity I hadn't come back by then," René had said as Rosalie told him at dinner that evening about the American psychopath who, in his state of perpetual agitation, had harassed her twice already that day, after first accusing her of plagiarism and then knocking the postcard stand over in a fit of rage. "I would have shown the guy what's what. I'd have enjoyed it."

Yeah, pity, thought Rosalie, taking a gulp of red wine. A rumble between René—strong, athletic, and fitness trained, and Sherman—tall, lanky, and not looking exactly as if he played for the legendary New York Yankees, would definitely have calmed things down very quickly. Still, it was all very strange. Either the guy really had a screw loose, or . . . The "or" was making her uncomfortable. It could, after all, no matter how unlikely it seemed, have been deeply felt indignation, righteous anger, so to speak, that had driven the stranger so crazy. At first sight he hadn't looked at all like a lunatic, she had to admit. He'd actually seemed more astonished than anything else.

Either way, the accusation was outrageous. Not to mention the tone of voice it was delivered in.

Try as she might, Rosalie could not imagine Max Marchais copying someone else's story. She still clearly remembered the evening in Le Jules Verne when he'd given her the first copy of *The Blue Tiger,* and how proud and moved she'd been by the "For R." And his embarrassment as she thanked him for the dedication.

She shook her head. No one could be so deceitful. She thought of the old author's eyes, how they had suddenly lit up. No one dishonest could look like that.

Then she sat bolt upright, because something had struck her. Hadn't that Sherman guy said that he'd known the story for years—"since I was five, to be exact"? She guessed he was about thirty. Yet Max Marchais had sent her a very modern computer printout, which could only mean that the story was not one that anyone could have known since he was five. And what exactly did he mean by saying that the story was his? Had the arrogant attorney written the story himself when he was five? None of it made any sense.

She leaned forward, wrapping her arms round her knees. Unless . . . unless there was a common source they had both had access to. It was always possible that there was an old fable about a blue tiger. She nodded pensively, then wrinkled her brow again. Even if that was the case, the stories could not have been, as that arrogant New Yorker insisted, identical word for word.

Rosalie felt her thoughts beginning to get muddled. She was probably racking her brains for no good reason at all. René was right. First thing the next morning she would call Max Marchais to sort the matter out. But she'd have to approach it very sensitively—after all, she didn't want to antagonize the old man.

There was probably very little likelihood that the madman would turn up at the store again, but you never knew. She finished her red wine and climbed back through the window into the apartment.

By the time she closed her eyes to sleep, the following entry was in her blue notebook:

The worst moment of the day:

The number of strange men who come into the store and knock over the postcard stands is increasing alarmingly. Today there was a horrible American who was rude to me and is going to sue me because *The Blue Tiger* has apparently been plagiarized.

The best moment of the day:

Monsieur Montsignac called and asked me if I would illustrate a book of fairy tales for his company. A really big contract. I said yes.

Twelve

....

Marie-Hélène had been in the house all morning, making a hell of a din. Her excessive bustling derived from a certain basic nervousness that was itself based on the fact that she was intending to go away for two weeks. She and her husband wanted to go to Plan-d'Orgon, their home village near Les Baux, where the rest of her family lived—especially her eldest daughter, who had just had a baby.

"Just think—I'm going to be a grandma, Monsieur Marchais!"

Max couldn't remember how many times he'd heard those words over the last few months, coupled with reports on the current state of mother and child. Three days previously, the daughter had actually given birth to little Claire ("she weighs seven pounds twelve ounces, monsieur, and she can already smile"), and Marie-Hélène Bonnier was beside herself with delight and announced to him that she was going to Plan-d'Orgon that weekend and that he would unfortunately have to look after himself for two weeks.

"You will be all right, won't you, Monsieur Marchais?" she had asked with concern, wiping her hands on her apron. Over the years, Madame Bonnier had developed the illusion that he would be completely at a loss if she didn't shop, cook, and clean for him three times a week.

"Of course I'll be all right, Marie-Hélène; after all, I'm not in my dotage yet—am I?"

"That may well be, but you're a man, Monsieur Marchais, and it simply isn't good when a man is left alone in the house, everyone knows that. He doesn't eat properly, the papers pile up, the dishes are left in the sink, and everything goes to pot."

"You're exaggerating as usual, Marie-Hélène," said Max, burying himself in his newspaper. "I can assure you that the house will still be standing in two weeks' time."

Even so the housekeeper had insisted on coming again the Friday before her departure and going over the rooms, doing the washing and freezing some meals that he would only need to thaw and heat up. On the counter there were at least fifteen Tupperware containers that she'd filled so that he wouldn't starve during her two weeks away.

Max had nodded resignedly. There was no point at all arguing with his housekeeper and explaining to her that he was perfectly capable of frying himself an egg or going into the village to eat a snack in the Bar du Marché. Which would even have been quite useful, because that way he could buy himself some pain relief gel from the pharmacy next door.

That morning he had woken up early with a rather unpleasant pain in his shoulder. He'd probably been lying awkwardly. That's how it was. In the mornings you woke up earlier and something was always hurting.

Max Marchais stretched out luxuriously in the bathtub and listened to Marie-Hélène rampaging around, zealously vacuuming the carpets. The bathroom was his only refuge.

A few minutes later Madame Bonnier was audibly bustling about outside the bathroom door. After a while she called out: "How long are you going to be, Monsieur Marchais?"

With a sigh he climbed out of the green shimmering water—like every morning, he'd put in two scoops of Aramis, his favorite bath salts—and got dressed.

Later on she drove him out of the kitchen, then the library. There were hums and bangs, mops clattered on wooden flooring; something in the kitchen fell with a rattle. The whole house smelled of orange cleaning fluid, mingled with the scent of freshly baked cake. Marie-Hélène seemed to have mastered the miraculous art of bilocation: wherever he retreated to, she would appear a minute or so later, armed with vacuum, mop pail, and dusters.

When she finally began to clean the windows in his office, Max took a book down from one of the top shelves with the aid of the library ladder and fled outdoors to sit in the shade in the garden. The sun was shining and it was already pleasantly warm as he immersed himself in Blaise Pascal's *Pensées,* a book whose pithy sayings about life he always enjoyed reading. It was Blaise Pascal, too, who had said that "all of humanity's problems stem from man's inability to sit quietly in a room alone."

A wise and insightful remark, which was even more relevant when you were prevented from being alone in a room, thought Max as the howling of the vacuum came to a stop. Seconds later his housekeeper appeared on the terrace, looking around as if searching for something. "Monsieur Marchais?" she called, and he raised his head reluctantly to see that she had something in her hand.

"Telephone for you!"

IT WAS ROSALIE LAURENT—her voice sounded a bit strange, he thought. Like the voice of someone trying to sound as normal as possible.

"*Bonjour,* Max! How are you? I hope I'm not disturbing you."

"Not at all," he said. "My housekeeper's been rampaging around the house since seven o'clock. There's nowhere to hide here, so I've retreated to the garden." He heard her laugh. "And how are you, Rosalie? Everything okay?"

"Oh yes, I'm fine." She hesitated a moment before continuing. "Montsignac called yesterday. He wants me to illustrate a big book of fairy tales for him."

"Congratulations! That's great!" Perhaps she wanted to ask him something, he thought.

"And it's all because of you. And *The Blue Tiger,* of course."

"No false modesty, Mademoiselle Rosalie. Your illustrations are simply excellent." He put Pascal down beside him and leaned comfortably back in his wicker chair as she told him about her new book project and his thoughts wandered a little.

Whenever he talked to Rosalie Laurent, and she shared the little things that made up her day, asked him something, or requested advice, he felt revitalized. Since their collaboration on the book, they had met regularly: sometimes she came to Le Vésinet, at others he took the RER train to Paris and they went for coffee or took her little dog for a walk.

Since Marguerite's death his life had been lonely; for a long time he hadn't really noticed it, and when he finally did, it hadn't bothered him much. He'd entrenched himself with his books and thoughts behind a wall not unlike the stone wall around his garden. But since his friendship with this young woman he sensed something new developing that was gradually putting the past in its place, making it really something that was past. Cracks were appearing in the old wall, and light was shining through the cracks.

Rosalie had entered his life like a ray of light, and to his great surprise Max Marchais realized that he'd begun to look to the future and make plans again.

The hum of the vacuum cleaner boomed out of the house, then gradually moved away, and Max gazed at the roses in his garden, which were still in bloom.

"I'm so happy every morning when I see the book in the display window," he heard Rosalie saying—she seemed somehow to have returned to the subject of *The Blue Tiger*. "How did you actually get the story?" She corrected herself hastily. "I mean, how does someone get an idea like that?"

Max returned from his musing and considered for a moment. "Hmm—the way you always get a story. You see or hear something, there's a thought in the air, you go for a walk in the bois de Boulogne and suddenly you begin to weave a story. There's always a particular moment that triggers the story and sets it in motion." He paused for thought. "It could be a sentence or a conversation. . . ." He fell silent.

"And what triggered your story?"

"Well . . ." For a moment he thought of telling her the truth, but then rejected the idea. "I'd say it was good old Montsignac," he said, somewhat irrelevantly. "Without his prodding the book certainly wouldn't exist."

She laughed—a bit embarrassedly, it seemed to him. "No, no, that's not what I mean. What I'm wondering is . . . is there perhaps a folk tale that is the basis of the story of the blue tiger?"

Max was taken aback. "Not that I know of," he said. "And if there is, it's not one I'm familiar with."

"Oh."

There was a slight pause.

Max felt a growing sense of unease. What was the real reason for this strange telephone call? He cleared his throat.

"Come on, out with it, Rosalie, what's bothering you?" He finally ended the silence. "You're not asking me these questions for no reason."

And then she actually came to the point and told him—carefully and a little despondently—about the disagreeable incident with the stranger who had turned up in her store and claimed that the story of *The Blue Tiger* had been stolen.

"What utter nonsense," Max Marchais roared. "You don't believe that madman, do you?" He laughed and then shook his head in disbelief at the absurdity of it all. "Well, my dear Rosalie, I beg you, forget this idiocy at once. I can assure you that I am the creator of the story, and you are welcome to tell that to the gentleman from New York if he ever returns. I thought the story up—word by word."

He heard her sigh with relief.

"I never doubted it, Max. It was just that this man insisted he could prove it was his story. He was completely out of it, and even threatened to take us to court."

Max snorted with rage. "Monstrous!"

"His name is Robert Sherman. Do you know him at all?"

"I don't know anyone called Sherman," retorted Max Marchais curtly. "And I have no particular desire to make the acquaintance of this gentleman, who is obviously a lunatic."

And that was that as far as he was concerned. At least, that was what he thought.

Thirteen

....

A ray of sunlight fell diagonally into the room. A summery gust of air swelled the drapes at the window. Robert Sherman blinked and listened to the gentle clattering of crockery, which seemed to be a long way away and didn't disturb the pleasant restfulness that enveloped him. The peace of the morning reminded him of the lazy Sundays of his childhood in Mount Kisco.

He stretched, and tried to find his way back into his dream, which was fading fast. It had been a pleasant dream, from which he'd awoken feeling good. Some woman or other had been in it—he'd been sitting on a bench in a little square with her.

He tried to remember more clearly, but the images were too fleeting for him to catch hold of. Not important. He turned on his side, pulled the bed covers up, and dozed off again. For a few happy moments everything in Robert Sherman's world was in order.

Then the shrill tones of an electric drill shattered the silence.

Robert sat up in bed, yawned, and took a sip of water. He looked at his cell phone and saw that there was a text.

> *Well, my dear, that all sounds very exciting. I hope you'll think again. Didn't I tell you that it was crazy to go to Paris. Shall I transfer some money for you? Love, Rachel*

And then he suddenly remembered everything. The witch from the card store, the book, the steak restaurant, his wallet. All at once he was wide awake and his feeling of well-being had vanished. He glanced at his watch. Ten thirty! He'd slept for almost twelve hours.

It was Friday, his wallet was missing, and the blasted card store opened at eleven.

As, after a hurried breakfast (consisting of strong coffee and a hastily swallowed, though very crisp, croissant), he squeezed past the two workmen who were standing arguing by the elevator with their toolboxes and ran up the sunny rue Bonaparte, he thought of the bossy tone of Rachel's text. Even if it hadn't been the very best of ideas to go to Paris, there was no need to rub it in like that.

IT WAS JUST AFTER eleven when he clicked the latch on the door of Luna Luna and warily entered the store. This time there was no bell to fall on his head—just the dog, who was back lying in his basket, and gave him a sleepy growl. As a precaution, Robert took a step to the side.

There were no customers in the store yet. Rosalie Laurent,

who was sorting something on one of the shelves by the wall, turned round.

"Oh, no. Not you again!" she said, rolling her eyes.

"Yes, it's me again," he replied sharply. "Unfortunately you wouldn't let me in yesterday evening." At the thought of the way she'd left him standing outside the door the previous evening and how he'd made a fool of himself shouting on the open street, he felt a cold rage rising within him.

"I think we have a little matter to sort out," he said.

"Oh yes?" Her smile was pure provocation. "What brings you to me today, Monsieur Sherman? Have you taken out a summons already, or did you just want to knock another postcard stand over?" She raised her dark, prettily curved eyebrows.

He took a deep breath. There was no point picking a quarrel with this little postcard cow. He had to remain in control. He was a professor of literature and he knew his Shakespeare. "First things first."

"Neither," he said as calmly as possible. "I would just like my wallet back."

She laid her head to one side. "Aha. Interesting. And what has that to do with me?" She was obviously *trying* to be difficult.

"Well," he looked studiously past her at the table with the till where a few leaflets were lying. "I assume that I forgot it here."

"Is that why you tried to break my door down last night?" She smiled sardonically.

"Does that surprise you? I mean, you lock the door in my face and show me your middle finger. If that's what passes for fine French manners—"

"It was already locked, monsieur." She took a step toward

him, looking him up and down with her dark eyes. "Do you know what your problem is? You obviously have the greatest difficulty taking no for an answer."

"No, I don't," he said firmly. "At least . . . not normally. But yesterday it was an emergency. I can assure you that it's not particularly amusing to discover in a restaurant that you've lost your money and all your cards."

"Oh, and am I to blame for that, too?" The eyebrows went up again. She was really good at that.

"Well, at any rate it's no wonder that I lost my wallet here in all that kerfuffle."

"'Kerfuffle.' You said it. It took me nearly an hour to remove all the traces of the devastation you caused." She looked at him reproachfully. "I don't suppose you thought of helping me to tidy up all that mess?"

"Can I help it if you keep a little beast in your store to attack your customers?"

"That's ridiculous. Just listen to yourself. Now it's my sweet little William Morris's fault?" Rosalie gave a hoarse laugh.

William Morris heard his name, raised his head with a little whimper, and wagged his tail happily.

"See for yourself. He's a perfectly friendly, sweet little dog. I think you're suffering from paranoia, Monsieur . . . what was your name again . . . Sherman from—New York. And not only where it concerns how dangerous dogs are."

She folded her bare, slim arms over a delicate blue silk blouse with little white polka dots and looked at him pointedly.

Robert Sherman grabbed his forehead. Why on earth had he come back here again? Of course. Because of the wallet.

He shouldn't get sidetracked. This woman was an eternal arguer. The wallet was the most important thing.

"Just give me my wallet, and I'll be off," he said brusquely.

"There's nothing I'd like better," she replied scornfully. "But your wallet just isn't here."

He looked at her suspiciously. For a moment he wondered if this contrary creature with the big, dark eyes was capable of keeping his wallet from him—out of pure spite and to cause him difficulty.

She shook her head as if she'd guessed what he was thinking.

"And no, I'm not just saying that to annoy you, though I must admit that the idea is very tempting."

"I wouldn't put anything past you," he said crossly. Perhaps she was lying anyway. He was 100 percent sure he'd lost his wallet in the store.

"Monsieur!" She stood with arms akimbo. "That's enough of your accusations. After all, I tidied the whole store yesterday—*after* you stomped out and knocked the postcard stand over . . . but I didn't find a wallet. Perhaps you lost it somewhere else. Or someone stole it."

"No, no. That's not possible . . . it *must* be here," he insisted. "The last time I took it out of my pocket was here in this store—when I paid for the book."

"Oh, yes . . . the tiger story. That was stolen from you, too. You're really being dogged by bad luck, monsieur. Perhaps Paris just isn't your city. Perhaps you should just get back to New York as quickly as possible." She took a couple of steps backward and went behind the counter. "But . . . be my guest. You can take another look for yourself." She directed her whole attention to a squared notebook, pretending to write something on it with an aggrieved expression.

Robert looked around and tried to remember what direction he'd taken as he exited so hastily. Had he left the brown leather wallet on the shelf by the counter? But it clearly wasn't there. Or had he still had it in his hand when that yappy little mutt circled round him barking and he fell over the postcard stand in fright? Had the wallet fallen out of his hand without his noticing it in all the commotion?

He looked in every corner of the little store, searched under the big wooden table that stood in the middle, inspected the area around the entrance, and even looked carefully at the window display. But there was no sign of the wallet.

All this time Rosalie Laurent watched him with a bored expression, winding her long hair into a bun that she fastened at the back of her head with a single hairpin.

"Well?" she said, yawning.

"Nothing," he replied, with a shrug of his shoulders.

"I could of course give you the thirty euros you overpaid yesterday," she said, and he might even have accepted the offer, if she hadn't immediately added: "It's not much, but it'll be enough for a Coke and a couple of Big Macs."

"I appreciate your generous offer, but no," he said with a growl. "I'd rather starve than take any money from you."

"Huh. As you wish. Then I'm afraid I can't help you, Monsieur Sherman."

"Oh, it'd be a great help to me if you'd just keep your mouth shut for a moment," he replied. "I'm trying to concentrate."

"*Charmant, charmant,*" she chatted on unperturbed. "That's a favor I'll be glad to do you, monsieur. I've got better things to do than talking to you, you know." She smiled triumphantly. "But you won't find your wallet here, *mal-heu-reuse-ment*."

Robert racked his brains. The way it was looking at the moment, he would really have to accept Rachel's offer. He didn't have a cent in his pockets. And that was not just in the proverbial sense. He would have to work out an emergency plan. Rachel would have to cancel his cards immediately and he would have to go to the consulate to get a replacement passport. He'd ended up in every tourist's favorite nightmare. Except that he hadn't even been mugged.

"Funny, I was absolutely certain . . . ," muttered Robert, more to himself than anyone else, and chewed his knuckles thoughtfully. In the absurd hope of a miracle he stood at the display window and stared at the black-and-white tiled floor.

And the miracle happened.

Outside, a racing bike was parked with panache. A tall, sporty guy in shorts and a T-shirt took off his helmet and opened the door to the store.

SO FAR ROBERT SHERMAN had only ever experienced unfortunate chains of circumstance. But here, in a postcard store in Paris, where he was standing not entirely by chance and certainly not voluntarily, he experienced for the first time in his life a fortunate chain of events.

For example, it was fortunate that a client of a certain René Joubert, a fitness trainer by trade, had canceled her coaching appointment that Friday because of a migraine, as a result of which that young man was parking his bike outside Luna Luna at the very moment that Robert was in the process of learning the pattern of the tiled floor by heart. Also fortunate was the fact that the cyclist greeted his girlfriend with a hearty "My appointment was canceled, so I thought I'd drop in! There's great news!" And even more fortunate was the fact that—while Rosalie came out from behind the counter to welcome René—the little dog also felt himself compelled to climb out of his basket wagging his tail and jumping up at the muscular legs of the man in the green shorts.

While René bent down to scratch William Morris's fur, Robert and Rosalie looked almost simultaneously into the dog basket, which, as they could easily see, wasn't *totally* empty.

They looked at each other in surprise, then, against their will, grinned, one of them with a feeling of boundless relief, the other with a slightly guilty expression, and then remarkably said the same thing:

"I think I owe you an apology."

Fourteen

·····················

That very evening Rosalie Laurent was, to her own surprise, walking through the Tuileries beside Robert Sherman in perfect harmony. After the discovery of the wallet, which had inexplicably landed in the dog basket, she had apologized shamefacedly. But the American had also done the same. For his unacceptable behavior. Then an embarrassed silence had fallen.

René, in some confusion, had looked from one to the other. Then amazingly the connection between the wallet and the stranger with the American accent had struck him.

"*Non!*" he shouted. "*C'est pas vrai!* Is that the psychopath?"

Rosalie went bright red.

"Eh . . . yes . . . sort of," she stuttered. "This is Robert Sherman." She glanced quickly at the American, who seemed to be enjoying her embarrassment. "We . . . we were just sorting something out. Let me introduce you. Robert Sherman—René Joubert."

"Glad to meet you," said Sherman with great presence of mind.

René drew himself up to his full height. "I don't share your gladness, *connard*," he thundered. He took a threatening step toward the surprised Sherman, who seemed momentarily not to understand the meaning of the word *connard*, and looked him straight in the eye. "Listen very carefully; I will say this only once. If you hassle my girlfriend again, I'll break every bone in your body."

Sherman regained his composure surprisingly quickly. A thin smile played at the corner of his mouth. "Oh, is this your boyfriend?" he asked Rosalie, who at that moment simply wished that the earth would swallow her up. "What is he then? A bouncer in a club?"

He ducked smartly behind one of the postcard stands as René took a swing at him. The blow hit thin air and René spun completely around and shouted at the smirking Sherman: "Come here, you coward!"

"René . . . stop!" Rosalie threw herself between them before it developed into a brawl in the shop that would surely have knocked over more than just a couple of postcards.

It cost her some effort to explain to her outraged boyfriend that she didn't need protection anymore, and that Monsieur Sherman had only returned because he wanted to get his wallet back. He'd lost it in the shop, and it had actually—believe it or not—been in the dog basket the whole time.

"Just think, William Morris was lying on it, which is why we couldn't find it at first," she said, laughing to defuse the situation.

René frowned and looked suspiciously at the American. "What's this all about? A wallet? I thought it was all about your book? You told me yesterday that this lunatic kept insulting and threatening you. He trashed your store and then in the evening rampaged around so wildly in the street that you almost called the police, is what you said!"

Sherman raised his eyebrows expressively. Rosalie squirmed uncomfortably as the two men looked at her in confusion. Perhaps she'd been so angry that she'd exaggerated a bit when telling René.

"Well . . . I suppose 'threatened' is a bit too strong," she said eventually. "But anyway I didn't get the feeling that you were on a peaceful mission yesterday, Monsieur Sherman."

"I may have gone a little too far," Sherman conceded. "Yesterday one thing just led to another—the whole day was more than unpleasant. But as far as the authorship of the children's book is concerned, I am one hundred percent in the right, and if you hear the whole story, you'll understand why."

Rosalie coughed. "I'm all agog." She thought back to her telephone conversation with Max Marchais. "I have my own contribution to make. We should discuss the matter once more—calmly. Perhaps not here in the store, where customers could come in at any moment."

They had finally agreed to meet in Le Café Marly that evening. "Now that I have my wallet back," Sherman had added; finding the wallet had obviously made him feel generous, "we can continue our discussion over a civilized meal. Your friend is also very welcome to come, of course, and can then personally convince himself that I wouldn't harm a hair on your head."

ABOUT HALF PAST EIGHT they were sitting under the arcades of Le Café Marly and had ordered their meal—but without René, who had arranged to meet a friend that evening.

"If you ask me, he actually seems quite normal," René had said after Sherman had left the shop again.

That's what Rosalie thought, too, as she now unobtrusively examined the American who was admiring the view of the Louvre with its illuminated glass pyramid.

"That wasn't there the last time I was in Paris," he said. "But that was a long time ago. I was still a kid then, and the only thing I can remember about the Louvre is the Mona Lisa with her strange smile. Did you know that her gaze follows you everywhere? That really impressed me at the time." He cut a chunk of his club sandwich, and Rosalie tried to imagine Robert Sherman as a little boy.

"How come you speak French so well?" she asked. "I always thought that Americans don't learn any foreign languages on principle, because they think they can get along anywhere just using English."

"Strange, I've heard the same about the French," he retorted, and there was no mistaking the mockery in his voice. "I've heard that they absolutely refuse to speak anything but their mother tongue. But only out of narrow-mindedness—not because they speak a world language." He grinned.

"Let's not start arguing again, Monsieur Sherman, okay?" Rosalie speared a piece of chicken in red-wine sauce. "So, what's the reason? Or is that top secret?"

He laughed. "No, no. There are no secrets in my life. The whole thing has a rather boring explanation. My mother insisted that I learn French because her family originally came from France. She spoke French to me even when I was very little. I have to admit, if it had been left to me I would never have thought of it. In those days I found the language . . . well . . . how shall I put it . . . kind of unmanly—for a true American."

"You don't say!" Rosalie sat up in her chair. "That shows how long you've been harboring your prejudices. But I can assure you that the French language is not unmanly—and nor are French men!"

"That makes me very happy for you, Mademoiselle Laurent. I assume you're speaking from experience." His eyes gleamed.

"No, don't be impertinent, Monsieur Sherman. My private life is none of your business. And I'm also very happy for you."

"Why? Because French men are so manly?"

"No, because your mother had her way. She seems to be a very bright woman."

"Well . . ." He reached for his wineglass, and looked into it thoughtfully. "Bright . . . she certainly was, my mother." He lowered his gaze. "But not anymore, unfortunately. She died a couple of months ago."

"Oh." Rosalie was disconcerted. "I'm sorry about that."

"That's all right." He nodded a couple of times, putting his glass down with a jerk. You could see that the wound still hadn't healed. "Well—at least I'm happy, too, that she insisted on it. And not only because it will make my stay in your city so much easier."

When he mentioned the guest professorship he'd been offered, Rosalie could hardly conceal her surprise.

"A Shakespeare specialist? But I think the legal profession suits you perfectly," she declared.

"Why? Because I insist on my rights?"

"No, because you always insist on being right," she riposted, chewing contentedly on her chicken.

"And you're at least as quick on the trigger as Shakespeare's Kate."

She swallowed the chicken. Shakespeare's Kate meant nothing to her. "Aha. And is that good or bad?" she asked.

"Have you never heard of *The Taming of the Shrew? La Mégère apprivoisée?*" he added in French with a smile.

"Of course I have," she replied. "But I don't know the details."

"I'll give you a copy to read sometime, then you can decide for yourself," he said. "I bet Kate will appeal to you."

He smiled as if he'd just cracked a great joke, then he looked at her, becoming serious.

"So, Mademoiselle Laurent, we have something to discuss. Which of us should start?"

Rosalie laid her cutlery aside and dabbed at her mouth with her napkin.

"*Bon.* Then I'll come straight to the point," she said. "Your strange accusations allowed me no rest, and so I called Max Marchais this morning. . . ."

"And?" Sherman leaned attentively. The color of his shirt matched his blue eyes perfectly—the thought shot through Rosalie's mind. Then she brushed it aside and shook her head.

"It was exactly as I thought. Marchais assured me that he thought up the story. And—I quote—'word by word.' To be on the safe side I also asked if there was possibly a fairy tale, some kind of source that his book is based on, but that is not the case, either. He became extremely annoyed when I told him about the accusation of plagiarism. And the name Sherman means nothing at all to him. It's Marchais's story, and I believe him, no matter what you say."

"But Mademoiselle Laurent, that cannot be."

"Then what?! Are you seriously trying to tell me that you wrote the story? When you were five years old?"

"I've never claimed to be the story's author," responded Sherman in surprise. "I've only said that it cannot possibly be by this guy Marchais."

"What makes you so sure?" Rosalie set her elbows on the white tablecloth, linked her hands together, rested her chin on them, and looked at him quizzically. "It can't just be the fact that you're the great Shakespeare specialist."

"Okay then." Sherman shoved his plate aside. "I'll give you my version of the story."

ROBERT SHERMAN TALKED for quite a while. He left nothing out. Not the fact that the story of the blue tiger had been his favorite as a child, or that his mother had told him it didn't exist in book form. When he talked about her death and that she'd mentioned a passage from *The Blue Tiger* in her very last moments, without his realizing it at the time, Rosalie's eyes turned black as ink. And as he then told her—his voice breaking—how he'd found the manuscript among the papers his mother had left behind— with the dedication and her final handwritten message—she couldn't prevent the tears from welling up in her eyes.

Listening to him, she was very moved. What a sad story. And yet, how much love there was in it. It was only when Sherman mentioned the dedication that she realized that his name began with an R just like hers. "Rosalie" . . . "Robert." Strange.

"Well, I always thought that the 'R' was meant for me," she said in some embarrassment. "But the way you tell it, that's hardly possible."

Sherman looked at her with surprise before continuing. "No, that's out of the question, the 'R' is for 'Robert.' After all, my mother did attach that note to the manuscript, and that makes it quite clear."

Rosalie listened to him in silence, trying to master her confusion. She had naturally assumed that the "For R" in the book had been for her, and Max Marchais had said nothing to the contrary. Nevertheless, she was suddenly less certain.

She tried to recall the moment when she'd thanked Marchais for the dedication. What exactly had he said then? She thought a moment, and then it came back to her: "Don't say anything."

Of course she'd interpreted it as meaning that he didn't want to make a big deal out of it, but perhaps it had just been difficult for him when she discovered the *R* and assumed it was meant for her. The old man's obvious embarrassment had touched her, because she'd imagined that his heart beat a little too strongly for her and that he was ashamed of it, even though there was no reason to be. You should never be ashamed of love. But now she asked herself if there could be another reason for the author's strange reaction. For example, that she'd caught him out in a lie?

Rosalie played thoughtfully with her glass. If Sherman was telling the truth—and she now saw no reason to doubt it—there was an old manuscript that his mother had left him. With a story that Mrs. Sherman had thought up for her little son.

Poor Sherman! No wonder he'd been so shocked when he discovered the book in the window display. And so hurt and furious when he found "his" story between the covers of the book.

By the time Sherman had stopped talking, the Marly was already quite empty. There were only a few isolated customers sitting at the tables conversing quietly. Rosalie said nothing for a while, allowing the literature professor's words to work on her. What she had just heard made her feel ashamed. She believed the man who was sitting opposite her and who, all at once, had all her sympathy. But she also believed Max Marchais, whose outrage had been totally unfeigned. This was all more than strange.

And what if they were both right? What if there were two truths? she thought.

"What's up? Don't tell me you're lost for words." Sherman was looking attentively at her.

Rosalie smiled thoughtfully and looked up at him.

"Yes," she said. "Just imagine, that's exactly what's happened."

"Will you help me to find out the truth anyway?" He had instinctively reached for her hand.

She nodded. "I think the key to all this must lie in the manuscript. Do you think you could get it sent here?"

Night had fallen as they left Le Café Marly. The pyramid outside the Louvre shone through the night like a mysterious spaceship that had been stranded in Paris.

Just after midnight, Rosalie slipped into bed. Drunk with sleep, René muttered *"Bonne nuit"* as she snuggled up to him, and then carried on sleeping.

And the following entry found its way into her blue notebook:

The worst moment of the day:
    René calls the American an asshole and there is almost a fight. Lucky there weren't any customers in the store at the time! This was really embarrassment day: first of all, Sherman finds his wallet in the dog's basket, even though I'd previously insisted it wasn't in the store, then René asks, out loud, if that is the "psychopath"!

The best moment of the day:

René has been invited to a seminar with Zack White-man in San Diego—he once worked with Jack LaLanne, the famous fitness guru. Never heard of him, but it appears to be something very special—René is completely over the moon. The seminar lasts four weeks, and René swung me in the air and asked if we shouldn't move into an apartment together when he comes back. He's never asked me that before!

PS: Another strangely nice moment in Le Café Marly: Sherman asks me if I'll help him to find out the truth about the tiger manuscript, and briefly takes my hand. The glass pyramid shines and everything is kind of unreal. I said yes, of course, and suddenly had the feeling that I'm an altogether good person. Actually, he's not such an odd-ball after all, this American. Even if his image of the French is so ludicrous. The story about his mother moved me deeply.

Fifteen

....

In the middle of the night his cell phone rang. Drunk with sleep, Robert Sherman fumbled around on the bedside table and held the phone to his ear. Strangely enough, he'd thought it would be Rosalie Laurent, and so he was really surprised when he heard a voice that at first seemed completely unknown.

"It's me," said the voice.

"Who is this?"

"Don't you recognize your own girlfriend anymore?" Rachel asked sharply.

"Rachel!" He grabbed his forehead with a sigh. "Sorry. I was asleep. It's"—he glanced at his little brown travel alarm—"a quarter past one. What's the matter? Why are you calling me in the middle of the night?"

"I've been trying to reach you all day, darling, but you never answer." He heard the crackling on the line. She seemed to be waiting for an explanation.

"I'm sorry. The battery was dead. I didn't notice it in all the excitement. But it's charged now."

"Thank God for that." She seemed to be a little friendlier. "I was worried, Robert. What's the situation with your wallet now? Didn't you get my text? Should I transfer some money to you? I've already spoken to the bank." That was typical Rachel. Efficient as always.

"Oh . . . yes . . . right." He rolled back onto his pillow. "Yes, yes, I got your text. Thanks! But I got my wallet back this morning. Just think, I'd dropped it in a store; I went back yesterday evening, but the owner wouldn't let me in." Strangely enough, he felt able to laugh about it now.

"And you didn't think to tell me?" He heard her making a little annoyed sound.

"I'm so sorry, darling—in all the excitement it completely slipped my mind," he said sheepishly.

"Excitement? What excitement—I thought you'd just gotten your wallet back! And it took a whole day to do it, if I understand things rightly."

"Oh, it's not just the wallet. You have no idea what's going on here, Rachel."

"What's going on? To be perfectly honest, I didn't understand half of your text yesterday. Why is Paris full of surprises and puzzles? And what about the French bitch?"

Robert sat up in bed with a sigh. He probably did owe Rachel an explanation. As he summarized the events of the previous day, it surprised him to think that he'd only been in Paris two days.

"Can you imagine how shocked I was to suddenly find the

blue tiger story in the stationery store in the rue du Dragon?" he ended up.

" 'Shocked'?" she repeated dubiously. "I think you're exaggerating a little, Robert. It's not a matter of life and death after all."

"You may not think so. But I absolutely have to find out what's behind it, and Rosalie Laurent's promised to help me. The strange thing is that she was completely convinced that the author had dedicated the story to her, because she'd done the illustrations—and then the 'For R.' But of course the 'R' stands for 'Robert.' You get it?" he said urgently.

"Who knows, it might even stand for Rachel," said Rachel, who seemed not entirely to share his excitement.

"You don't have to make fun of it. If that Marchais guy has simply stolen the story, I'll sue him!"

Rachel sighed. "Jesus, Robert! You really scared me! There was I thinking God knows what had happened! There's no need to get so worked up about an old story like that." She laughed with relief—sounding a little reproachful. "I thought you'd gone to Paris to make your mind up about some important matters."

The nonchalance with which she was dismissing the whole affair annoyed him a little. As if he were a little boy whose toy had been taken from him.

"Well, for me the matter is important," he replied, a bit hurt. "Quite important, in fact. Even if you obviously don't understand."

"Come on, don't be so huffy, Robert," he heard her say. "That's not how I meant it. The matter will be cleared up quickly enough, I'm sure. And if not . . . my God! Nothing good usually comes of it when people dig around in old stories." She laughed.

That's exactly what he would do, thought Robert silently. Dig around in old stories. "Would you do me a favor, Rachel?" he asked.

"Sure," she said.

"Send me my mother's manuscript. It's still in the envelope the attorney gave me. You'll find it in the bottom drawer of my desk. Would you do that for me? It would be best if you could do it tomorrow morning—express."

He gave her the exact address of the hotel once more and thanked her.

"No problem," said Rachel. "The manuscript will be on its way tomorrow."

She wished him good night, but before ending the call she suddenly asked, "And what was that about the French bitch you got to know?"

"Oh, that's just the Rosalie Laurent I was telling you about. The owner of the stationery store where I found the book and knocked over the postcard stand. But in actual fact," he thought aloud, "she's not all that bad."

She's actually quite nice, he thought before his eyes drooped and he fell into a dreamless sleep. *Even if she knows nothing about Shakespeare.*

Sixteen

....

The woman who knew nothing about Shakespeare had, contrary to her normal custom, gotten up early in the morning. It was Monday, and Rosalie felt that she needed to sort out her thoughts by taking William Morris for a long walk. She walked toward the Place Saint-Sulpice, passed to the right of the church with its angular white towers, and carried on along the rue Bonaparte, where all the stores were still closed, finally reaching the Jardin du Luxembourg.

She was met by the scent of a summer garden. The flowers and the greenery of the trees exuded a delicate fragrance that mingled with the dust of the paths and the morning dew. Two lonely joggers loped past her on the outer paths with extended strides: they wore little earphones whose thin white cables disappeared into their sweatshirts. Without much thought, Rosalie struck out along one of the many paths. The broad avenue she entered was still deserted. A ray of sunshine fell diagonally through the rustling leaves on the trees, bathing the path with light. The gravel crunched pleasantly under her feet, passing between rows of iron benches that lined both sides of the path beneath the trees, inviting passersby to stop and relax.

She made sure that she was on the side of the park where dogs were allowed, then let William Morris off the leash. He stormed off before stopping to sniff excitedly at the trunk of a tree.

René had already gone back to his own place earlier in the morning. When he had told her a few days before, his eyes shining, about his invitation to Zack Whiteman's seminar, she hadn't realized that he would be flying to San Diego so soon. But René had only managed to get the sought-after spot because a friend from the fitness club had had to drop out of the seminar, leaving room for him. So it was a matter of striking while the iron was hot, or losing out. He would have to leave in a few days, and René still had a lot to do. "This is a really lucky break," he had said. "Whiteman is *the* fitness guru."

Rosalie had nodded absentmindedly. To be honest, she had not really been on the ball since the evening with Robert Sherman. "Don't you think it's all very strange? I wonder what's behind it?" she had said as she reported her conversation with the American to her boyfriend the next morning.

"Why are you getting so worked up about other people's business?" René had asked as they sat at breakfast on the little roof terrace. "Don't get me wrong, Rosalie, but you only painted the illustrations after all. Even if it does turn out that Marchais stole the story, you're not guilty of anything. Let that crazy literature professor find out for himself."

"Firstly, he's not as crazy as I thought—his story even seems quite credible—and secondly, it's my book, too, in a way," Rosalie had objected. "And apart from that I don't want Max Marchais to get into any trouble."

"Well, if everything turns out right, your beloved children's writer won't be in any trouble. Why didn't you just give Sherman Marchais's telephone number? I mean, that would have been the simplest way of dealing with it. They're both grown men—let them sort it out between themselves who sues whom." René took a great gulp of his carrot, apple, and ginger juice and wiped his mouth. He couldn't see that there was any problem.

"Hey, listen, I can't just give someone an author's number," Rosalie had said, laughing a bit awkwardly. "And anyway, if I know Max he'd only hang up when he heard who was on the line. When we last spoke on the phone he was already so worked up about the whole affair that he said he hoped he'd never have to meet the guy." She took a sip of her hot café au lait and shook her head thoughtfully. "No, no, I don't think it would be a good idea for the two of them to meet. All hell would break loose. And anyway, this business is beginning to interest me. Even if I do find it a bit disturbing."

In her mind's eye she could see a pair of azure-blue eyes looking quizzically at her, and tried not to think more deeply about what the most disturbing element of this whole mysterious story was.

"I promised Sherman I'd help him to find out the truth," she had said, thinking of the American's hand, which had touched hers for a fraction of a second. "It would be best if I call Max again. I really can't imagine that he's lying, but I still have a feeling he's hiding something from me. But what?"

• • •

DEEP IN THOUGHT, ROSALIE had reached the massive pond that glittered in the sunshine in the middle of the park in front of the chateau. She sat down on one of the iron benches and watched a model yacht that a young boy was steering over the water with his remote control. He was standing on the other side of the pond beside his father, and he shouted with joy as the boat with its white sails made a wide curve to the right.

How simple life was when you were a child. And how could such a simple life later develop into such a complicated business? Was it all the half truths, the unspoken words, all the suppressed feelings and everything you kept to yourself that clouded and so confused the wonderful clarity of childhood days, because sooner or later you realized that in life there was more than one truth?

As Rosalie looked at the open face of the boy, the untroubled play of expressions revealing every change in his feelings, she was almost a little envious.

William Morris had returned to her bench, and she put him back on the leash. He sat up in front of her, looking at her with lolling tongue and an expression of devotion. She absentmindedly stroked his soft coat as she continued to watch the sailboat.

Had she told René the whole truth? Was the fact that she was the illustrator of the book or was worried about Max Marchais's reputation really the reason for her excessive interest in this story, which seemed to be attracting her like a magnet? Was Robert Sherman telling the truth? Would they find a clue in the mysterious manuscript, which was meant to be the proof that what he was saying was true? Could you be honest and still not tell the truth?

And what about Max, who also claimed the authorship of the book so vehemently? Had he perhaps been lying?

At their dinner in the Marly, Sherman had quite justifiably pointed out that the author hadn't written a book for more than seventeen years. Perhaps because his ideas had dried up? Could it be that Marchais had gone back to an old story, possibly even one that wasn't his?

And who was really meant in the dedication in the book? The whole weekend Rosalie had been trying to reach Max to ask him that vital question. But he hadn't answered. She hadn't been able to reach him on his landline or his cell phone. She'd left a message on his cell phone asking him to call her back, even saying that it was urgent, but he hadn't replied.

That Monday, too, she had tried to call Le Vésinet from early on in the morning. Every time she'd let the phone ring until the ringing tone broke off to be replaced by a hectic busy tone. Marchais hadn't even switched on his answering machine, as he usually did when he left the house.

The author seemed to have vanished from the face of the earth, and Rosalie began to have a strange feeling about it. She would have preferred to go to Le Vésinet herself to see what was going on, but that day of all days was the one where three applicants who had replied to her advertisement for some help in the store would be turning up in the afternoon.

Max Marchais had not traveled away for years, and if he'd intended to go anywhere he would surely have mentioned it. Rosalie remembered her last telephone conversation a few days ago, the unpleasant questions she'd asked Max, and how gruff and irascible the old man had finally been.

Was he mad at her? Was that why he wasn't answering his

phone? Or did the American's accusations—which she had told him about—have anything to do with his disappearance?

She leaned forward, picked up a little pebble, and threw it out over the water. It plunged through the silvery surface that reflected the light like an impenetrable mirror and created a central point from which concentric circles spread out in little waves until they reached the edge of the pond. *Cause and effect,* thought Rosalie suddenly.

Every lie produced its effects, created its circles, made waves. And sooner or later its circles reached the edge. Even if the lie was as tiny as a pebble.

THE UNEASE THAT HAD taken hold of Rosalie and had even spread to William Morris, who kept getting under her feet in the store so that she finally had to banish him to the apartment upstairs, bothered her for the whole of that day.

She did her shopping in a daze, dealt with some office matters, and then held the interviews, first with the pretty Mademoiselle Giry, who never stopped chewing gum, then with the misanthropic Madame Favrier, who never smiled once during the whole conversation and did nothing but complain about the terrible people on the subway, and lastly with the warmhearted Madame Morel. The decision had not been a difficult one. She chose Claudine Morel, whom she had liked from the very first moment. She was a rather well-padded woman in her early fifties with chin-length brown hair, lovely big hands, and gold-brown freckles on her arms. She had two almost grown-up children and had previously worked in a bookstore that had long since closed down. Claudine Morel was looking for a job that would provide three afternoons' work a week, and they agreed that she would start in Luna Luna the following week.

After she left, Rosalie tried Max again several times, but always in vain. She even briefly considered calling Jean-Claude Montsignac. Perhaps he would have some idea of where his author was. She already had the publisher's business card in her hand when she realized that her search for Marchais might lead to some unpleasant questions that, if answered honestly, might possibly show the author in a dubious light. No, it was not a good idea to drag other people into the affair. She would speak to Max first of all. He was her friend, and she owed him that at least. She hesitantly put the card down again.

THE PHONE WAS TO ring three times that evening. Each time Rosalie snatched the handset from its cradle expecting to hear Max Marchais's voice. But the author had veiled himself in silence.

The first time it was Robert Sherman, who wanted to tell her that the manuscript was already on the way, and would probably arrive in Paris sometime in the course of the next day. The second time it was René, who told her, his voice full of regret, that he would be unable to make it to her place that evening because he still had to work out the schedule for his replacement at the fitness club, and that would take him until very late. "So I'll see you tomorrow, *chérie*! I have an appointment at the Place Saint-Sulpice in the morning, and could drop in at your place straight afterwards."

When the phone rang for the third time, Rosalie had already put on her sleeveless white nightdress. It was just before ten, and up there in the little apartment the heat of the day was still tangible.

Rosalie had opened all the windows and had then climbed out of the window to sit with a cigarette on her favorite place on the roof. "If that's Maman . . . ," she muttered with a sigh, as she jumped up, stubbed out the cigarette, and climbed back into her apartment. Ten o'clock at night was her mother's preferred time for calling: the rest of the day she was far too busy to telephone.

"Yes?" Rosalie picked up the handset and waited. But it wasn't her mother. It was Max Marchais, who apologized in a strangely husky voice for disturbing her so late.

What he then told her was so hair-raising that she had to sit down on her bed in alarm.

"Oh—my goodness," she stammered. "That's terrible. Yes . . . yes . . . of course I'll come. I'll come first thing tomorrow morning."

After the call, which only took a few minutes, Rosalie sat on the bed for a while, her heart racing, before getting out her blue notebook.

The worst moment of the day:
Max has just called. He's had an accident and has been in hospital for three days.
A fractured thigh. Surgery. He apparently fell off a ladder and was lying helpless on the ground for hours until the gardener found him, entirely by chance. Does he really need to climb trees to pick cherries at his age? The doctors say he was very lucky.
The nicest moment of the day:
This morning a little boy smiled at me in the Jardin du Luxembourg.

Seventeen

....

Ultimately it was all Blaise Pascal's fault.

If Max Marchais hadn't taken the book down from the shelf that Friday and then (to escape Madame Bonnier) read it under the trees in the garden—disturbed only by the low humming of the vacuum cleaner and a rather strange telephone conversation with Mademoiselle Rosalie—then he wouldn't have had any reason to put it back on the high shelf in the library after reading it, which as always had given him great pleasure. And if the place where the *Pensées* belonged had not been on the very top shelf, then Max would not have had to climb up the library ladder.

A stable wooden ladder, movable sideways on rollers, which enabled its users to reach any book on the shelves with very little trouble, no matter how high up it might be.

Unfortunately Blaise Pascal's book was *very* high up—or rather *had been* very high up.

That Saturday Max had read the last pages over a peaceful

breakfast, and, being the tidy man he was (Madame Bonnier had a completely false impression of him), he was hovering a little later beside the library shelves, his leather slippers on the third highest step of the ladder, his silver-gray hair almost brushing the ceiling. As he reached upward to the right to put the book back in its proper place among the philosophers, pesky Blaise Pascal somehow managed to slip out of his hand. In the attempt to prevent the inevitable fall of this first edition (he hated dog-eared pages, which is why he seldom lent books out) Max grabbed out into thin air. The ladder moved sideways under this unexpected impulse, and the tall man in the blue cardigan and light cotton pants lost his balance, slipped out of his left slipper, tried to stop the ladder sliding sideways (without success), and a few seconds later—like Blaise Pascal—crashed to the parquet floor.

He fell directly on his back, and the shock of the first impact winded him. If it had been a stone floor, he would probably never have drawn another breath. He stared up at the wall of books, tried to breathe, and panicked when he felt that his chest just would not expand, denying oxygen to his lungs.

An excruciating pain shot though his hip and deep into his right leg, and his head rang as if the bells of Notre-Dame were ringing their knell inside his skull.

At least I'm dying surrounded by books, thought Max, before falling into merciful unconsciousness.

WHEN HE CAME ROUND, the light seemed to be shining into the room from a different angle—but he wasn't sure. It could have been three hours or just a quarter of an hour—he wouldn't have known. Stupidly, his watch was in the bathroom. And he was still lying on his back like a helpless beetle, and any movement, no matter how careful, was painful.

The telephone rang several times, but it was impossible for him to cross the few yards to his desk—the pain was so strong that everything went black every time he tried to sit upright. Later he heard the trilling ring tone of his cell phone, which always made him think of Hitchcock's *Dial M for Murder*. He could really have used the damned thing right now—but it was in the pocket of his summer jacket, which was hanging in the hall.

He groaned. If he'd only had a little luck, the jacket would have remained where he took it off the day before—over the arm of the sofa, an arm's length from him. But unfortunately Marie-Hélène, with her love of tidiness, had—before she left for her vacation in the early afternoon—taken it out into the hall and hung it in the closet. It was enough to make you weep!

When his landline rang again, Max tried to roll over onto his stomach and push himself toward the desk. But once again he was struck by that stabbing pain, and he had to gasp for breath. He'd definitely broken something—his leg was sticking out at an awkward angle from his hip.

An old villa in Le Vésinet was many people's dream. But if you lived alone and something happened, a house like this could become a trap. The gardens were big, the houses detached—the chances of being heard by a neighbor were very slim, unless you were playing a saxophone or a trumpet, which Max had never learned to do, and at this particular moment he couldn't have done so even if he had been able to play either of those instruments.

Marie-Hélène would come back in ten days' time. First she would be surprised that none of the meals she'd prepared had been touched, and then she'd find his rotting body lying beside the bookshelves.

The first thing she would probably say would be that this proved it wasn't good for a man to be alone in the house.

When the doorbell rang a little later, Max Marchais thought, in spite of all reason, that his housekeeper had returned to save her "Monsieur Proust." He needed her more than he ever had in his life.

But no key turned in the lock, no dark voice called, "Monsieur Marchais? Are you there?" He straightened up and shouted for help with all his strength, but there was obviously no one to hear him. Then he remembered that no one who rang his bell did so right at the front door; they did so using the bell on the outside wall of the front garden, which itself was not small. The cast-iron gate could admittedly be opened relatively simply by reaching through the bars and pressing the latch—but who was aware of that?

Oh well, thought Max with a certain degree of fatalism before he slipped back into unconsciousness. *Now the only thing that can save me is a burglary.*

THE SUN WAS ALREADY low in the sky and the gnats were dancing at the big living-room window, which was slightly open, when Max suddenly heard the sound of a lawn mower. He turned his head toward the window and peered out into the garden.

A man in green overalls was walking up and down the lawn with the lawn mower. Max had never been so glad to see his gardener. Sebastiano—a Costa Rican, who was living proof of a study claiming that people from Costa Rica were the happiest in the world—had his own key to the back gate of the garden and to the shed behind the wall where the gardening tools were stored. Among them the lawn mower.

For years Max had refused to acquire an electric lawn mower. It wasn't because of avarice—Marchais had always been an extremely generous man, even in the days when he had been a freelance journalist and was only just making ends meet. It was just that he somehow liked the smell and the loud rattle of the gasoline motor. It reminded him of his childhood in the country near Montpellier, where every Saturday his father had with shouts, curses, and bitter pulling of the starting cord set the mower in motion: its contented puttering then rang in the weekend.

So you could see that nostalgia was of little use; quite the opposite—in many cases it could even be life threatening. He lay on the parquet floor, shouting in vain against the crazy clatter of the mower which came and went in rhythmic waves, as the evening air filled with the smell of newly mown grass.

And then suddenly it was still.

"Help! Help!" shouted Max as loudly as he could in the direction of the living-room window. "I'm here . . . here in the library!"

He twisted his neck and saw Sebastiano stopping and looking over toward the house. Hesitantly, he came nearer, looking with surprise at the table on the terrace, where the breakfast dishes had not been cleared.

"Hola? Señor Marchais? Hola? Hola?"

A few hours later Max Marchais was lying on a smooth green

operating table in the nearby private clinic in Marly, slipping into the gentle, pain-free embrace of a general anesthetic. As well as a minor concussion and a big wound on the back of his head, which had been stitched up straight away, he had bruises on his hip and leg and a compound fracture of the thigh.

"You've been very lucky indeed, Monsieur Marchais. This could all have ended very differently. How old are you? It would be best if we fit you with a new hip at once," the surgeon in the emergency room had said. "Otherwise you'll be lying in hospital too long. And then—bang!—pneumonia." He gave him a knowing look. "In the old days elderly people died by the dozens after a fracture like this. Of pneumonia. But today it's not such a big deal. A new hip and—bang!—you'll be able to walk around again very soon, Monsieur Marchais. Should we let anyone know? The man who found you said you live alone. Do you have any next of kin?"

"My sister. But she lives in Montpellier," groaned Max, still dazed with the pain. "Am I really in such a bad state?"

The thought that Thérèse—always disappointed with her life—and her know-it-all husband and their appallingly spoiled son might turn up in the hospital turned him even paler.

Monsieur Bang, who actually answered to the name of Professeur Pasquale, smiled. "Not at all! Don't worry, Monsieur Marchais. It's a routine operation. Not life threatening at all. In a few hours you'll be as good as new—and that's a promise."

WELL, MAX WASN'T EXACTLY feeling like new. The operation had been three days ago, but there was still a hellish pain in his skull and his hip and his leg hurt as well. But thanks to the drug that was patiently dripping from the thin tube over his bed, ending in a needle in the back of his hand, things were getting steadily better.

Everyday life in the hospital was not exactly designed to help a sick person recover. He had less peace here than on the days when Marie-Hélène was whirling through the house. Even at night the door was opened every two hours, blood pressure was taken, the drip was changed, his arm was pulled about so that they could take blood—they seemed to take pleasure in doing the latter as often as possible—and if this didn't wake him up they would shine a glaring flashlight in their patient's face to make sure he was still alive.

Well, Max Marchais was still alive, but he wasn't getting any sleep. At six o'clock in the morning the cleaners reached his room. A couple of delightful women from the Ivory Coast laughed and gossiped as they cleaned the floor, constantly knocking against his bed, said, "Oh, sorry! Sorry!" and then continued chatting in convoluted sentences that he couldn't understand, giggling all the while.

The delightful ladies from Africa had slept well, it was easy for them to be in such a good mood, thought Max grimly, wondering if he would ever be granted that privilege again.

After the cleaners came, Julie, the trainee nurse, arrived with a smile, a frugal breakfast, and the weakest coffee he'd ever drunk. As she left, she would always point to the dish of tablets. "Don't forget those, Monsieur Marchais!"

Then came the ward sister. "Well, Monsieur Marchais, how are we today? Have we slept well?"

"I don't know how you slept, Sister Yvonne," growled Max. "For my part, I haven't slept at all—how could I when they keep waking me up?"

"That's fine. So we'll take a little walk today, Monsieur Marchais, then we'll feel a lot better," said Sister Yvonne with a broad smile. *"On y va?"* She seemed to be relentlessly cheerful.

Hadn't she been listening? Was she deaf? Or was the hospital using intelligent robots that looked like women but kept on playing the same script?

Max looked dubiously at the nurse with the short blond hair who now tightened the blood-pressure sleeve around his arm, pumping it like mad to fill it with air. She narrowed her eyes, stared at the display, and pumped again. "Hmm, your blood pressure seems a little high—but we'll soon get it down again."

She nodded and smiled her relentless smile and Max was absolutely sure that no blood pressure on earth would ever dare to resist Sister Yvonne's orders. "We'll soon get it down again." In spite of all her annoying familiarity, that at least was reassuring.

He hadn't believed his eyes when a wiry little physiotherapist had arrived to take him for a "little walk."

"There must be some mistake," he had said. "I've only just had an operation."

He frowned, a vertical wrinkle appearing between his eyebrows. You were always hearing about patients being mixed up in hospital. He supposed that in that case he could be pleased that he'd been given a new hip and not a new heart valve.

"No, Monsieur Marchais, there's no mistake." She looked at him pertly from under her short Jean Seberg bangs and smiled. "Nowadays we get our patients out of bed straight after the operation. You were allowed a little more rest than normal because of your concussion." Was he imagining it, or could he discern a trace of sadism in her smile? "Come along then, Monsieur Marchais—we can do it."

However, only one of them walked behind the walker that she put in front of him—and it was him.

SO, IN BRIEF—AFTER three days in hospital Max Marchais was longing for nothing so much as his own bed and people who were not hospital personnel. When he'd had him taken to hospital, Sebastiano had shown the presence of mind to grab his employer's trench coat—with his cell phone in the pocket. On Monday evening Max had used the last reserves of his battery to call Rosalie Laurent, who had promised to come and visit him.

Still, Monsieur Bang aka Professeur Pasquale had held before him the prospect of returning home at the end of the next week if he did his exercises properly and his blood pressure was acceptable.

"Our blood pressure is still a little too high, Monsieur Marchais," he had said on his round that morning, looking with concern over the rims of his little spectacles at the chart, and Max had replied, "No wonder, if we don't get any sleep at night, *hein?*"

He noticed that he was developing an allergic reaction—to the careless way they used the word *we,* to doors that opened every couple of minutes, to light switches that were always turned on and never off, and more than anything to the permanent squelching of rubber soles as they walked around him, seeming to stick to the linoleum floors like Spiderman's webs (what did they clean the place with?), only then to come unstuck with a squeaking noise.

Squelch, squelch, squelch. Squelch, squelch, squelch.

Squelch, squelch, squelch. Squelch, squelch, squelch.

Trainee nurse Julie bustled around the room. She was clearing his lunch away and asked if we'd enjoyed it and if we'd remembered to take our tablets. Then she propped the window open on the latch, pulled the curtains shut so that we can have a little afternoon nap, Monsieur Marchais, and left the room. The door closed quietly behind her.

As Max wearily let his head droop onto the pillows, closing his eyes in the hope of having that afternoon nap, the hazy dream images were penetrated by the delightful clatter of high heels, which came up the corridor and came to a halt outside his door.

Eighteen
....

"What on earth have you been up to, Max dear? How are you? What were you doing up a ladder, for heaven's sake? And what's happened to your head?" Rosalie put the bunch of tea roses down on the bedside table and leaned over Max Marchais with an expression of concern. Her old friend looked rather run-down, she thought, with the bandage on his head and the dark shadows beneath his eyes.

A delighted smile flashed across his wrinkled face. "Which question should I answer first, Mademoiselle Rosalie?" he asked. "I'm an old man, you're demanding too much of me." He was trying to sound cheerful, but his voice was hoarse.

"Oh, Max!" She pressed his bony hand, which was lying on the thin bedspread. "You look really terrible. Are you in pain?"

He shook his head. "The pain is bearable. Today I even managed to take a couple of steps, thanks to a friendly drill sergeant pretending to be a nurse. It's just that I can't get any sleep. The door constantly opens and one of those white coats comes in for something. And they all ask the same things. I wonder if any of them ever talk to each other."

He sighed deeply, smoothed the bedspread, then pointed to a chair standing in the corner.

"Get yourself a chair, Rosalie. I'm really very glad you could come. You're the first normal person I've seen for days."

Rosalie laughed. "You shouldn't be so impatient, Max. You've only been here a few days, and the doctors and nurses are only doing their job." She pulled the chair over to the bed, sat down, and crossed her legs.

"Yes, I'm afraid I'm a very impatient patient." His gaze followed her every movement, finally coming to rest on the graceful, light-blue sandals that clothed her feet with their painted toenails. "Pretty sandals," he said unexpectedly.

Rosalie raised her eyebrows in surprise. "Oh, thanks. They're just ordinary summer sandals."

"Oh, well . . . you know, you get to appreciate normal things when you've spent a couple of days on the other side of the river," he replied philosophically. "I hope I can get out of this joint soon."

"I hope so, too. You really had me scared. I'd been trying to call you all weekend without success, but I never reckoned we'd meet up again in hospital."

"Yes, I heard all my phones ringing. Foolishly enough, I was in no position to pick up," he joked. "What was it that was so important?"

Rats! Rosalie gnawed her lower lip. This really wasn't the right moment to bring the book up again and ask about the mysterious dedication. That would have to wait until Max had recovered a bit more.

"Oh . . . I just wanted to see if you could come to Paris next week and have lunch with me," she said deceitfully. "I've got help in the store for three afternoons every week, and René's off to a training seminar in San Diego at the end of the week. I thought we could help the time to pass together."

At least the last two statements corresponded to the truth. A pity Madame Morel couldn't have started work that day. Rosalie had hung a sign on the shop door that morning: CLOSED DUE TO A FAMILY EMERGENCY.

She smiled. It may not have been a family emergency in the strictest sense, but it felt like one. She stared at the tall man with the bushy eyebrows. All of a sudden he seemed so helpless and frail. There was only a thin veneer covering the signs of mortality. How quickly an old person's facade crumbled when they were catapulted out of their normal routine and no longer able to look after themselves, she thought. She looked at his thin hospital gown and his pale face, noting that he was unshaven, moved by the sparse gray stubble that was visible in the reflected light. Strange, this old man seemed as close to her as a grandfather. And at that moment he actually looked like a grandfather. Rosalie was happy he was still alive, relieved that no worse had happened to him. There was no way she was going to bother him with the business about Sherman. It was clear that he was not in very good condition.

"Well, I'm afraid the lunch in Paris is off the menu for the immediate future, my dear Mademoiselle Rosalie, no matter how tempting the idea might be," said Max, as if he had read her thoughts. "You can see for yourself the state I'm in. And if it weren't for my artificial hip I'd be spending several weeks in bed." He pointed at the outline of his legs under the bedspread. His right foot was sticking out at the bottom of the bed.

"My goodness, did you break your toe as well?" asked Rosalie, pointing at Max Marchais's little toe, which was quite a dark color.

"What? No!" Max wriggled his toes. "I've got several things wrong with me, but my little toe is completely in order. It's always been that brown—it's a mole." He grinned. "My dark spot, if you like."

"You're really full of surprises, Max," responded Rosalie, leaning back in her chair. "And now tell me, please, what you were doing up a ladder? Were you picking cherries or what?"

"Picking cherries?" His eyebrows shot up in surprise. "What on earth gave you that idea? No, no, I was standing on my library ladder putting a book back on the shelf. Do you know Blaise Pascal, Mademoiselle Rosalie?"

She shook her head. "No, but it seems to be a dangerous book!"

AFTER MAX MARCHAIS HAD told his story, in which the thoughts of a philosopher, an old ladder, a Costa Rican gardener, and a gasoline lawn mower provided the requisite drama, he gave Rosalie the key to his house in Le Vésinet and asked her to bring him some things that he needed.

"I'm sorry to trouble you, Rosalie, but Marie-Hélène is away, as you know. Sebastiano has already informed her, and I think she's coming back earlier than she had planned—if only to say 'I told you so'—but I don't know exactly when." He shrugged his shoulders with a sigh. "Sebastiano did admittedly save my life, for which I'm eternally grateful, but he's not particularly good when it comes to packing. And he doesn't really know his way around the house." He smiled. "I don't want to seem ungrateful—and he did remember my coat and my cell phone. Otherwise I wouldn't have been able to call you—that's the result of the fact that no one writes down telephone numbers these days. Fortunately, yours was stored in my contacts. So I hope you won't mind collecting a few things for me."

Rosalie shook her head. "No problem at all," she said. "I'm here in the car—just tell me what you need and where I'll find it. Then I'll bring it all over later. I imagine your departure in the ambulance was a little hasty."

"It was indeed. I don't think I've ever left the house so quickly. I don't even have my pajamas or my dressing gown here—you can see what a stupid nightshirt they've stuck me in."

He pulled a comic grimace as the door opened and a nurse with short blond hair and softly squelching shoes came in with a kidney dish in her hand.

"Time for your thrombosis jab, Monsieur Marchais," she trumpeted. "Oh! We have a visitor, do we?" She looked busily at Rosalie as she filled the syringe. "She'll have to leave us for a moment. Your granddaughter?"

"No, my girlfriend," riposted Max, winking at Rosalie as she stood up. "And, Sister Yvonne—could you put the flowers in water?"

Sister Yvonne was audibly gasping for breath as Rosalie left the room while suppressing a laugh.

IT WAS EARLY IN the afternoon when she stood outside Max Marchais's villa and pressed the latch of the garden gate. The sun was shining warmly on the narrow gravel path that led between hydrangea bushes, lavender, and sweet-smelling heliotrope.

The rectangular white house with the red-tiled roof stood there peacefully, as if painted by a child, and as Rosalie unlocked the front door she was in no way prepared for what was awaiting her there.

Nineteen

....

There was always something eerie about coming into an empty house. It was as quiet as a museum, and only the click of Rosalie's summer sandals on the parquet floor disturbed the solitude as she walked carefully through the rooms and looked around a little. Although she had already visited Max several times, she really only knew the library with its big fireplace and two massive sofas, and the terrace with its reddish round tiles, which was directly outside the library and led to the garden. The traces of his hasty exit were still apparent all around her.

In the kitchen with its milky stone floor the used breakfast dishes were standing on a tray next to a white sink. The gardener must have brought them in before he closed and locked the big living-room window. Rosalie found the dishwasher and put in the dishes. In the library, the book that had caused the fall was still lying on the floor beside the tall wooden ladder. She picked it up and put it on the rectangular coffee table between the two sofas.

The afternoon sun shone brightly between the opened drapes.

A squirrel was sitting on the terrace nibbling at something until, scared off by the movement behind the window, it ran across the lawn and scampered up a tree.

There was a single men's leather slipper on the floor next to one of the two wide, light-colored sofas that stood opposite each other between old-fashioned saffron-yellow floor lamps. Rosalie had already found the other one in the hall, almost tripping over it.

She walked past the book-lined wall and turned right where the library opened into a study. In front of the window, which also had a view of the garden, stood a desk with a dark-green leather surface. Next to the desk lamp was a framed picture of a smiling woman with friendly eyes. That must be Marchais's late wife. Rosalie looked around on the desk, quickly finding the little book Max had asked for. Raymond Radiguet, *Le diable au corps*. Then she opened the right-hand desk drawer where the cell phone charger was kept.

She glanced at the list they had just made in the hospital. Toiletry bag and aftershave—upstairs in the bathroom, on the right in the little closet. Before she left the study, she noticed an old, black Remington typewriter standing on a cabinet beside a five-armed silver candelabrum and a round silver tray with a water carafe and matching glasses. Above it, between two antiquated wine-red floor lamps, hung a large oil painting of a southern French landscape in shades of blue and ochre, just as Bonnard might have painted.

Rosalie leaned forward with interest, but she couldn't decipher the artist's signature. She took a step back and stood for a while, absorbed in the painting, which captured the bushes and the soft fall of the cliffs over a gleaming summer bay so well that you almost felt you could hear the chirp of the crickets.

When her cell phone rang, she started with fright as if she'd been a burglar. *"Oui? Allô?"* she asked as she pulled herself away from the picture.

It was Robert Sherman, calling her from a café. The manuscript had arrived, and he wanted to meet her and show it to her.

"Where are you, Mademoiselle Laurent? I've already been to the store, but it was closed. Due to a family emergency. Has something happened?" He sounded concerned.

"I'll say it has! I'm in Max Marchais's house at the moment. He's had an accident."

She quickly told Sherman about the writer's unfortunate fall from the library ladder and ended with: "I'd actually intended to ask Max about the tiger story again, and about the dedication, but I'm afraid we'll have to postpone that until he's better. I wouldn't want to press him or possibly upset him. You do understand, don't you?"

"Yes . . . of course." His voice sounded disappointed.

"It's only a couple of days, Robert. Then we'll know more. Listen, I have to pick up a few more things here, and I don't have much time. I'll call you later when I'm back in Paris. Then we can meet and you can show me your manuscript, okay?"

"Okay," he said.

It was only when Rosalie was putting her phone back in her purse that it dawned on her that that was the first time she'd called him Robert.

HALF AN HOUR LATER she had collected all the things that were on the list. Toiletry bag, Aramis aftershave (which she'd finally found on the bedside table in the bedroom), blue-and-white-striped pajamas, a thin dark-blue dressing gown with a little Paisley pattern, underwear, socks, a pair of light leather moccasins, slippers, some other clothes, and some books. The only thing she hadn't found was the dark-green cloth travel bag, which according to Max was somewhere right at the back of the wardrobe. She took another dive into the three-doored, polished, dark-wood wardrobe and rummaged around among shoe boxes and other cardboard boxes.

Finally she gave up and swept the room with her gaze. Where else could the bag be? She looked in the other drawers in the wardrobe, she looked under the wide bed, carelessly covered with a bright quilt with a rose pattern, she looked in the little storeroom next to the bathroom where the cleaning things were kept. Hopefully she wouldn't have to search the whole basement!

She looked at her watch and tried to call Max, but he'd switched his cell phone off. He was obviously trying to have his much postponed afternoon nap. With a sigh she went back into the bedroom. She thought about where she herself might put a bag, and looked instinctively up to the top of the wardrobe.

Bingo! Behind a couple of shoe boxes she could see two brown leather handles that obviously belonged to a travel bag.

She took a chair from beside a chest of drawers that stood under a big mirror and put it beside the wardrobe. On tiptoe she groped for the handles, and as she tried to pull the bag forward, she dislodged a large cardboard box which slid forward, spilling its contents all over the floor.

"*Zut alors*—what a mess!" she cursed as she got down from the chair and set about collecting all the papers, letters, pictures, and cards that were strewn all over the floor. She had to smile as she glanced briefly at an old black-and-white photo of Max Marchais as a young man. He looked really damn good sitting there so coolly outside a Parisian café in his light chinos and a white buttoned shirt, a cigarette between his thumb and index finger. He was leaning back in a wicker chair, laughing straight into the camera.

Something about the picture seemed odd to her. She looked at it more closely. Was it the fact that he had no beard—or just seeing Max with a cigarette? She hadn't known that he used to smoke.

She carefully put the picture back in the box with the others and tidied the letters. Most of them seemed to be from Marchais's wife, Marguerite; on one of the envelopes she saw the name of his sister, Thérèse. Max had once briefly mentioned to her that he had a sister in Montpellier, and his tone had given Rosalie to understand that the relationship between the siblings was not particularly close. Photos of Max as a child in short pants, a couple of faded pictures of his parents, Max as a young journalist at his typewriter in a newspaper office.

As she was hastily putting away these mementos of a time long past, these fragments of a lived life, her eye was caught by the faded color photograph of a young woman. She was wearing a red summer dress with white polka dots and was standing under a big tree in a park. She had obviously been caught in a shower, because her shoulder-length blond hair, held back by a headband, was wet and she was shivering as she folded her arms over her dress with its round neckline. She was leaning forward and laughing. Her mouth was full and red, and for a moment Rosalie almost felt she was seeing herself in this young woman who was laughing so heartily. The whole picture exuded an infectious joie de vivre. Was it Thérèse? She actually looked quite nice. Rosalie turned the picture over and saw a date that someone had scribbled on the back in pencil:

Bois de Boulogne, 22nd July, 1974

Rosalie smiled thoughtfully as she put the pretty young woman's photo back in the box. Perhaps it was a childhood sweetheart of Max Marchais's? "I wasn't always an old man, Rosalie," was what he'd once said to her.

You did actually tend to forget that even old people were once young. It seemed almost as unimaginable as the certainty that you would yourself—soon, or at any rate quicker than you thought—be old. It was only with people you had known from earlier times that you could see through the layers of all the years that had settled on body and soul, extinguishing the glow of expectation in their eyes—or a wonderful smile like that, which was absolutely fixed in the moment.

Rosalie looked around the floor once more: there was nothing left lying around. Then, just to be sure, she looked under the bed, and discovered a bundle of papers whose pages were just barely held together by a rubber band. She lay down on her stomach and, with some difficulty, pulled the papers out from under the bed.

It was an old manuscript, or rather the carbon copy of an old manuscript in which a mechanical typewriter had etched delicate blue imprints on the paper.

Rosalie sat up with the parchmentlike bundle in her hands. She carefully smoothed the pages and then removed the red, almost crumbling rubber band very delicately so as not to snap it.

She felt her heartbeat becoming irregular as she looked at the title page. And then her thoughts became so confused that in the end she wasn't thinking at all.

She sat there like that for a while on the wooden floor of the bedroom, which was bathed in the warm light of the afternoon sun, and stared at the pale blue letters on the faded paper.

On the thin, yellowing page she read THE BLUE TIGER. And beneath it: FOR R.

Twenty

....

He was beginning to like Paris. There was something wildly exhilarating about strolling through the little streets of Saint-Germain, which—totally unlike Manhattan—suddenly curved off to the left or the right, taking you past countless stores and boutiques, cafés and bistros. Everything was so colorful and varied, exuding an almost alarming cheerfulness that was one thing above all: life affirming. Yes, Robert Sherman was feeling particularly lively that sunny Tuesday.

That may have had something to do with the encouraging conversation he'd had with the dean of the English faculty the day before. The dainty little man, whose hands seemed to be in perpetual motion, had intimated to him that he could not think of anything more delightful than the idea of Sherman giving his Shakespeare lectures as guest professor for the upcoming semester.

"Since I read your articles on the *Midsummer Night's Dream,* you 'ave me 'ooked, Mr. Sherman," Professeur Lepage had said in his comical English. "*Non, non,* no false modesty, monsieur.

We are all burning to 'ear you. I 'ope you will agree?" And, noticing Sherman's hesitant expression, he'd added: "Do not worry, we will 'elp you find somewhere to live."

Perhaps the reason for the sudden burst of energy that had gripped Robert like a fresh breeze also had something to do with the simple fact that he'd slept very well for the first time since his arrival in Paris. And perhaps he had just surrendered to the charm of the city by the Seine, which, as his mother had said, was always a good idea. Yes, Paris had him " 'ooked."

Robert smiled contentedly as he ate his breakfast—calmly and without any rush—in the secluded courtyard of his hotel, sitting in the shade and studying the *Figaro*.

The café crème—invigorating. The crisp baguette, which he spread thickly with strawberry jam—invigorating. The delicate scent of roses that permeated the courtyard of the Hôtel des Marronniers—invigorating. The receptionist's charming smile—invigorating.

As he set off with his manuscript, which had arrived in the hotel that morning, toward the Luna Luna stationery store, he admitted to himself with some surprise that the prospect of once more seeing the attractive and somewhat prickly owner of the store, with her long brown braid, was also invigorating.

Strangely enough, the store was closed—due to a family emergency—and when he reached Mademoiselle Laurent on her cell phone, it turned out that, to cap it all, the shady writer had fallen off a ladder and was in the hospital. She was in his house at that very moment to collect some things for him and seemed extremely concerned.

Come on, a fractured thigh wasn't that serious. What did she see in that old man who wasn't even a relative and was in all probability a liar as well? Robert felt a twinge of jealousy. He was annoyed that their investigation—had the word *investigation* really popped into his mind?—was being held up. He would have had no problem beating Marchais round the head with his mother's manuscript, and then they'd see what was what.

Robert strolled on without any particular goal, turned into the winding rue de Buci, which was lined with bistros where people were sitting outside in the sunshine, chatting and eating. He passed boulangeries, greengrocers, and stalls selling oysters and grilled chickens, suddenly realizing that he was hungry, too. He bought himself a baguette from a *traiteur*: tuna, lettuce, and slices of boiled potato, a strange combination, but it tasted excellent.

Then he glanced at his watch. Mademoiselle Laurent had promised to call when she got back from Le Vésinet, but that might take quite some time.

He took out his map and decided to take a walk to Shakespeare and Company, the legendary American bookstore on the Left Bank, where Sylvia Beach had once hosted the authors of the Lost Generation, and which still existed—even if the owner (still an American, however!) had changed and it had moved from rue de l'Odéon to the rue de la Bûcherie. And even today, or so Robert had read, young writers or would-be writers could still find a place to lay their heads if they were prepared to help out in the bookstore for a couple of hours.

It was astonishing, and absolutely anachronistic, but the spirit of Shakespeare and Company had survived down the decades, even if there had never again been such a throng of great writers as there had been in the golden age when T. S. Eliot, Ezra Pound, and Ernest Hemingway had walked through the door.

Some things just couldn't be repeated, but it was good that they had once happened.

As Robert now walked along the rue Saint-André-des-Arts, he was reminded of Hemingway's words. He'd once said, "If you are lucky enough to have lived in Paris as a young man, then wherever you go for the rest of your life it stays with you, for Paris is a moveable feast." Admittedly, Robert had never lived in Paris—and if you really thought about it, what was Paris compared with New York?!—but still, he had been here once as a child, which was not something Americans took for granted. And perhaps even he had a little piece of Paris somewhere in his pocket.

In high spirits, Robert marched part of the way along the boulevard Saint-Michel and then turned right onto the rue de la Bûcherie. A few paces more, and he was standing in front of the little bookstore—which had an old-fashioned wooden bench and a couple of little tables and cast-iron chairs outside it— looking through the window with its dark-green frame.

The incredible abundance of books he saw there was impressive and made him feel pleasantly at home. He walked in through the open door, looking forward to browsing in the store.

That was easier said than done.

The little store, with its narrow passageways winding between ceiling-high bookshelves and walls of books, was as full as if they were giving things away. And that was what they were doing, in a way.

The magic of this very special bookstore, which was dedicated to books both old and new and which had supported and lodged great writers, was still there for those who had enough imagination to see it. If everyone who was crowding into the store succeeded in doing so was questionable, but at least outwardly it seemed as if everyone wanted to take home some reflection of its glory days—even if it was only a Shakespeare and Company cloth carrier bag or a labeled paperback.

Robert squeezed past three giggling Japanese girls. They were holding English books in their hands, pretending to read them, while an older Japanese man in horn-rimmed spectacles photographed them—in spite of the notices saying that photography was forbidden in the store. But no one complained about their behavior. And even the good-tempered and rather bleary-eyed student at the register—he had an unmistakably British accent and was obviously one of the help that were allowed to spend the night there—ignored their faux pas with great insouciance.

Robert worked his way to the back of the store and found a narrow wooden staircase that led upward. In one of the rooms on the first floor he could hear music being played. Individual notes were interwoven to produce Debussy's *Prélude à l'après-midi d'un faune*. Robert stood aside to let the customers who were coming down pass, and then he climbed the stairs curiously and turned into the room on the right, where the slightly clangy piano music seemed to be coming from. An older woman with chin-length ash-blond hair and narrow shoulders was sitting at an old piano with her back to the door, not letting herself be disturbed in the slightest by the people who looked curiously around the room, stepping first this way and then that, before disappearing again. She had something of the reckless nonchalance of Djuna Barnes, thought Robert as he quietly left the room with the hammering pianist.

Directly opposite the stairway there were two adjoining

rooms full of secondhand books. There were also old tables with old typewriters and worn sofas. On the walls hung faded photographs of the previous owner and his little blond daughter. In the corners there were mattresses; faded blankets that might once have been red were carelessly thrown over them.

No one here was ambitious to move with the times. The pleasant, unhurried atmosphere that reigned here seemed to spread to the people in the rooms who, as Robert noticed with a smile, moved around more carefully and considerately than normal.

It was only when he went back to the stairs and looked around that he became aware of the notice—in English and in big black letters—over the door frame:

BE NOT INHOSPITABLE TO STRANGERS LEST
THEY BE ANGELS IN DISGUISE

All at once Robert felt totally welcome in the bookshop. And in Paris.

Lost in thought, he went back downstairs and stepped over to a shelf at the back of the shop where the drama section was to be found.

He was just looking for an edition of Shakespeare's *Taming of the Shrew* when his cell phone rang.

It was Rosalie Laurent. She sounded very excited. And she had sensational news.

Twenty-one

....

Paris flew past him. After the seemingly interminable dark tunnel, a few really ugly apartment towers came into view in Nanterre, between them gray concrete walls sprayed with graffiti—a touching attempt to defy the dreariness of the Parisian suburbs. It was only on the last stretch that the landscape gradually grew greener, and the train tracks that led to Saint-Germain-en-Laye were lined with old houses and enchanted gardens.

Robert Sherman was sitting in an RER train heading for Le Vésinet Centre and looking out of the window. In his lap he held his leather briefcase with the manuscript and, following an uncontrollable compulsion, kept continually checking that the envelope with its pages was still there. It was hard to imagine what would happen if he were to lose the manuscript now that Rosalie Laurent had found its counterpart. Or rather its carbon copy.

"I don't understand it," she kept on saying as she told him about her discovery, her voice trembling with her confusion. "So

Max did actually lie to me. But before I confront him with it, I'd like us to compare the manuscripts. Perhaps the whole affair has another explanation."

The way she kept on defending the old scoundrel was really touching. After a short discussion they had come to the conclusion that it would be best for Robert to take the train to Le Vésinet—the journey was only thirty minutes—while Rosalie drove to the hospital and delivered the things Marchais wanted. She would then return to Le Vésinet.

The key to the house was a problem. She could hardly keep it without giving a reason. And she vehemently refused to ask the old man for an explanation yet.

"Oh, do you know what? I'll just leave the terrace door open a crack," she said finally. "It's easy to slide the big French window to the side, and then we can get into the house unseen from the garden side."

Although Robert had never doubted that he was in the right, he could feel the excitement rising up in his stomach like a snail as he got out of the train a little later in Le Vésinet and saw Rosalie Laurent standing on the platform in her brightly colored dress. She was paler than usual, and her deep blue eyes had an expression that was difficult to interpret. She shook his hand hesitantly.

"My car's over there," she said.

They drove through the quiet streets of the little town in silence. After the excited telephone conversation that afternoon there was a strange embarrassment in the air. Rosalie glared determinedly to the front, chewing her lower lip. There was not much room inside the car for a tall man with long legs, and Robert could feel the nervousness of his silent driver like a series of pinpricks. Once, as Rosalie changed gear, her hand brushed his knee briefly, and she hastily apologized. He shook his head.

"No worries," he said, smiling to lighten the tense atmosphere.

The sun was already low in the sky as they crept though the bushes in the garden of the old villa with the red-tiled roof to get to the rear terrace door. Rosalie looked back to make sure there were no undesired observers, then she pushed the frame of the sliding door with all her strength, and the huge pane of glass slid silently aside.

"We must be very quiet," she warned, totally superfluously.

"Don't worry. I have no intention of playing a trumpet solo," said Robert in a muffled voice.

They both started as the tune of "Fly Me to the Moon" suddenly burst out in the evening silence.

Rosalie turned around. "What's *that*?" she hissed.

" 'Fly Me to the Moon,' " answered Robert automatically.

"Comment?!" She looked at him as if he'd lost his mind as the melody trilled on interminably. "Switch your cell phone off, now! You'll alert the whole neighborhood!"

"Yes. Sure. At once." He reached into his pocket, and in his confusion pressed the Accept button.

"Robert?" Rachel's clear voice sounded metallic as he held the phone at hip level. "Hello . . . Robert . . . can you hear me?"

He raised the phone and pressed it to his lips. "I can't talk to you now, Rachel, it's not a good time," he muttered. "I'll call you back later."

"What's wrong with you, Robert—you sound as if you were in a confessional. Why are you whispering like that?"

He sensed Rosalie's look of exasperation and raised his hand apologetically.

"We're in the process of breaking into a house," he whispered as loudly as he could. "It's about the manuscript. I've got to go, Rachel. Sorry."

"What?!" Rachel seemed to be losing her cool. "You're breaking into a house? Tell me, have you completely lost it? And who is *we*? Robert? *Robert?!*"

Ignoring the protests from the other side of the Atlantic, Robert ended the call as Rosalie dragged him in to the library.

"We made it," she said with relief and quickly pushed the door to. "*Mon Dieu,* who was that hysterical woman?"

"Oh . . . that was just . . . Rachel. Someone I know!" he said quickly, and immediately wondered a little guiltily why he was disowning his girlfriend. On the other hand—wasn't it Rachel who'd threatened to break up with him if he took the job in Paris? So you could say that their relationship was hanging in the balance, and a girlfriend who was possibly soon to be an ex-girlfriend might very well be described as "someone I know," he thought rather casuistically.

"Robert?"

Rosalie had obviously asked him something.

"Er . . . yes?"

"The manuscript!"

He hastily opened his briefcase and took out the brown envelope. "Here." He held the pages out to her. "Rachel . . . that is, the woman who just called, sent it to me."

She glanced at it, leafed through a few of the pages, and then shook her head. "I don't believe it," she said. "Wait down here, I'll be right back."

Robert sank down on one of the sofas and listened as Rosalie ran up the stairs.

Shortly afterward she was back with her own sheaf of paper in her hands. She sat down next to him on the sofa, out of breath.

"Here," she said, taking a deep breath and putting her manuscript down on the coffee table beside his. "It looks as if both versions are completely identical."

Robert leaned forward and excitedly studied the individual pages. "No doubt about it," he said and picked up two sheets to compare them. "The same alignment, even the same typeface. And look here"—he pointed to some places in the text—"the lowercase 'o' always has the same little smudge in the upper-left part of the curve." He looked at her. "And where exactly did you say you found the manuscript?"

"Upstairs in the bedroom," said Rosalie, red faced. "A cardboard box full of old photos and letters fell off the wardrobe, and among other things there was also this manuscript." She joined her hands and put them to her lips. "I still don't understand it," she said. "How does your mother come to be in possession of a manuscript belonging to Max Marchais?"

Robert shrugged his shoulders and looked at her knowingly. "In fact, a better question would be: How does Marchais come to be in possession of my mother's manuscript?" He watched Rosalie as she played uncomfortably with her braid. "I don't wish to offend you, but it is perfectly obvious which is the original and which the carbon copy."

She nodded and cleared her throat. "I'm afraid you're right." Then she gave him a sideways glance and her eyes sparkled. "I bet that pleases you, doesn't it?"

He grinned. "Of course it pleases me. I'm the son of a famous lawyer, remember?" He saw that she was trying to suppress a smile and was glad that he'd been able to make her laugh. Then his look became more thoughtful. "No, to be perfectly honest, it's not a matter of being right. At least, not just a matter of being right. Of course it's disgraceful that old Marchais tried to pass my mother's story off as his own in any case. Whether you like it or not," he added, as Rosalie shook her head energetically. "But of course I'm beginning to wonder what the story behind the story is. How did Marchais get hold of the carbon? Did he know my mother? New York isn't exactly just around the corner."

"Didn't you tell me that your mother has French relatives? And that she was in Paris once herself?"

"Could be, but that was long before I was born. The story of the blue tiger didn't exist then. After all, Mom made it up for me."

They were both silent for a moment, each lost in their own thoughts, and failed to notice that the sky outside the big living-room window was gradually turning all sorts of shades of lavender.

Suddenly Rosalie broke the silence. "Don't you find it a bit unusual that your mother wrote the whole story in French?"

He looked at her in surprise. "No, not at all. In fact, she spoke French fluently. Quite the contrary, when I found the manuscript among her papers, I had the feeling that it was meant to remind me of Paris. After all, she had made sure that I'd be able to read the story in French, hadn't she?" He smiled wryly and ran his hands brusquely through his hair.

Rosalie had stood up and gone over to the cabinet near the door with its two dark-red lamps. She switched on the light.

"And if we just let the whole thing rest?" she asked, running her fingers hesitantly over the keyboard of the old black typewriter that was also on the cabinet. "To be honest, Robert, I have a very strange feeling. Perhaps we'll be waking sleeping dogs. Perhaps we'll conjure up ghosts—"

"Utter nonsense," he interrupted her, sitting up straight. "You can't seriously ask that of me, Rosalie. No, I must find out the truth. I owe it to my mother. I'm sorry, but if you don't speak to Marchais then I'll do it myself."

Her shoulders slumped. "Why did he never tell me that it's an old story?" she said unhappily. "It always sounded as if the idea had just come to him."

Robert pushed himself up out of the soft cushions with both hands and went over to her. "It's not your fault, Rosalie. But no matter how much sympathy you feel for your old friend and author, you have to understand me, too."

She nodded imperceptibly, and stood there lost in thought, her fingers continuing to stroke the keyboard of the old Remington as if it could, like Aladdin's lamp, produce a genie that would fulfill all her wishes. Then she turned and strode decisively over to the desk in front of the window near the library. She took a blank sheet from a ream of paper and came back.

"Wait a moment," she said, and loaded the paper into the old machine. Robert watched her in some surprise as she now began to peck a short text on the machine with two fingers. She looked carefully at the page, and then let out a little cry of triumph.

"I knew it," she said with relief, nodded a couple of times, and then pointed to the page on which he recognized the first lines of the tiger story.

"What's this supposed to be?" he asked, somewhat puzzled. "Are you going to produce a third version of *The Blue Tiger*?"

"Look at it carefully," she said excitedly. "What do you see?" Her eyes shone.

The girl was a bit worked up, but okay! Robert sighed resignedly, and took a closer look at the page again. A guessing game, why not? Everything was quite complicated enough already.

So, Robert, he thought to himself, *what can you see? Concentrate, please.* He felt an impulse to laugh.

A moment later he frowned. Again and again his gaze ran over the few lines that stood out in pale blue from the white paper.

"Now you can see it, too, can't you?" Rosalie had come over to him.

Robert nodded. "Yes, now I can see it," he repeated in amazement.

He could see it all: the old typeface, the blue ribbon, the letter *o* with its smudge in the upper left.

The text on the paper that stuck in the typewriter was exactly the same as his mother's manuscript. Or to put it another way: the story of the blue tiger had been written on the old Remington he was standing beside. He shook his head slowly as it became clear to him what that meant.

Rosalie raised her eyebrows and pursed her lips. "That rather blows your theory out of the water, doesn't it, Robert?" she asked.

"But . . . the original . . . was in Mount Kisco," he objected.

"Oh please!" Rosalie's eyes shone with indignation. "You're not going to suggest that Max Marchais didn't just steal the story from your mother, but the typewriter as well? *C'est ridicule!*"

Robert said nothing. He was totally at a loss.

"This is Max Marchais's old Remington. There can be no argument about that. I've even seen it in one of the old photos. Whoever wrote the story, one thing is certain: it was written on this typewriter. And that can only mean . . ."

She fell silent, a little embarrassed.

Robert tried to finish her sentence. What, yes, what could it mean? His mother had written that story for him when he was a little boy—on a typewriter that was in Paris at the time and belonged to a Frenchman? Ludicrous. He thought very hard. Or that the story hadn't been written by his mother, but by Marchais, who was after all the author of numerous children's books? And yet . . . the story seemed so clearly designed for him, Robert, and his mother had always said that the story was just for the two of them. She'd loved the story of the blue tiger as much as he did. So why had she lied to him about it?

But on the other hand—had his mother ever said that she had written the story? That she had made it up? He thought awhile, but could not remember—only that she had said she was giving him the story as a gift. And apart from the question of its author-ship, the real and more interesting question was how it had come about that this Marchais and his mother had the same manuscript if they had never met. Had they never met?

He felt Rosalie's eyes on him and looked up.

"I'm still trying to work out what the 'R' means," she said thoughtfully.

He didn't understand immediately. "What?"

"Well—the dedication! I thought the 'R' stood for 'Rosalie.' You thought it stood for 'Robert.' The way things look, it can't be either, can it?"

He pressed his lips together and nodded. She was right, absolutely right. The dedication was not for him, even if it filled his heart with sadness.

Then he felt a gentle touch. Rosalie had put her hand on his arm, and her eyes seemed to him to be bigger than ever before.

"Robert," she said. "What was your mother's name?" It took a moment for him to see what the question meant. Then he slapped his forehead.

"Ruth," he said. "My mother's name was Ruth."

Twenty-two

It was always astounding how blindly and carelessly you could overlook the obvious, thought Rosalie, as she watched Robert Sherman blanching beside her. Although they had so frequently talked about the dedication, attempting to find someone to fit the mysterious initial, it had obviously never ever occurred to him that his mother's first name began with the letter *R*.

Robert was so perplexed that he was unable to speak for a moment. And then when he was finally about to say something, they heard the noise.

It sounded like a key turning in a lock. Seconds later the front door opened, and then swung shut with a soft click.

Heavy footsteps crossed the hall. A rustling noise. A closet was being opened. Clothes hangers rattled against each other.

They stood frozen on the spot beside the cabinet and looked at each other. The steps approached the library, and Rosalie felt her heart beginning to race. Who was it, there in the hall? For one mad moment she thought it was not impossible that it could be Max returning—and that he would catch them red-handed. Then she heard a sniff, and the muttering of a deep but clearly female voice. The steps passed the living-room door and went into the kitchen, where something was put down.

In a panic, she reached for Robert's hand.

"Come on!" she hissed. "Upstairs!"

They heard clattering from the kitchen and hastily grabbed the two manuscripts, crept out of the library, and went up the staircase that led upward from the hall. "This way!" She led Robert into the bedroom where the cardboard box of letters and photographs was still standing in the middle of the floor. They listened in silence to the noises that came up to them from downstairs.

Who would come into Max Marchais's house in the evening? wondered Rosalie. A neighbor? The gardener? As far as she knew, the housekeeper was the only one who had a key, and she was far away in Provence with her daughter.

"Let's wait a moment. Whoever it is, they're sure to go away soon," she whispered to Robert. He nodded, clutching the two manuscripts tightly.

"I can't understand why I didn't work it out for myself," he said softly. "The 'R' stands for 'Ruth.' Ruth Sherman. How could I be so dumb?"

"You just couldn't see the forest for the trees," she whispered back. "These things happen. And anyway, I'm sure you didn't call your mother Ruth."

He nodded and then put his finger to his lips. "Damn! She's coming upstairs."

They listened carefully to the creaking of the wooden stairs as they were trodden by a person of some weight. Rosalie looked around. In the open bedroom there were no real places where they could conceal themselves, and they would no longer be able to reach the little storeroom next to the bathroom. "Under the bed!" she hissed, dragging a surprised Sherman to the floor.

By the time the bedroom door opened and Madame Bonnier—Rosalie had no difficulty in recognizing the housekeeper—came panting in, they had disappeared from view. Hidden under a big, old, wooden bed, whose dark and dusty depths offered them a kindly refuge. Holding their breath and pressed so tightly together that barely a single manuscript page could be slipped between them, they looked into each other's eyes like a couple of conspirators, each listening to the other's heartbeat, which they were sure could be heard in this seemingly endless moment of suspended motion, danger, and intimacy. They listened to the housekeeper's footsteps and saw her flat-heeled sandals and meaty calves moving up and down beside the bed, as she began to smooth out the sheets and blankets and shake out the scatter cushions and pile them up at the head of the bed, grumbling as she did so.

Rosalie looked directly into Robert Sherman's azure-blue eyes, which were unsettlingly close to her, as too was his mouth, surprised once more (and totally inappropriately, given their current situation) at the extraordinary color of this man's eyes, which had struck her the first time that Robert had appeared outside her window display. She swallowed, feeling a tingling as if a thousand ants were walking over her.

She would surely have been somewhat surprised if she had known that the man from New York, who was pressed against her in complete silence in the deepest part of their hidey-hole, was at that very moment thinking something similar—that is, that he'd never looked into such midnight-blue eyes as Rosalie Laurent's.

And so it was no surprise that neither of them was able to work out what the humming, vibrating sound was that suddenly burst out between them.

Madame Bonnier had heard it, too, because her sandals, which had moved away from the bed, stopped immediately, offering Rosalie an unencumbered view of the rosy backs of the housekeeper's knees.

Madame Bonnier listened intently; even the backs of her knees seemed to be listening as the constant humming tone pierced the silence like the buzzing of a particularly fat fly.

Rosalie breathed in inaudibly, staring reproachfully at Robert. Her lips soundlessly formed the word "idiot!" as he dumbly begged forgiveness with a guilty expression, because it was his cell phone: he had of course switched it to silent mode, but stupidly had not switched it off entirely. She realized that it was impossible for him to get it out of his pocket without making yet more unnecessary noise.

Fortunately it was beyond the bounds of Marie-Hélène Bonnier's imagination to think that there might be people of the kind who would hide themselves under Monsieur Marchais's wonderful Grange bed.

She stamped over to the reading lamp on the bedside table, examined it carefully, jiggled it about, and then switched it on and off a couple of times.

"Damn electricity! A good thing I came this evening to make sure everything was all right," she muttered as the buzzing tone finally came to a stop. "Lights on all over the house, cardboard boxes on the floor, the whole place is going to the dogs." She shook her head disapprovingly and switched the lamp off. "That gardener could at least have switched off the lights!"

She bent over to pick up the box of photos and letters, and for one terrible moment Rosalie was absolutely certain that the housekeeper would discover their hiding place under the bed.

She held her breath.

But Madame Bonnier had better things to do. She had to restore order. The housekeeper got a stepladder from the storeroom, took the box, and, with a groan, put it back where it belonged. On top of the wardrobe.

When she disappeared into the bathroom to dust the washbasin with scouring powder, they left their hiding place as if at a secret word of command and ran down the stairs in their stocking feet, their shoes in their hands.

"Wait a moment—my bag is still in the library," whispered Robert softly as Rosalie headed for the front door.

"*Bon.* Let's escape through the garden." They crept into the library past the wall of books and the two sofas, pushed the heavy glass door aside, and then closed it behind them from the outside.

As they ran through the garden seconds later like Bonnie and Clyde after a successful bank job and disappeared between the hydrangea bushes, Rosalie felt an overwhelming urge to laugh.

"'Damn electricity!'" she burst out hilariously, fighting for breath as she leaned with her hand on the trunk of a cherry tree that overhung the old garden wall. Robert fell forward, his hands on his thighs, as he joined in her suppressed laughter.

And then—Rosalie could not afterward have said exactly how it happened—he kissed her.

That evening she wrote in her blue notebook:

The worst moment of the day:

Robert's damn cell phone begins to buzz as Madame Bonnier is standing beside the bed we are hiding under. I nearly wet myself with agitation. It doesn't bear thinking what would have happened if she'd found us!

The nicest moment of the day:

An evening kiss under a cherry tree that left us both a bit disconcerted.

"Sorry, I just couldn't help it," says Robert. And I say, as my heart performs a backward somersault, "That's okay, it was probably the result of all that tension." And laugh as if the kiss had been nothing.

During the ride home we continue to talk about our discovery, trying to puzzle out what it could mean. I talk and talk to cover up the beating of my heart. Then Robert makes a stupid remark, and we fall silent. The silence is embarrassing, almost unpleasant. A hasty parting outside the hotel. No further kiss. I'm relieved. And strangely also a bit disappointed.

René was still awake when I got home. He didn't notice anything—well, nothing had happened. A little slipup. *C'est tout!*

Twenty-three

....

Something had happened.

And by that Robert Sherman did not mean the series of surprising events that had happened to him since, a good week before, he had made a remarkable discovery in the window of a store in the rue du Dragon. A discovery that had since proved to be somewhat confusing, had thrown him off balance, and had thrust the actual reason for his trip (clarity about his professional and private life) into the background.

He meant something else: he could not get that hasty, unexpected, completely irrational kiss in an enchanted garden in Le Vésinet out of his head.

As he walked along the rue de l'Université early the next morning, heading for the Musée d'Orsay, where he wanted to see the Impressionists, images from the previous evening rolled up like the waves in a painting by Sorolla. He kept seeing Rosalie in her slim-waisted blue summer dress in front of him as she stood, laughing and breathless, her cheeks warm and rosy, under the cherry tree whose branches spread out over her like a roof. The air was full of the scent of lavender and twilight had fallen on the garden where the shapes of the bushes were becoming indistinct as the sky grew darker. Her hair had fallen loose, and her laugh, too, had something of a glorious release about it and for one intoxicating moment that knew neither day nor hour the woman with the lovely smile was for Robert the most desirable creature on earth.

She had been too surprised to defend herself. He had caught her unawares and she had abandoned herself to that impetuous kiss which fired a thousand particles of light through his body and tasted as sweet as a wild strawberry.

He instinctively ran his tongue over his lips and rubbed them briefly together as if that could bring back the taste of the kiss, which now seemed totally unreal to him, almost as if he had dreamt it. But he hadn't been dreaming. It had happened, and then suddenly everything had gone wrong.

Robert stuck his hands deep in his pockets and stamped along the narrow street with furrowed brow.

It must have been unpleasant for her rather than the reverse—he shouldn't pretend otherwise. After the moment had flown, he had sensed her pulling away from him in embarrassment. "It must have been the tension," she'd said, and then laughed as if nothing had happened.

His kiss had obviously not been exactly overwhelming, and she had obviously been kind enough to gloss over the embarrassing situation so that he wouldn't feel like an idiot.

He sighed deeply. On the other hand, when they'd been lying there together so silent and motionless under that bed, as if they were in a cocoon—hadn't there been something in her eyes? Hadn't he read a sudden attraction in her unwavering gaze? Hadn't there unexpectedly been a closeness that made them completely oblivious to the hard parquet floor and the fear of being discovered?

Had he really just imagined all that? Was it due to that special moment? He had no idea anymore.

He just knew that he could have continued to lie under that bed forever. But then his cell phone had made its presence felt, and its low buzzing had rung in his ears like the trumpets at Jericho. They were within a hair's breadth of being found out.

He grinned as he thought of the heavy footsteps of the housekeeper, and how she'd kept on shaking the bedside light suspiciously.

The drive back to Paris had been peculiar. They'd hardly taken their seats in the little car when Rosalie began pouring out words like a waterfall, literally bombarding him with questions ("And you're sure that your mother never mentioned the name Max Marchais? Perhaps he visited your mother in Mount Kisco sometime? But they must have known each other, since he obviously dedicated the story to her!"), had continued to address him formally as *vous* in spite of the kiss, and had gone on inventing new scenarios which ranged from Max Marchais as his mother's long-lost brother to Max Marchais as her secret lover.

Robert had begun to feel uncomfortable and had become quieter and quieter. All these discoveries and the questions they threw up were just too much for him. It would have been simpler to sue an ageing, somewhat arrogant French writer for plagiarism. But then Rosalie had found the manuscript in Marchais's house and immediately everything became far less simple. It had then become clear—or at least seemed to be clear—that his mother had not made up the story of the blue tiger for Robert, but rather that it had been dedicated to her—as seemed very probable—by (of all people) a Frenchman, whom she had never mentioned (at least, not to him). All this made him uneasy, but he hadn't begun to think deeply about it or, if he were honest, hadn't wanted to start thinking about it.

After all, it was a matter of *his* mother and *his* feelings, and whatever the background to this strange story was, it would affect him far more strongly than it would affect the blithely chattering woman behind the wheel, whom he found both annoying and baffling.

Eventually it got too far-fetched for him.

"Your speculation is all very fine, Rosalie, but it's not taking us a single step forward. It's about time we finally spoke to Max Marchais himself," he had interrupted her harshly. "He's not going to drop dead simply because we ask him a few questions."

"Oh, fine. Absolutely fine. Excuse me for trying to help you," she had retorted. "Fine, then I'd better just keep my mouth shut."

Upset, she had fallen silent, even though he had immediately assured her that he hadn't meant it like that, and finally a tense silence had filled the cramped space in the little car.

When she later dropped him outside the hotel, he hadn't dared to touch her again. They had parted with a brief nod of the head, and Rosalie had promised to call him as soon as Max Marchais was in a fit state to be asked certain questions.

"We should at least wait until he's back home," she had said, and Robert had sighed inwardly. "Perhaps we could visit him together, I'm sure that would make things a lot easier, don't you think?" She had looked at him with a hesitant smile.

"As long as we don't have to lie under a dusty bed again," he had said, in a failed attempt to be funny. He could have immediately slapped himself for such a boneheaded remark.

She had clammed up like an oyster. Of course. He looked unhappily at her pale face, which betrayed no emotion.

"Well, then . . . I've got to go," she had said finally, with a strange little smile, fiddling with her safety belt. "I'm sure René is waiting for me."

René! The thrust had hit home.

Grouchily, Robert kicked a pebble, which fell into the constantly running water of the Paris gutter. He had completely failed to remember that Rosalie had a boyfriend—the bodyguard, who was only too ready to defend her with his outsize fists. Robert smiled wryly, thinking of his first and hopefully last encounter with the French giant, who had already made it clear he wanted to beat him up because he had ostensibly insulted his girlfriend. A fitness trainer, well, well. ("He's a sports graduate and yoga teacher," Rosalie had explained to him earnestly that evening in the Marly. "He's even worked as personal trainer for a famous French actress.") So what? Admittedly the guy, thanks to his size and his velvet-brown eyes, was certainly not the kind of man women would fail to notice. Okay, he wasn't bad-looking. But what else did he have to offer? thought Robert with a degree of defiant arrogance. He couldn't quite work out what it was that Rosalie saw in the pragmatic René, and in fact he didn't really even want to try—it was certainly not a union of kindred souls. It was as clear as daylight that the pair were not suited for each other.

And then, strangely, he thought of Rachel.

Rachel: sensible, efficient, assertive, slick as a fashion plate, gorgeous. It had been she who had called him a second time as he was hiding under the bed with Rosalie. At a really awkward moment. She hadn't left a message, which made it clear that she was really displeased with him. He'd call her that afternoon when it was morning in New York.

If he told her all about the manuscript and explained to her that he had crept into a stranger's house to follow the trail of a mystery that closely concerned him, she'd surely understand why he had broken off her call to him. It would probably be better not to tell her that he'd been lying under a bed with Rosalie Laurent when she'd called the second time. And he wouldn't mention the kiss either. The whole business was already complicated enough.

He speeded up and arrived at the Quai d'Orsay. As he took his place in the line outside the museum and patiently edged forward bit by bit, he saw Rosalie once more in his mind's eye, standing laughing under the tree like Shakespeare's Titania. He tried to dismiss the vision and think about something else, but he couldn't help asking himself if he'd ever seen Rachel laughing as uninhibitedly as that capricious, contrary, willful and—yes, he had to admit it—exceedingly enchanting woman, who was only linked to him, if you looked closely at it, by the story of the blue tiger.

Was that a little or a lot? Or perhaps even everything? "How happy some o'er other some can be," he thought briefly. Was this going to be his personal *Midsummer Night's Dream*?

The fact that, of all people, it was this young French graphic artist who had illustrated his favorite story and that he had only gotten to know her because of that seemed all at once to be a matter of fate.

And, as they worked together to uncover the mystery of an old story, hadn't a new story begun to develop—one that was far more exciting?

Deep in thought he went up to the window in the entry hall of the museum and bought his ticket.

As he put his wallet back in his bag, he came across the book, bound in red-and-white-striped leather, that he'd bought in Shakespeare and Company and completely forgotten. *The Taming of the Shrew.* The book was still in his shoulder bag.

He'd wanted to hand it to Rosalie with a witty remark when the right moment arrived. But it seemed somehow not to want to arrive. Robert sighed. At that moment the omens were, it seemed, not looking too favorable for Petruchio.

Twenty-four

....

After more than two weeks in hospital, Max Marchais was exceedingly delighted to be back at home. He was so thankful that he even put up with Marie-Hélène Bonnier's reproaches with a smile.

"On a ladder with open leather slippers, really, Monsieur Marchais! How careless! You could have broken your neck."

"You're right, as always, Marie-Hélène," replied Max, happily cutting himself a slice of the crisp-roasted *confit de canard* that Madame Bonnier had prepared for him on a bed of salad.

"Really delicious, the duck. No one does it better than you." He thought of the tasteless health food he'd been served in hospital and relished the tasty, tender meat of the duck breast that his housekeeper had, as he well knew, bought fresh at the market in Le Vésinet. "Simply divine." He swallowed the duck and took a great gulp of Saint-Émilion from his balloon glass.

Madame Bonnier glowed red with pride. She didn't often hear such hymns of praise from her employer. "Well, yes, I know it's your favorite dish, Monsieur Marchais. And of course we're all glad that you're back here with us."

Somewhat flustered, Madame Bonnier retreated to the kitchen, while Max asked himself with amusement who this "all" might actually be. It was not exactly the case that he knew hordes of people who had sorely missed him, old curmudgeon that he was.

It had moved him to think that Marie-Hélène had insisted on returning early from her stay with her daughter and grand-daughter in order to take care of the house and oversee some urgent building work. Now that it was really important she would not leave him in the lurch, she had said. And you couldn't trust that gardener who had left all the lights in the house burning and hadn't even locked the sliding door in the living room properly. Anyone could easily have broken in!

That was rather strange, because Sebastiano swore to high heaven that he had locked all the doors properly—including of course the big sliding door in the living room. Now it could be that in all the upheaval he'd forgotten to, but even so Max would be eternally grateful to him, and not only because he kept the garden in impeccable order. It had also been Sebastiano who had picked him up at the hospital and driven him home.

"Clément could just as well have done that," Madame Bonnier had said, somewhat offended. Clément was her husband, and these minor hostilities that had flared up between the housekeeper and gardener both surprised Max and made him smile.

When he got home, he found a bunch of flowers from Ro-salie Laurent. How thoughtful. On the delightful get-well card she sent with it was a message: She was very much looking for-ward to visiting him in Le Vésinet very soon.

Rosalie had visited him twice more in hospital, each time waiting patiently until the energetic physical therapist who dealt with him every day (they never knew exactly when beforehand) had finished with her exercises.

She had brought a lavender-colored box of little cakes from Ladurée and told him that she was getting on well with the illustrations for the fairy-tale book and that having help in the store had turned out to be a godsend. She had also told him about René, who was obviously enjoying himself immensely in sunny California and was really inspired by the seminar and the mentality of the people there, all of whom were very sporty and health conscious.

Nevertheless Max had not failed to notice the searching looks Rosalie occasionally cast in his direction when she thought he wasn't looking.

"Is something wrong? Or do I look that awful?" he asked finally, and she had shaken her head in embarrassment and laughed.

"No, no, what could there be? I'm just glad that you're getting so much better." He'd still felt that something wasn't quite right. Rosalie seemed more pensive than usual, turned in upon herself. As if she was waiting for something.

Well, yes, perhaps she's just missing her boyfriend, he said to himself. He himself was by now used to living alone and valued the advantages brought by not having to take other people into account. But recently he had noticed with increasing dismay that even he felt something was missing from his life.

As he lay in his hospital room he had had enough time to think things over. Just a couple of years ago, his peace had been most important to him; he quickly felt irritated or bored by other people and had always thought that he would never feel lonely, because there would always be interesting books for him to read.

But when the people who meant something to you were no longer there, books strangely began to lose their meaning, too. Deep inside, and in spite of all the arrogance he sometimes showed, Max regretted not having a family. And by that he didn't mean his sister in Montpellier with her constant complaints. She had actually telephoned the hospital, because Madame Bonnier had gone over his head to let her know about the accident ("She is your sister after all, Monsieur"). As might have been expected it had not been a very pleasant conversation. Thérèse had first (for decency's sake) asked how he was getting on, and then she'd had nothing better to do than to tell him that a neighbor of hers, some tottering old fogey whom he didn't know from Adam, had just recently died as a consequence of a broken hip.

That was typical of his sister who, no matter what happened to you, could always come up with an even more horrific story. After the gruesome story about her neighbor she'd complained that he never came to Montpellier to visit her. And she used all the rest of the call to tell him in great detail about the *terrible* burst water pipe they'd had in the spring. "You can't imagine what that ended up costing, and the stupid insurance refused to pay anything because they claimed the pipe was already in a very poor condition."

Who knows, perhaps the family in Montpellier was already speculating about his will. But they were making a very big mistake.

Family wasn't necessarily something positive, Max thought as he put the phone down grumpily after another quarter of an hour. And yet—he sometimes caught himself thinking that old age would certainly be easier to bear if there were someone with whom you could expect to share the future, in the certainty that it would continue and that something would always remain.

And yet again he thought what a great stroke of luck it had been that he'd given in to his publisher's importuning.

Without *The Blue Tiger* he would certainly never have met Rosalie Laurent, who had for him taken on something of the role of a daughter. Never mind the fact that he would never have set foot in the little postcard store on the rue du Dragon if Montsignac had not been so insistent about it.

Good old Montsignac! At the important moments in his life, whether good or bad, he had always been there. And this time, too, he had visited him in hospital.

Without any warning, as was his custom, he'd suddenly appeared in the room one morning in a dazzling white shirt that, as always, was stretched rather precariously over his belly.

"Well, well, you keep on inventing new ways of avoiding answering the phone, eh?" he joked. Then he'd sat down beside him, waved Sister Yvonne out of the room with a lordly gesture, and as soon as she had left the room with squeaking soles and a mistrustful look, he'd calmly taken a bottle of pastis out of his bag. "Never do that again, Marchais, my old friend! How could you give me such a fright? All the hopes of our publishing house rest on you." He poured the pastis into two water glasses and they toasted each other. *"Santé!"*

"I might have realized that you've only come because you want something from me," Max had said mockingly, trying to conceal his emotion. "If you've got another idea up your sleeve, Montsignac, just forget it! I'm not going to write another line for you, I'd sooner fall off the ladder again."

"Well, we'll see about that. There's a time for everything, that's what I say. And anyway you've got to do your exercises with that . . . *delectable* nurse"—Montsignac pointed at the door and grinned—"so that we can get you back on your feet, *n'est-ce pas?*" His eyes shone with amusement.

"But a little Christmas story, illustrated by your friend Rosalie Laurent—you can write that between soup and pudding."

"Not if they both taste as disgusting as the food in this hospital."

"You've been spoiled, my dear Marchais—I wish my wife could cook as well as your Madame Bonnier. Stupidly, she much prefers reading."

They'd laughed, and now he had actually been home for several days and was just spooning in the rich crème brûlée that Marie-Hélène had served him in the dining room. With a sigh of satisfaction, Max wiped his mouth with his damask napkin and limped, leaning on his crutches and taking very small, careful steps, into the library. It was a wonder that he could move about so well so soon after the operation. The word "progress" had taken on a new dimension. Even Professeur Pasquale had been surprised how well the "Ward 28 hip" was doing and had finally given in to Max's constant pressure, allowing him to go through the necessary postoperation rehabilitation phase as an outpatient.

So now Max took a taxi every day to a physiotherapist's practice near the hospital where he could do the necessary exercises. A bit laborious, perhaps, but still far better than being stuck in a rehabilitation clinic getting depressed. Professeur Pasquale had also advised him to remove anything in the house that might cause him to trip and to have handholds and a bath seat fitted in the bathroom—as well as to avoid ladders for a while.

Max put his crutches to one side, dropped into his desk chair with a groan, and looked out into the garden which was bathed in the midday sun. Then he picked up the phone and dialed Rosalie Laurent's number.

She was in the store when he rang, and there were customers there, but there was no mistaking her delight at his call. It wasn't a long conversation, but long enough to deal with what was most important: to invite Rosalie to Le Vésinet for coffee on Saturday.

"How lovely that you're home again, Max. I'd love to come," she had said. "Should I bring anything?"

"No need, Marie-Hélène will bake us a tarte tatin. Just bring yourself."

Max put the phone down with a smile and sat at his desk for a while, lost in thought. At the end of the call Rosalie had said that there was something she wanted to discuss with him when she came to Le Vésinet. What could it be?

Max sat thinking for a while, and then noticed that he was gradually succumbing to a pleasant weariness. Since his time in hospital he'd gotten into the habit of taking a little afternoon nap. And fortunately no one would disturb him at it here in the peaceful silence of the old villa. He reached for his crutches and heaved himself laboriously out of his chair. Montsignac had probably won Rosalie over to the idea of the Christmas story, and she was now meant to persuade him to do it. The old fox!

Shaking his head, he went over to the door. As he passed the old cabinet, glancing with pleasure at his favorite picture, a southern French seaside landscape, he suddenly saw something that brought him to a stop.

In the old black Remington, that he hadn't used for decades and kept more out of nostalgia than anything else, there was a sheet of paper.

Startled, Max turned the little wheel at the side and pulled the paper out of the roller. What he saw made him feel strangely uneasy. The pale blue lines seemed to him like a message from the past. Could there be such a thing?

His heart beat faster and he felt like a time traveler hurtling through space at breakneck speed.

On the page in his hand were the first sentences of the story of the blue tiger. Written almost forty years before. On that old Remington.

Twenty-five

....

"Sometimes in life things happen that you just weren't expecting," he had told her when they spoke together on Skype as they did every Friday. His voice had sounded a little guilty, but also very definite, like the time-delayed pictures of his face, which had taken on a golden-brown coloring under the California sun. "I thought it was better to tell you right away," he added ingenuously, smiling at her from the screen in his boyish way. "I hope we can still be friends." Rosalie had indeed expected many things. But definitely not that René would end their relationship on Skype. Nothing like that had ever happened to her before—still, she should have seen it coming, and if she hadn't been so bound up with the events and emotional upheavals of her own life she would certainly have noticed the signs earlier.

Almost three weeks had passed since she had taken her boyfriend to the airport in Paris. From the very beginning she'd gotten the impression that René was taking to his seminar in San Diego like a duck to water—whenever she spoke to him, this was the old-fashioned phrase that popped into her mind. In every telephone conversation his voice had brimmed over with enthusiasm. Zack Whiteman—a god. The participants in the seminar—outgoing, laid-back, all with the right spirit. The long, golden beaches—unbelievable. The climate—fantastic. Everything was perfect; she'd already understood that.

"The latest trend is roga," René had told her. "The best thing you can do for your body."

"Roga?" she repeated suspiciously, sitting in bed with her cup of coffee, hoping she'd never have to try a sport that was so demanding just to pronounce. "What on earth is that?"

"A combination of running and yoga," he explained. "I'll show you when I get back."

She'd laughed and thought, *No thank you!* When he'd then told her about the blond long-distance runner who accompanied him on his "fasted training" first thing in the morning before sharing a papaya with lime juice, she'd put it down to "sporting enthusiasm" and thought no further of it.

In subsequent calls the name Anabel Miller had cropped up again a couple of times, and then the long-distance runner suddenly disappeared from their conversations. But not, as it turned out, from the life of her roga-practicing boyfriend.

For a couple of days she heard no more, and when they then spoke again and René materialized on her computer screen looking visibly sheepish, Rosalie could see that he had something on his mind. His permanent enthusiasm had given way to embarrassment, and the gaze of his brown eyes into the camera was rather anxious.

"Can we talk?" he had asked.

"Of course. We're talking already, aren't we?" she'd said, unaware of what was going on.

"*Alors* . . . well . . . I don't really know how to tell you this . . . humph!" He scratched the back of his head. "It's not so simple. You're . . . such a wonderful woman, Rosalie . . . even if you definitely eat too many croissants." He gave an embarrassed grin. "But what does that matter, you can afford it, you've got a good metabolism. . . ."

"Eh . . . so?" Disconcerted, Rosalie bent forward, trying to find some sense in her boyfriend's babbling.

"Well . . . I mean, it has nothing to do with you, there's no way I want to put you down, you're too important to me . . . and even if we sort of . . . well . . . how should I put it, aren't such a good match in terms of our interests," he hemmed and hawed, "it was always very good with you. . . ."

And then finally the penny dropped.

"The long-distance runner," she said and he nodded in relief because it was all out in the open at last.

And then he said those words about the things that sometimes happen in life even when you're not expecting them.

STRANGELY, IT HADN'T HURT at all. Well, not much. Of course she'd felt a little strange as the years she'd spent with René rolled past her inner eye like a film. There were many things she would not have wanted to miss, not even that solitary early-morning run through the Jardin du Luxembourg and certainly not that first night on the roof of her little apartment.

Rosalie smiled as she thought of it. She hadn't been totally destroyed or outraged at René's confession that he'd fallen head over heels in love with a sporty blonde called Anabel Miller, who ate papayas for breakfast and with whom he could now practice roga—or anything else—to his heart's content.

René's honesty was disarming, as usual, and she couldn't be angry with him. Surprised at how quickly he'd fallen in love, yes of course. But when she got dressed after their conversation and stood in front of the mirror in the bathroom putting on a touch of lipstick, she realized to her surprise that she was even a little relieved. That could have been because some things that she hadn't been expecting had occurred in her own life.

The previous Tuesday Robert had, to her surprise, turned up at the store to find out "how things were." It was the first time they'd seen each other after their dubious adventure in Le Vésinet and their unfortunate parting outside the hotel. When she saw the tall, lanky figure with his mop of blond hair appear at the door of the store at midday, something approaching a shock of joy ran through her limbs.

"Am I intruding?" Robert had asked, flashing her a hopeful smile that was difficult to resist.

"No . . . no, of course not. I just have to . . . ," she had stammered, self-consciously removing a lock of hair from her face, "deal with this lady's purchases." Her cheeks red, she'd turned to her customer. "So . . . what do we have here? Three sheets of gift wrap, five cards, a rose stamp . . ."

"Oh, do you know what? I think I'll also take one of those pretty paperweights that you have in the window," said the customer, a red-haired woman in an elegant yellow shirtwaist dress—obviously an Italian—clumping over to the window on her breathtakingly high heels. "That one there . . . with the writing." She pointed into the window.

"Yes, of course, with pleasure." Rosalie followed the customer, pushing past Robert who was leaning on the store doorpost. "Which paperweight would you like—*Paris* or *l'Amour?*"

"Hm . . ." The Italian woman thought for a moment. "*Molto bene*—they're both very pretty. . . ." She pursed her lips indecisively as Rosalie took both the oval glass paperweights out of the display and held them out to the customer.

"Why don't you take both?" they suddenly heard from the direction of the door, and both women turned round in surprise. Robert Sherman stood there smiling, his arms folded over his water-blue polo shirt. "Excuse me for intervening—but Paris and love—they suit each other perfectly, don't you think?"

Flattered, the Italian woman smiled back, and it was not difficult to see that she found the "intervention" of this good-looking foreigner pleasing. Her gaze lost itself for a moment in his eyes and then slid down over the suntanned arms with the little blond hairs that emerged from the polo shirt, the bright, slightly too loose-fitting duck pants, and the brown suede moccasins.

She seemed to really like what she saw.

"*Sì, signor*, that's a good idea," she purred. "After all, Paris is the city of love, isn't it?" She laughed, tilted her head back a little, and fluttered her thick black eyelashes. She obviously interpreted Robert's remark as an invitation to flirt. She nodded curtly to Rosalie. "Wrap them both for me, please!" Then she directed her undivided attention back to Robert. "You're not from here, are you? No, let me guess!" Another throaty laugh. "You're . . . an *American!*"

Robert raised his eyebrows and nodded with amusement, while Rosalie stood beside the till in silence, wrapping the paperweights in tissue paper and following the banter with furrowed brow. What was all this idiotic billing and cooing about? Luna Luna wasn't a dating café.

"An American in Paris—how romantic," cried the Italian woman with delight. Then she lowered her voice.

"So we're both foreigners in this beautiful city." She held her slim hand out to him, and it wouldn't have surprised Rosalie if he'd kissed it. "Gabriella Spinelli. From Milano."

Robert took her hand with a grin. "Robert Sherman, New York."

Gabriella Spinelli took a step backward. "No!" she breathed, opening her already outsize eyes even wider. "You aren't by any chance from the law firm Sherman and Sons? My uncle, Angelo Salvatore, who lives in New York, was represented in a very complicated case years ago by a Paul Sherman. A lot of money depended on it. The best lawyer he ever had—Uncle Angelo still says so. He was more than satisfied." She straightened the sunglasses in her hair.

Robert nodded in surprise. "That was my father."

"Well what do you know! *Madre mia!* My goodness, is it possible!" Gabriella laughed ecstatically and all at once Rosalie felt a violent urge to wring the scrawny neck of this red-haired lady from Milan, whose uncle—Angelo Soprano? no . . . Salvatore—was obviously the godfather of the New York Mafia.

"It's-a small-a world-a," she said with her appalling Italian accent. "Do you believe in coincidence, Mr. Sherman?" She tilted her head coquettishly, and Robert couldn't help shaking his head with a smile.

Rosalie felt that the moment had come to intervene. "*Et voilà*—that makes seventy-three euros and eighty cents," she said, thrusting a pretty sky-blue bag with a white ribbon under the nose of a rather shocked Gabriella.

The Italian woman rummaged quickly and without thinking in her canary-yellow Prada bag and took out a massive wallet, while still keeping an eye on the American, who had not moved from his place near the door.

When she had paid and stopped right in front of Robert to continue their conversation, Rosalie came up behind her. "*Au revoir,* madame, I'm very sorry, but we close for lunch," she said, opened the door, and shoved the red-haired Italian gently but firmly out onto the street.

"Oh, just one moment!" Gabriella swooped elegantly round and was back beside Robert.

"How lucky we met, Mr. Sherman," she twittered. "Do you have time for a coffee? I'd really like that."

"I'm afraid Mr. Sherman has an appointment," said Rosalie with a grim smile. She folded her arms and blocked the lovely Gabriella's path back into the store. "*Bonne journée, madame!*"

"Oh, what a pity! Such a pity!" The Italian woman retreated regretfully with her shopping, but not before giving Robert a visiting card and a longing look. "Call me, Signor Sherman, I'm sure we have a lot to talk about."

"So I have an appointment?" asked Robert with some amusement after Rosalie had slammed the door behind Gabriella Spinelli.

"Yes," she said with a challenging look. "With me."

"Oh!" He raised his eyebrows with an amused smile. "That is of course . . . *much* better."

"Very witty. If you've only dropped in to flirt with foreign women, then you might as well go at once," she blurted. *Too dumb!* She chewed her lip.

"Do I detect jealousy here?"

She rolled her eyes theatrically. "Don't flatter yourself, my friend. I merely wanted to save you from the relentless twittering of an Italian robin redbreast."

"An extremely attractive robin redbreast." He grinned. "Great legs."

"Oh, I didn't know you had a penchant for Italian robins," she mocked.

He shook his head. "No need to worry, my dear. When I think about it, I much prefer French mockingbirds." He looked at her, the corners of his mouth twitching. "So what's up—do I have an appointment or not?"

"If you behave yourself—maybe." Rosalie looked at him meaningfully. She still hadn't forgiven him for the remark about the dusty bed. "Perhaps later, when Madame Morel comes—my assistant," she added. "I can't get away until then."

"Didn't you just say you were closing?" He pretended to be surprised.

"If you don't stop asking dumb questions right away, you'll be thrown out," said Rosalie. "Why are you here anyway?"

"Well, I just happened to be in the neighborhood and wanted to ask if you'd heard anything from Max Marchais. You haven't been in contact since . . . since we came back from Le Vésinet, and I wasn't sure . . ." He was silent for a moment, and she wondered what he was thinking. "I mean, you were pretty mad . . . in the car. . . ."

"Okay." She felt herself going red and looked to one side.

"Max Marchais left hospital a few days ago, but he hasn't called back yet. As soon as he gets in touch, I'll let you know, and then we'll go to Le Vésinet. As we agreed."

He obviously thought she was an overly touchy shrinking violet who wouldn't keep her word if she felt offended.

"I didn't intend to annoy you, Rosalie. It's just that I was quite confused myself that evening. After all, for me this whole business is of great personal importance and not just a kind of . . . exciting treasure hunt, as I'm sure you understand?"

Rosalie nodded. Of course she understood. Robert gave her a searching look.

"And when I said I didn't want to be under a bed with you, that was just—"

"Stupid," they both said simultaneously and laughed.

"So, when does this Madame Mortel arrive?"

"Morel. And she comes at two o'clock. If you like, you can pick me up then and we'll go for a walk with William Morris."

William Morris raised his head when he heard his name and the word *walk* and wagged his tail happily.

Robert bent down and carefully scratched the little dog's head. "Well now, who knows," he said, "perhaps this will be the beginning of a beautiful friendship."

THE AFTERNOON TURNED OUT totally differently than expected. Except perhaps for William Morris, who hardly cared how many people took him for his walkies.

Instead of two, in the end there were three of them walking along the bank of the Seine. And the greater part of the conversation was taken up by her mother.

Rosalie had been quite surprised when, just before two, not only did Madame Morel come into the store, but also just a little later Rosalie's mother, with whom she'd had dinner quite recently.

"Bonjour, mon enfant," she said, immediately claiming the maximum possible attention for herself. "Well, aren't you going to say hello to your mother?" As usual she was extremely elegantly dressed—light-gray suit, white silk blouse, pearl necklace—and she had obviously come straight from the hairdresser, because her ash-blond hair was freshly streaked and wound into an elegant chignon at the back.

Rosalie, who was actually involved in a conversation with Madame de Rougemont, who even on this summery day insisted on wearing her gloves and even outdid Madame Laurent in elegance, smiled and stopped to briefly greet her mother.

"Hello, Maman!" Mother and daughter exchanged the obligatory air kisses. "I'll be with you right away. Would you like to sit down?" She pointed to the leather armchair in the corner.

"Oh, no, I'd rather stand—I've just spent hours sitting at the hairdresser's." Madame Laurent gave a dainty little sigh and, with a quick movement of her hand, checked her artistically stacked hair. "Don't you worry about me, *ma petite,* I can wait."

She walked up and down in the store, running her gaze over the goods on show. It finally came to rest on Madame Morel who was restocking some shelves with colorful cards and envelopes.

"Ah, you must be the new assistant. How sensible that my daughter has finally thought about getting some staff—she really does work too hard." She nodded regally to Madame Morel and continued to wander around the store, humming a little tune, her heels clicking on the tiled floor.

Rosalie felt a degree of uneasiness rising within her. With half an ear she listened to Madame de Rougemont, who was telling her in great detail about her wishes for a hand-painted card for the round-numbered birthday of her oldest friend, Charlotte. "It must be something with a gondola," she mused aloud. "Charlotte loves Venice, and I'd like to gift her a weekend in Venice. What do you think of the idea?"

"Oh, I think that's absolutely great," Rosalie hastened to assure her, keeping an eye on her mother, who was circling round the store with her hands clasped behind her back and her heels clattering.

"But the text on the card must be . . . original, I'd like something *original*." Madame de Rougemont waved her gloved hand in a delicate spiral and pursed her lips with their hint of pink lipstick thoughtfully.

"I'm sure I'll think of something, Madame de Rougemont." Rosalie straightened up in an attempt to bring her conversation with the old lady to a conclusion.

"Good, then I won't keep you any longer, my dear." Madame de Rougemont reached for her purse and looked curiously over at Cathérine Laurent. "You have a visitor, I see. Your mother?" she chirped.

Rosalie nodded and the old lady obviously saw it as a sign that she could introduce herself. She tripped over to a surprised Madame Laurent and said, "I love your daughter's store, such lovely things."

"Maman—may I introduce Madame de Rougemont, a very dear customer of mine. She lives in the seventh arrondissement, too," Rosalie explained quickly. "My mother—Madame Laurent."

"Enchantée," said Cathérine Laurent with a measured nod of the head. But before she could come up with a reply that would certainly have implied that she was a de Vallois by birth, the door opened yet again. It was on the dot of two o'clock.

Robert came in. He was carrying a gigantic bouquet of flowers.

"Oh—am I too early?" he asked, looking at the collection of ladies of varying ages, all of whom were staring at him with great interest.

A quarter of an hour later—the bouquet, which had been admired by everyone in the store, had by then found its place in a large vase—they set off on a walk together: Robert, Rosalie, and—Maman.

Cathérine Laurent had insisted on accompanying her daughter and this interesting American, who obviously had perfect manners and brought her daughter flowers.

"Oh, I think I'll come along for a little of the way, the weather is so wonderful and I've been sitting down a lot today," she had said after Rosalie had introduced her to Robert Sherman briefly as an "acquaintance."

Madame de Rougemont would certainly also have had nothing against a little walk if anyone had asked her. She kept on inspecting the tall man with the American accent who seemed somehow familiar—an actor, perhaps.

"Such a lovely bouquet," she had said as she finally, hesitantly turned to go, not without giving Robert Sherman a charming smile. Then she suddenly stopped, opening her eyes wide. *"Parbleu,* now I know where I recognize you from, monsieur! You've been here before, haven't you? You're . . . aren't you the lawyer who—"

"Oh, Monsieur Sherman is a *lawyer*?" cried Cathérine Laurent delightedly.

"—knocked over the postcard stand?" Madame de Rouge-mont continued undeterred. "Well, I see that you've come to regret your behavior." Her little hand waved in the direction of the bouquet as she stepped out of the store. "It's always good when a man knows how to say sorry—my husband never could."

"What behavior?" Rosalie's mother asked with interest, while Robert raised his eyebrows in astonishment and Madame Morel hovered deferentially behind the counter.

Rosalie decided to bring an end to the general confusion by putting William Morris on his leash.

"Let's go," she said, waving to Madame Morel, who would now watch over the little postcard store until the early evening.

As they walked in perfect harmony along the bank of the Seine and Cathérine Laurent engaged Robert in conversation, Rosalie could hear the cogs rattling in her mother's brain.

A male acquaintance whom she'd never heard of, flowers, a quarrel, an apology, her daughter clearly embarrassed, and René far away and out of the picture.

Rosalie saw a satisfied smile playing round the corner of her mother's mouth. Maman was obviously coming to the totally wrong conclusion. That it was ultimately not such a wrong conclusion, because the whims of Fate had decided to enter a long-distance runner into the race in far-off San Diego to take René's heart by storm, was something that Rosalie was as yet unaware of on that Tuesday afternoon.

"And how did you meet my daughter, Monsieur Sherman?" she heard her mother asking. Madame Laurent had adopted an intimate tone of voice that was completely inappropriate, and

Rosalie wondered how long it would be before she took Robert's arm. My goodness, the way she was interrogating Robert was really embarrassing. Almost as if she saw him as a potential son-in-law. "Your French is absolutely fabulous, if I may say so," she now added approvingly.

"Yes . . . your daughter has already discovered that," replied Robert with a grin at Rosalie. "In fact you could probably say that we met because of a book that we both . . . um . . . value very highly."

"Oh yes, literature . . . it's something that so often brings people together." Madame Laurent began to rhapsodize. "I love books, you know."

Rosalie looked at her mother in surprise. What was going on here?

"Are you staying long in Paris, Monsieur Sherman? Then you must definitely come and have tea at my house with Rosalie."

"Well, I—"

"Monsieur Sherman and I are working on a project together, Maman," interrupted Rosalie and bent down to release William Morris, who was tugging energetically at his leash. "And that is all." She tried not to hear the little voice inside that mockingly asked if she herself really believed what she was saying.

Anyway, her mother seemed not to believe it. "Well, well," she said, not allowing herself to be diverted from her chosen course, and playing with her pearls. "So you are a lawyer, Monsieur Sherman?" she continued her interrogation. "An interesting profession. Are you here on business?"

Robert dug his hands deep in his pockets and smiled. "Yes and no. I'm still a bit undecided." And then he explained to a deeply impressed Madame Laurent that, although he had studied law, he had ultimately decided on a university career in the humanities and that he was in Paris because he had been offered a guest professorship at the Sorbonne for the coming semester.

"A professor for Shakespeare, how wonderful," exclaimed Madame Laurent. "*Hamlet, The Taming of the Shrew, Romeo and Juliet!* 'What love can do, that dares love attempt,'" she declaimed to Rosalie's chagrin, before darting a meaningful glance at Robert. "And you still haven't decided?"

Twenty-six

·····················

"The game is on," she had said. "We're invited to Marchais's place on Saturday. That is—" She interrupted herself and laughed softly into the phone. "Actually it's only me that has been invited. We'll have to think something up for you."

"Why didn't you just say that I was coming with you? What's the cloak-and-dagger business for? After all, I have a right to find out—"

"Yes, granted," she'd choked him off. "It's just not that simple to explain everything on the telephone. If he'd heard that you were coming, too, he might have canceled the visit from the very start. Max Marchais has only been back home for a few days, and I can assure you that he's not particularly keen on meeting you. At the time he said in so many words that he hoped he'd never have to meet 'that lunatic.'"

"I can imagine. If you told him the same sort of horror stories you told your boyfriend, I'm not at all surprised."

"Yes, yes, leave my boyfriend out of it," she replied somewhat sharply. "What I meant was: Just hold back a little, okay? The old man is not as easily impressed as my mother."

Before he could respond, she'd hung up. Robert grinned. Cathérine Laurent was indeed somewhat easier to impress than her rather standoffish daughter. The interest that the elegant Madame Laurent had shown in him had been almost inexhaustible, while Rosalie had pointedly played with her braid to show her boredom and failed to contribute anything to the conversation. Clearly the epitome of contrariness. It was astounding how different mother and daughter were—and not only in terms of their outward appearance. Rosalie, with her dark hair and her deep blue eyes, obviously took more after her father.

Even if Robert would have preferred to take that afternoon walk beside the Seine alone with the daughter, he had two things to thank Madame Laurent's sharp motherly eyes for: for her, there was no question about his taking his guest year in Paris as a "Shakespeare Professor," and—this pleased him even more— about his being the right man for her daughter, even if the daughter herself had not yet realized this, and had finally said something about René, with whom she had a date on Skype the next Friday.

"Don't give up, Monsieur Sherman," Cathérine had whispered furtively to Robert as they parted. "My daughter is sometimes a little difficult, but she has a heart of gold."

The woman with the heart of gold was visibly nervous when they parked that Saturday outside the white villa with the dark-green shutters at about four o'clock. And Robert himself felt a certain excitement. He was holding his big leather shoulder bag with the two manuscripts in his lap. What was awaiting him in this house? Was there something his mother had concealed from him?

Rosalie pulled a little too hard on the hand brake and took a deep breath. "So, this is where it gets exciting. *On y va!*" she said, nodding to him. "And, as I said, leave the talking to me."

"Okay, okay. You don't have to tell me every two minutes." They got out and walked through the front yard. The gravel crunched softly under their feet; the air was warm and smelled of grass. In the distance they could hear the hum of a lawn mower. A bird twittered. A perfectly normal Saturday afternoon in Le Vésinet on a warm, late-summer day in September. Outside the dark-green front door they looked at each other once more. Then Rosalie raised her hand and pressed the brass doorbell that was set into the wall on the right-hand side.

A bright *ding-dong* rang out from inside the house. Shortly afterward they heard light, shuffling steps and the clicking of walking sticks.

Max Marchais opened the door. His gray hair was combed back and his beard neatly trimmed. His face seemed to Robert to be a little more gaunt than in the author's photograph in the book. The eyes lay deeper in their sockets: the strain of the last weeks was clear to see.

"Rosalie—how nice of you to come." He stood in the doorway, resting on his crutches, and gave her a warm smile. Then his eyes looked toward Robert, questioning, but completely friendly.

"Oh, you've brought someone with you?" He took a step backward to allow them in.

"Yes. I'm sorry. I . . . I didn't know how to explain it to you on the telephone," said Rosalie. "This is Robert, a . . . a friend of mine . . . well, yes, he's become one, I mean . . . and we . . . we wanted . . . I should . . ."

She was floundering, and Robert saw a smile flash across the old man's face.

"Oh, please, my dear Rosalie, that's no problem at all. You don't have to explain anything. I have eyes in my head, even if my eyesight is beginning to go." He looked Robert up and down with obvious approval. "Your friend is naturally just as welcome here."

Robert saw that Rosalie was about to protest, but the old man had turned round and was walking gingerly on his crutches in front of them toward the library. The big glass sliding door of the living room was open, and on the terrace they could see a table set for coffee, shaded by a big white umbrella.

Marchais went out onto the terrace and waved them over.

"*Venez, venez,* there will be enough cake for everyone. Excuse me, but I must sit down. I'm still a bit shaky on my legs. I'm sure Rosalie has told you about my unlucky accident." With a sigh of relief, Marchais sat down in one of the wicker chairs, propping his crutches against the table.

Hesitantly, they followed him. Robert looked challengingly at Rosalie, but she just shrugged her shoulders and hissed something at him that was probably meant to be "soon!"

"So: you're Robert. Are you American?" asked Marchais guilelessly after he and Rosalie had also sat down. He looked toward Robert, who was sitting opposite him, and Robert had to admit that the tall bearded man—though at the moment looking a little helpless—had at first glance something about him that encouraged you to trust him.

Uncertain, he looked quickly over at Rosalie, who was sitting between him and Marchais and wasn't saying anything. It looked as if he was going to have to do the talking after all.

"Yes, that's right," he answered firmly. "I'm Robert. Robert Sherman." Good grief, he sounded like some kind of imitation James Bond. He watched Marchais attentively: his face showed no visible reaction. "I think Rosalie has already mentioned me to you." From the corner of his eye he saw Rosalie, who had just picked up the silver coffeepot to pour the coffee for them all, involuntarily freeze.

"Sherman?" The old man shook his head. He obviously didn't remember. He took his cup and raised it to his lips. And then he suddenly put it down, as if he'd choked. "Sherman—you are Sherman?" he repeated, and a deep furrow of anger appeared between his silver-gray eyebrows. "You are the impertinent American who accuses me of plagiarism and wants to sue me?" He sat up in his wicker chair and looked at Rosalie in annoyance. "I don't understand. . . . What does this mean, Rosalie? Why have you brought this madman to my house? Are you trying to insult me?"

"Hold on a moment! No one here is mad, Monsieur Marchais. I certainly am not," interrupted Robert. "We just have a couple of questions for you. And anyway, I have the original manus—ouch!" With a pained expression Robert reached for his left shin, which had just been given a violent kick under the table.

Marchais looked in confusion from one to the other as Robert rubbed his sore leg and Rosalie turned fiery red.

"I can explain everything," she said.

Marchais stared at her incredulously. "Are you going to tell me that you've taken up with this guy?" He shook his head in disbelief.

"No . . . yes." The color of Rosalie's face changed astonishingly quickly. "It's not what it looks like," she said cryptically.

"So what is it then?" asked Marchais.

As if to gather strength for the long explanation that was to follow, Rosalie hastily took a large gulp of her café crème. Then she put her pretty cup with its fine flowered pattern firmly down on her saucer.

"Monsieur Sherman's manner may occasionally be a bit presumptuous—but he is definitely not mad," she began. "He's simply looking for the truth, because the story of the blue tiger connects with him in a very . . . well . . . personal way." She cleared her throat. "And as far as this whole story is concerned, we have come across some . . . um . . . more than puzzling factors."

"We? Are you now in cahoots with this ignorant American to collect evidence against me?" Outraged, Max Marchais took a deep breath, looking contemptuously at Robert.

This guy Marchais can be really arrogant, thought Robert. *Typical Frenchman. They always think they're better than everyone else. God knows why.* He found it hard not to intervene, but Rosalie gave him a pleading look.

"So do you also now doubt that I wrote the story?" Marchais laughed in disappointment.

She shook her head. "Not at all. I am even absolutely certain that you wrote it." She nodded in the direction of the library. "On the old Remington that's there on the cabinet, wasn't it?"

Marchais narrowed his eyes and frowned. You could see the

whole business working on him. Finally he looked at Rosalie with a displeased expression.

"So that was you! You typed that text on my machine? I don't understand what this is all about. What sort of stupid game are you playing with me? I'd like an explanation. At once!" He slammed the table with the flat of his hand.

They'd thought of everything as they so hurriedly left Marchais's house, fleeing Madame Bonnier—but they'd forgotten that sheet of paper, thought Robert. Marchais must have been quite surprised to find it.

"I have to confess something to you, Max," said Rosalie. "That day when I brought you your things in hospital I came back here later, because I'd found something that I had to show to Robert. We were in your house, Max. We got in through the terrace door."

And then she told him—not in strictly chronological order—about the events of the past three weeks.

How Robert, after his first appearance in her store, had come back once again. How he had told her about his mother and the fact that she had told him the story of the blue tiger every night when he was a child. About the typewritten manuscript he had in his possession. About the box that had fallen off the wardrobe, and how she'd found the carbon copy. How she'd suddenly realized that the dedication could not have been for her, Rosalie (at this point Marchais blushed a little); how she'd called Robert and they had later compared the two manuscripts in the library. That they were completely identical, and that they'd then had the idea about the typewriter. "And that's how we established that the story had been written on the old Remington."

Rosalie nodded to Robert, and he took the two manuscripts out of his bag and put them beside each other on the table. Then they both looked at Marchais, who was sitting intently in his wicker chair and had grown ever more silent.

"Why didn't you say that this story had been written many years ago? Why did you let me believe that the dedication was for me, Max? It took a while, but when Robert finally told me his mother's name, I understood at last whom the story was actually meant for."

Marchais stared fixedly at the two manuscripts without answering. Then he turned to Robert.

"And what is your mother's name, may I ask?" His voice sounded fragile.

"Ruth," he replied. "My mother's name was Ruth. Ruth Sherman, née Trudeau. And I found the original manuscript among the papers she left me."

"Among the papers . . . she *left* you?" The old man was clearly taken aback. "Does that mean she's no longer alive?"

Robert nodded, once more feeling the tightness of the throat that still affected him when he talked about his mother's death. "She died earlier this year. At the beginning of May. A few days after my thirty-eighth birthday. She had cancer. It all happened so quickly." He gulped and smiled sadly. "As things do in life. She'd always wanted to come back to Paris with me. To the Eiffel Tower. I was there with her once, you know, as a little boy. And then all of a sudden it was too late."

Marchais turned pale. He was silent for a while and his gaze went blank. His eyes, which in the sunlight suddenly seemed almost glassy, were focused on a point that seemed to lie far off in the depths of the garden. Beyond the hydrangea bushes, beyond the old stone wall, beyond the little town of Le Vésinet, and perhaps even farther away. Infinitely far away.

"Ruth," he repeated then. "Ruth Trudeau."

He held his bent index finger to his lips and nodded several times.

Robert felt his heart beginning to beat faster.

"So you knew her?" Rosalie asked cautiously. "We've been wondering the whole time how it could be that Robert's mother never mentioned you, and yet the story of the blue tiger was so important to her. How did she come to have the story? What happened back then, Max?"

Marchais didn't answer.

For a few minutes they sat round the circular table without speaking—the golden-yellow tarte tatin remained untouched. It was as if time had stood still.

When Max Marchais cleared his throat, they looked up.

"They say," he began, "that every episode of our lives, no matter how small, contains everything—what we have left behind us and what lies before us. So if you ask me what happened back then, I can tell you: Everything. And . . . nothing."

He looked into Robert's eyes, which began to waver. "Yes, I knew your mother. Loved her, even. But it was only later that I realized how much." He reached for his coffee cup, his big liver-spotted hand shaking unmistakably. "I had a bad feeling straight away when I brought the blue tiger back to life. But please believe me when I say that the story means a great deal to me as well. It could be that it was a big mistake to let it out of its old box. But perhaps it was the best idea of my life. Because otherwise you two wouldn't be sitting here, would you?"

Marchais seemed to have regained control of himself. He looked warmly at Rosalie, and then fixed his gaze on Robert.

"Ruth's son," he said with a shake of the head. "I never thought I'd ever hear anything about Ruth Trudeau again. And now I'm meeting her son, who found *The Blue Tiger* in Paris purely by chance and is insisting on his rights to it." He smiled. "In one respect you are actually right, Robert: it is not in fact my story."

Robert and Rosalie looked at each other in astonishment.

"To be precise, I should never have published it. Back then in Paris, I gave it to a young woman as a gift—to your mother. That was a long time ago, and yet sometimes it seems to me as if it were only yesterday."

Twenty-seven

....

That afternoon Max Marchais took a trip through time. It led him back to Paris in the seventies. To a young man who hung around in the cafés, smoked too many cigarettes, and earned his living as a freelance editor for a daily paper. And to a young American woman with blond hair and sparkling green eyes who had been sent to Paris for the summer vacation by her parents and who had a hopeless sense of direction.

Max himself was surprised by the onslaught of images that flooded his retinas. He was so caught up in his own story that he hardly noticed the looks of the two young people, who were listening to him spellbound.

"I got to know Ruth because she'd gotten lost," he said. "I was sitting in a café not far from the rue Augereau, where I was living at the time in a two-room apartment on the fourth floor. It was really quite small compared with this splendid villa"—he raised his hand and indicated the house behind him with a smile—"but my goodness, what parties we had there. I often had friends there, and sometimes a girl, and when you woke up in the morning and looked out of the window, the first thing you saw was the Eiffel Tower looming in the sky a couple of streets away. That's something I never had later on—that magnificent view." He leaned back, lost in thought. "Sorry, I'm getting carried away—if you start to conjure up the past, all these memories flood back. . . ."

"You were just about to tell us how you met my mother, Monsieur Marchais," said Robert.

"That's right." Once more he could see Ruth as she walked along the street so charmingly in her red dress. "It was on a hot summer day that I first saw your mother. She was wearing a red dress with little white polka dots. She had a guidebook in her hand, stopped every few steps, turned the map in the book in every possible direction, and was looking out for street signs. When she passed the café for the third time, I got up and asked her if I could help in any way. She sighed with relief and looked at me with her green eyes, which were slightly aslant like those of a cat, and gave her delicate, heart-shaped face something really special. 'I think I'm totally lost,' she said and laughed. Her laugh was . . . wonderful. So optimistic and full of life that it conquered me immediately. 'I want to see the Eiffel Tower—it's somewhere in this direction, isn't it?'

"She looked at the guidebook once more, then pointed in completely the wrong direction. 'No, mademoiselle, you need to go the other way. It's really not far from here,' I replied. Then I clapped my book shut. 'Do you know what? I'll show you the way, otherwise you may never get there at all.'"

Max smiled. "That's how it all began. Over the next four weeks I accompanied Ruth on her walks through the streets of

Paris whenever I could. I showed her the city, and all the art museums." He shook his head with a smile. "*Mon Dieu,* I don't remember ever meeting anyone who was so obsessed with museums. By the end I'd seen museums that I didn't even know existed in my own city. Ruth loved pictures. Most of all she was taken by the Impressionists. Monet, Manet, Bonnard, Cézanne. We often went to the Jeu de Paume, where all those pictures were in those days. She could sit for hours in front of a painting, looking at it without saying a word. Then she'd turn her head and look at you with a smile. 'Absolutely beautiful, isn't it?' she would say. 'What a joy it must be to create something like that!' And I would nod, and think how happy it made me just to sit beside her, and occasionally stroke her arm or take her hand as if by accident, and breathe in the smell of her." He turned to Robert and Rosalie. "I don't know if it was a particular perfume, but she always smelled of mirabelles. Can you imagine it? Like mirabelle jelly. It was indescribable, kind of bewitching. After that I never met another girl who smelled of mirabelles." He sighed. "*Tempi passati.* So many things are irretrievable. That's why memories are so precious." He felt his throat becoming dry, and coughed. "It was a tender little romance that resulted in a couple of kisses, and yet it was all so much more intense than many things I experienced later. What great joy I felt as I looked into her lovely face or walked hand in hand with her on the weekend through the parc de Bagatelle, which she preferred to all the other parks in Paris."

Rosalie cast a meaningful glance at Robert, and the question of what the relationship was between these two young people passed fleetingly through his mind.

"You may find it difficult to believe nowadays, but it even made me happy to sit in a café just waiting for her." Then he suddenly noticed the untouched plates in front of them. "But please take a piece of the apple tart. I'm a very bad host."

Rosalie divided up the tarte tatin and served it on the plates. They tried the tart, with its slices of caramelized apple sitting smooth and gleaming on the puff pastry, while Max himself cut up his piece with a silver fork and then put it distractedly aside without eating any of it.

"Isn't it strange that you can sometimes experience such great happiness even when you know that the thing has no future?" he said thoughtfully. He looked over at Robert, who was excitedly shoving the last piece of his cake into his mouth. "Yes, no future. Because the love between your mother and me was an impossible love. It was limited to a few weeks, and we both knew it. From the very beginning. Even on that first day when I went to the Eiffel Tower with Ruth and afterward asked her if she'd drink a glass of wine with me, she told me that she had a fiancé waiting for her in America. Clearly a really nice man, likable, from a good family, a successful lawyer who would do anything for her. And that they were going to be married at the end of the summer. 'I'm afraid I'm already taken,' she said with a laugh. 'There's nothing to be done.' 'But now you're here in Paris,' I said, thrusting the thought of some fiancé on the other side of the Atlantic as far from my consciousness as possible. We knew that it would have to end sometime. And in spite of that I still held her hand, and still said, 'Give me a kiss,' as we took an evening trip in a *bateau mouche* along the Seine, with the Eiffel Tower outlined against the sky, so close you felt you could put your arms around it." He sighed happily. "And in spite of all that she did kiss me and we fell in love and enjoyed the moment as if it would never end."

"But then it did end," said Robert.

Max fell silent, remembering how Ruth had traveled to the airport by taxi in the pouring rain. She hadn't wanted him to go with her.

"I've always said that I have to come back," she had said on the morning she left, standing in front of him, her face pale.

"I know." His heart had clenched as if it had had icy water poured over it.

She chewed her lower lip, hardly able to bear his silence.

"We could write to each other now and again," she said, looking him beseechingly in the eye. *Don't make it so hard for us* was what her expression seemed to say.

"Yes, of course, okay," he'd answered, and they'd forced themselves to smile—though they both knew there would be no letters.

It was an infinitely sad moment. In the end she had stroked his cheek tenderly and looked at him for the last time. "I'll never forget you, *mon petit tigre*," she said. "I promise." And then she left, closing the door quietly after her.

Max smiled wistfully, and then noticed that Robert was looking at him because he still hadn't answered.

"Yes, the moment ended," he said simply. "Ruth vanished from my life just as she had entered it—with enchanting ease, and I was left with the two saddest words I've ever known: never again. I let her go, because I was not aware of the magnitude of what I was losing. Because I imagined that nothing could be changed. I was still young back then, I didn't know much.

I thought it was hopeless. Perhaps I should have fought for her. Of course I should. It's only when something is irretrievably lost that you come to realize what it meant to you."

Robert nodded and then said, "Then she married Paul, my father. And she never contacted you again?"

Max shook his head. "I never had any news of her again. Until today," he said. "But when I think back to that summer today, I know they were the best weeks of my life. It's impossible to describe how carefree those days were." He smiled. "They were the paint spots in my life. At least I did realize that even then."

A long silence followed. The sun balanced like a big red ball on the silhouette of the old stone wall at the bottom of the garden. Max felt his hip starting to hurt, but he ignored it. He kept looking at the young man who had silently joined his hands in front of his face and was staring out through the triangle formed by his fingers. You could see that Robert was trying to make some sense of what he had just heard.

"My mother never said anything to me," he said eventually. "I always had the impression that my parents were very happy together. They had a good marriage, never a cross word, and they laughed a lot."

Max nodded. "I'm sure they did. In life you can experience many different kinds of love, and I'm sure that your mother's heart was big enough to make several people happy. Your father was an enviable man, Robert."

"But what about the story then? When did you give her the story?" asked Rosalie.

"Oh yes, my little story—by the way, it was the first I ever wrote. I gave it to her on one of our last days when we'd gone to the parc de Bagatelle for a picnic. It was a glorious day, the air still smelled of rain, and we'd just gotten quite wet because there had been a short summer storm. But the sun quickly dried our clothes."

Max still clearly remembered how they'd lain on a plaid rug on the grass. Under an old tree on a little hill not far from the Grotto of the Four Winds. Ruth had found the spot and said that it was perfect for a picnic.

"Ruth had an instant camera—they were all the rage at the time—and I took a photo of her which she gave me afterwards. I think I still have it."

"Yes, you do. I think I saw it in the box," interjected Rosalie.

"That afternoon I gave her the story of the blue tiger," Max continued. "I'd had the original bound and kept a carbon copy for myself. The original title page had the words: 'For Ruth, whom I'll never forget.' But then I thought that that dedication was very revealing, and so I changed the title page and just wrote, 'For R.'" Max rubbed his beard in embarrassment as he looked over at Rosalie. "But that then led to a number of misunderstandings."

He saw that Rosalie was smiling and hoped that she had forgiven him for the little lie his vanity had made him tell. Of course he hadn't wanted to admit that he'd had to go back to an old story because he didn't have a new idea. And more than that, he had felt flattered because she was so delighted when she thought the dedication was meant for her.

"But if it had been a new story I would of course have been glad to dedicate it to you, my dear Rosalie. I also have something to confess to you."

"Yes?" she asked.

"The way you smile immediately reminded me of Ruth."

"Really?" She laughed.

Robert was squirming uncomfortably on his cushion and it wasn't hard to see that something was still bothering him.

"So the story that my mother used to tell me is really about you and her?"

Max nodded. "Of course only those who are in the know would recognize that. Ruth was Héloïse, the little girl with the golden hair who believes in her tiger—the cloud-tiger." He smiled. "And I was the tiger. She sometimes used to call me *mon petit tigre*; I really liked that."

"And the land that is so far away that you can't get there by airplane, but only by longing—," began Robert.

"—was our land." Max completed the sentence. "I hoped that this way Ruth would never forget me, and I see now that she never did." He nodded, and there was a strange gleam in his eye. What he did not say, however, was that the flight over Paris by night also had a deeper meaning.

One night they had flown. One magic, exhilarating, fairy-tale night that would have to be enough for a whole life, a night where they parted, intoxicated with love, in a dawn that already contained the bitter taste of separation.

She had kept her promise. A hesitant smile crossed his face. "I hope, Robert, you won't be angry with me if I'm glad that Ruth didn't forget me. Just as I am of course glad to meet her son. Your mother meant a great deal to me."

"Can I see the photo? The one of my mother, I mean."

"Of course. If Rosalie would be so kind as to get the box down from my wardrobe? I'm not really in a fit state for climbs like that."

While Rosalie got up and went upstairs to the bedroom, Max

gazed sympathetically at the young man who had intertwined his hands and kept stretching his fingers and pressing them against the backs of his hands. It was definitely not easy to have the past sprung on him like this. And more than that, a past on which he had had no influence at all.

"Why did she never tell me?" he said finally. "I wasn't a child anymore, and it was all so long ago. I would have understood."

"Don't brood too much, my boy. Your mother surely did the right thing, I just know that. She was a wonderful woman—even then—and she must have loved you very dearly. Otherwise you wouldn't be the person you are today."

Robert nodded gratefully. "Yes, perhaps you're right," he said, and his expression brightened.

A few moments later, Rosalie came back down.

"Is this it?" She put the faded color photograph of a young woman on the table, and both men leaned over it.

"Yes," said Max. "That's the photo from the parc de Bagatelle."

Robert pulled the photo nearer and nodded.

"Yes," he too then said. "That's Mom, no mistaking her." He looked at the young woman standing under a tree and laughing into the camera. "My goodness, that laugh," he said, wiping his eyes. "She never lost that laugh."

The sun was already going down when Max Marchais's guests departed. Robert had expressed a desire to see the place where the picture of his mother had been taken, and so they'd agreed that they'd all go to the bois de Boulogne together the next day.

"Finding the tree is not the problem," Max had explained. "I just hope I can get there with these stupid things." He pointed to his crutches.

"Oh go on, you can do it! If necessary we can push you there, I'm sure they rent out wheelchairs," Rosalie had said, and the laughter that followed was very liberating.

Then they had driven off in Rosalie's little car. Max had stood in the doorway a while longer, looking out after them. Life went on. It kept on going. A flame that was passed on by an endless team of runners until it reached its destination.

He hobbled back to the terrace and sat back down in his wicker chair. The cool of the evening descended on the garden. Deep in thought, Max looked at the faded photo that was still lying on the table.

He leaned back in his chair and shut his eyes for a moment. He saw two young people, full of the joys of summer, on a sunny day in the bois de Boulogne. They were stretched out under an old chestnut tree on a checkered woolen rug, joking with each other. The rug was scratchy, but only a little. Ruth was wearing her red dress with the white polka dots that he liked so much and her laughing mouth was almost as red as her dress. The light fell through the trees, casting tiny shimmering whirls on the rug and her bare legs. She had taken off her sandals. A bird chirped. The sky was bluer than blue. A white cloud drifted lazily by.

It had been a glorious summer day, and it was hard to imagine that it could ever end, it was so perfect. You could almost grasp the joie de vivre that filled the air with your hand. And suddenly Max felt his heart becoming light. So light that it could fly.

He opened his eyes and felt a long-forgotten love of life reviving in him. Yes, he loved this life, which was sometimes so much and sometimes less than nothing. But it was all there was.

He picked up the photo. Then he turned it over and looked at the note penciled on the back:

Bois de Boulogne, 22ⁿᵈ July, 1974

For a long time he just sat there, staring into the twilight. And a thought that had touched him that afternoon as gently as a young woman's hand suddenly became overpowering.

Twenty-eight

....

"Did you have to kick my shin like that?" asked Robert, as they drove along the narrow lane leading away from the old villa. "Is that the elegant touch you're always talking about?" He raised his pant leg to examine a bruise of considerable proportions.

"I thought an American feels no pain," replied Rosalie.

"An Indian, an Indian," corrected Robert. "I'm just another sniveling Yankee."

"Anyway, that was the only way to stop you. All I wanted to do was make sure you didn't beat each other's brains out." Rosalie smiled. She suddenly found the familiar *tu* tripping easily from her lips. While they were clearing the dishes together and carrying them into the kitchen, they had both moved to the familiar form without much ado. After that crucial afternoon, after everything they'd been through together, it would have been strange to continue using the formal *vous*.

Robert grinned. "Your Max Marchais isn't so bad after all. In fact he's actually quite nice. Though it's quite strange to suddenly come across an old man who . . . well . . . who was once in love with your own mother." He shrugged his shoulders helplessly.

"Even more when your own mother never said a word about it," added Rosalie. "On the other hand, she was already engaged to Paul of course; perhaps it was just a bit awkward for her. Or the whole thing just felt unreal when she was back in America in her familiar surroundings."

"So unreal that she later told me the story he'd written for her every evening?"

"Well, that's really kind of romantic. I mean, most people would ultimately like to look back at such an unusual story. And perhaps the special magic was due to the fact that their love was never fulfilled. And anyway *The Blue Tiger* is simply a very good story. At least, it moved me deeply when I first read it. Even if I didn't know the secret behind it. And even if the whole thing must have been very sad for Max back then—in a way he started writing because of your mother. Writing proper stories, I mean. You could say that Ruth was his muse." She glanced quickly at Robert. "Max has written a lot of other great books. You ought to read them. I used to devour them when I was a child."

"Hmm," said Robert. His eyes were half shut. Either he was too tired to answer, or he was lost in his own thoughts. At any rate he suddenly seemed to be far away, and Rosalie decided not to disturb him.

As she steered the car into the Nanterre tunnel, she could feel the last traces of tension vanishing.

She was glad, and relieved that the meeting between the two men had run so smoothly, which was by no means a foregone conclusion. Thank heaven the whole business had ended up being very friendly. After their first heated exchange, Max, who had been deeply moved by his memories and the sad fact that Ruth was already dead, had been genuinely glad to meet Ruth's son. As they left, he had hugged them both.

Rosalie had to admit that it would have made her sad, too, if Max and Robert could not stand each other. After all, she realized with surprise, they were both dear to her heart.

She signaled a turn, pulled out onto the expressway, and thought with horror of the hostile atmosphere that had prevailed at first. How the two of them had sat facing each other and accused each other—with anger in their faces and sparks in their eyes—of French arrogance and American ignorance! For a moment she'd actually thought that an outraged Max would throw them out before anything had been cleared up. But at the end of the day she had gained the impression that mutual concern and sympathetic candor was what had finally brought Max and Robert closer. Otherwise Robert surely would not have suggested that they meet the next day.

She was excited at the thought of their trip to the bois de Boulogne, where they would follow in the footsteps of Mrs. Sherman—or rather, of Miss Ruth Trudeau—who linked these two so very different men in a fateful way.

She looked over at Robert again as he sat silently beside her. These night drives with the "Shakespeare Professor" were gradually becoming a pleasant habit. But this time there was no uncomfortable silence separating them: this silence was companionable and a little exhausted.

All their misunderstandings and disputes, all the mysteries and speculations had led to that afternoon in the villa of an aging children's writer, who had told them his story. The story of a long-ago love that produced both joy and great sadness.

Rosalie leaned back on the headrest of the car and rolled her head back and forth. The car traveled through the darkness with a regular hum. As the cold lights of the tunnel flashed past her at regular intervals, blinding her for fractions of a second, she reviewed *The Blue Tiger* in her mind, trying to find further clues in the individual sentences. Although she had illustrated the book herself and knew it almost by heart, she would never have hit upon the idea that the heroes of the fairy-tale fable were in reality two lovers who should not have come together and who were left in the end with only longing—and memory.

She drove out of the tunnel and soon afterward reached the traffic circle that led onto the Champs-Élysées. She merged with the traffic and saw the black obelisk on the Place de la Concorde sticking up into the sky at the end of the broad avenue like a warning finger.

The search was at an end, the problem solved. But how would it continue? Would it continue at all? Rosalie caught herself wondering if the following day would also mean the end of their story.

At a red light she looked over at Robert, who had now opened his eyes again and was looking pensively out of the window, and studied his expression carefully. What could be going through his mind? The truth about his mother must have churned him up. Rosalie saw him frown and continuously tense his jaw. She would have liked to take him in her arms. She would have liked to say something that was appropriate to the situation, but unfortunately she couldn't think of anything.

"It's strange, the things that can happen in life, isn't it?" she finally said. "It must be funny for you." Without thinking, she took his hand and squeezed it.

"It's okay—it's not all that bad," he replied, holding her hand in his. It felt firm and warm. Like his kiss that time in the garden. "It's not bad at all, just . . . different," he continued. "It casts a new light on so many things." His fingers wrapped around hers as if their hands had discovered a language of their own. "Now it seems to me almost as if my mother wanted to give me a clue—with the story of the blue tiger and what she always said about Paris."

"And what did your mother say about Paris?"

"That it's a good idea?" He couldn't help grinning.

"You can leave out the question mark," replied Rosalie with a smile. "You know how it is: Paris is always a good idea." Regretfully, she took her hand away and changed down into second gear as she turned off the boulevard Saint-Germain onto a little side street, peering searchingly though the window. "That is, unless you need somewhere to park."

THIS TIME ROSALIE HAD not dropped him at the hotel. After she had succeeded, contrary to his prognosis, in squeezing the car into such a tiny space that there was not an inch of room left—naturally not without touching the cars in front and behind several times as she did so ("but why else do we have bumpers?" she had asked in astonishment)—they had gotten out of the car and he'd accompanied her to the rue du Dragon. Behind the door of the store they heard William Morris give a short bark and then whimper with delight.

"Would you like to come up for a glass of wine?" Rosalie asked as she unlocked the door. She tried to make it sound as casual as possible. "Or are you afraid of my little dog?"

Robert shook his head. "No, no. William Morris and I are the best of friends now." He twisted his mouth into a wry smile.

"And what about your personal bodyguard? I don't want him to challenge me to a fistfight again."

René! Rosalie felt herself going red and hoped that it couldn't be seen in the weak street lighting. In all the excitement she had forgotten to think about her boyfriend, though he—fortunately, as she immediately realized—was no longer her boyfriend.

She smiled like a sphinx. "My personal bodyguard has apparently found a long-distance runner in San Diego and prefers to guard her now," she replied curtly.

"Oh . . . what?!" Robert raised his eyebrows and smiled like the cat that's got the cream. "How did that happen?"

She left him without answering and he followed her up the spiral staircase to her little apartment. Upstairs he looked around curiously and stood for a moment by the big table to look at a couple of drawings that were lying there.

"Take a seat." She switched on the floor lamp and pointed to the armchair beside her bed. "I'll get us some wine from the kitchen." She took off her sandals, and he dropped his shoulder bag on the chair and wandered around the room, finally stopping in front of the framed photograph of her father that hung on the wall behind her desk.

"Your father?" he asked. She nodded.

"You can see that right away." He studied the photo. "The brown hair, the prominent eyebrows, the wide mouth. I like the look of him." Robert turned round toward her and ran his hand through his hair. "I take more after my mother."

"Of course." Rosalie smiled. "The *golden* hair!" The faded color photo of Ruth shot into her mind. Then she made an advance. "And who do you get those incredibly blue eyes from?"

"Oh, thanks a lot." He grinned and tried to conceal his embarrassment with a joke. "A historic moment!"

"In what way?"

"I think that's the first compliment I've ever received from a certain Rosalie Laurent."

"Could that be because a certain Robert Sherman hasn't so far given me much cause to compliment him?" she riposted. "But I bet you don't suffer from a shortage of compliments. I'm surely not the first woman to have noticed your blue eyes." She still remembered clearly how he'd stood at the store window and the color of his eyes had just knocked her out.

"Oh . . . well . . . I suppose . . ." He made a throwaway gesture and put on an expression of false modesty. "Not that many. About a hundred, maybe."

"Compliments—or women?"

He smiled in amusement. "Compliments, of course. I'm no Casanova, after all. But to answer your question—I don't have either my father or my mother to thank for my eyes. I get them from my maternal grandfather, whom I sadly never met. At any rate, our whole family was thrilled to bits with this"—he made quotations marks in the air with his fingers—"cute little Sherman with the blue eyes." He laughed, and Rosalie tried for a moment to imagine this big man in his blue-and-white-striped shirt as a little boy. "I think my aunt already had me set on a movie career—a kind of poor man's Robert Redford." He chuckled. "But I'm afraid I'm not that handsome."

"Oh, you know . . ." Rosalie tilted her head to one side. "Beauty isn't everything. I'd say there's enough for a professor of literature."

When she returned a few minutes later with two large,

brimming glasses of red wine, Robert was still standing in the middle of the room looking around.

She pressed a glass into his hand, and clinked hers against it.

"What are we drinking to?" he asked, the red wine swirling temptingly in his glass.

"How about: To the end of our search together?" she suggested.

"Yes, let's drink to the end of our search," he repeated, but in a way that suggested he meant something completely different. "And to the fact that after a rather unfortunate beginning we have still managed to become good friends," he added.

They both took a large sip. Rosalie felt the effect of the red wine straight away. No wonder: apart from a little piece of the tarte tatin she hadn't eaten anything since lunchtime. What had he meant by "good friends"?

"Is that what we are, then? 'Good friends'?" She quickly took another deep swallow and felt a relaxing warmth permeating her limbs.

Robert emptied his glass halfway and looked at her over the rim. "Perhaps," he said slowly, "we're more than that."

Rosalie smiled nervously, feeling slightly giddy. She watched Robert as he put his glass down on the little round table next to his chair.

"So this is where you disappear to when you're not down in the store," he said. "Very cozy." His gaze lingered involuntarily on the French bed with its blue-and-white Granfoulard bedspread and scatter cushions of all possible sizes and every shade of blue.

"Yes. My little refuge from the world." Rosalie threw open the window that led to the roof. "*Et voilà*—here is my second room." She put her wineglass down on the low bookshelf beside the window and looked out into the night. A cloud had passed in front of the sickle moon, and with a lot of imagination you might have seen a tiger in it. She remained by the window, took a deep breath of the cool air, and suddenly felt an overwhelming need to smoke a cigarette.

Robert had come up behind her, and she felt the nape of her neck begin to tingle. That morning she had fastened her hair at the back with a big tortoiseshell barrette.

"Really very, very pretty," he said softly, and Rosalie wasn't sure if he meant her little roof garden, where a wonderful tangle of flowering pot plants and bushes blocked the view of the surrounding houses. She felt his breath on her neck, and a pleasant little shudder ran down her back. "And it smells so good— like in an enchanted garden." He stroked a single wisp of hair from the nape of her neck, and his lips brushed her skin so imperceptibly that she almost believed she had imagined his touch.

"That . . . must be . . . the heliotrope . . . over there." With beating heart she pointed to a big bush with tiny dark-violet flowers whose delicate vanilla scent wafted over toward them.

"I don't think so," he said softly.

"What?" Hesitantly, she turned round. Robert was gazing at her tenderly.

"I smell wild strawberries," he murmured, burying his face in her hair. "Wild strawberries and fresh rain. I'd recognize that scent among a thousand others."

And then he gently took her face in both hands and kissed her.

That evening Rosalie didn't write anything in her little blue notebook.

She had better things to do.

Twenty-nine

Contrary to her usual custom, Rosalie woke up very early in the morning. It was Sunday, it was half past five, and her left arm had fallen asleep. The reason for that was an American literature professor who was sleeping blissfully with his whole weight on it and hadn't known what *Je te kiffe* means. His French was obviously a bit out of date. Rosalie smiled and tried to pull her arm out from under Robert without waking him. She stretched sleepily and sighed happily.

Her original plan to tempt Robert out onto the roof terrace to drink a glass of wine, smoke a cigarette, and look at the moon had sunk without a trace.

Someone else had taken over the reins and proved to her that life can sometimes—very seldom, but it did nevertheless happen—be far more romantic than anything you might possibly envisage.

Robert had kissed her, and after that they had never reached the roof.

After that kiss, which did not stop because neither Robert nor Rosalie would ever have had the absurd idea of wanting to stop something so wonderful, they had finally been compelled to tear themselves apart and breathe deeply to get some oxygen into their lungs.

The barrette had sprung open and fallen to the floor, along with many other unnecessary items they had dropped as they stumbled in an intoxicated embrace the few steps over to Rosalie's bed. Laughing and whispering, caressing each other with fingers and words, they sank into the blue cushions as if into a tumultuous sea of joy, where nothing more and nothing less could be heard but the beating of their hearts.

"Je te kiffe," she had said some time later, impulsively ruffling his hair. They were lying facing each other on the rumpled Granfoulard, as close as they had been almost three weeks earlier on the dusty floor under the bed in Le Vésinet.

"You've developed a lisp?" He'd looked at her in astonishment.

"Idiot," she had said. "That means that I like you."

"Oh, she *likes* me," he'd replied. And then he had pulled her to him with a swift movement and kissed her passionately. "You like me?" He lay on her and kissed her again. "And what else?"

She had laughed, then smiled and then simply looked at him. "I love you," she had said, and he had nodded with satisfaction and traced the line of her eyebrows, her nose and her mouth with his finger.

"That's good, that's very good," he had murmured. "Because this is how it is, *ma petite*: I just happen to love you, too."

He lay back and folded his arms behind his head. "My goodness," he said. "The day was exciting enough. But compared with the night . . ." He left the end of his sentence open and stared happily at the ceiling as she snuggled in the crook of his arm.

"Okay," she said happily. "We don't need a joint—but how about a cigarette?" She mentally apologized to René, but one cigarette wasn't going to finish her off.

"I'm just trying to give up," said Robert.

"Oh, that's good. Me, too," she said.

"In other words, a cigarette to break the habit."

"Exactly."

They'd exchanged meaningful looks, and then Rosalie had quickly gotten out of bed. "Before either of us changes our mind."

After she had lit his cigarette, and he was lying back on the cushions, smiling, with his right arm carelessly laid over his drawn-up knees, the cigarette between finger and thumb, she had started. It was like a moment of déjà vu.

"What is it?" he'd asked.

"Nothing. I think I knew you in another life." Rosalie had shaken her head and smiled in some confusion. She couldn't have said herself what had just moved her so strangely.

AS SHE NOW CAME barefoot out of the bathroom in her short nightdress and gazed lovingly at the sleeping man with his tousled hair, who was lying diagonally across the bed, tangled up in both the sheets and the Granfoulard with only his left leg sticking out, she suddenly knew what it was.

"I don't believe it!" she whispered, suddenly wide awake.

Wide-eyed, she bent over Robert's right foot which was lying on the covers with the left side upward. She frowned.

If you hadn't known better, you might have thought that the sleeper had banged his toe somewhere during a bout of passionate lovemaking. But if you looked closer, you could see that it wasn't a bruise or a cut.

On Robert Sherman's right little toe you could see a very noticeable big brown mark. Rosalie remembered seeing a similar one very recently on another man's foot.

She looked up and breathed deeply, and then a breathtaking cascade of images flooded over her: the light-blue eyes, the friendly catlike smile, the vertical anger line on the forehead, the powerful hands with their long fingers, the way he raised his eyebrows so arrogantly.

The truth had been there the whole time. Why hadn't she seen it before?

All of a sudden it was clear to Rosalie what had disturbed her in that old photo of Max. It wasn't the fact that Max was smoking, or that he didn't have a beard. It was the unmistakable resemblance to Robert, his son.

AFTER DISCOVERING THE TELLTALE birthmark in the early hours of the morning, Rosalie had first made herself a café crème. For over an hour she sat with her legs drawn up on the blue wooden chair in her kitchen and thought deeply. Would it be right to tell Robert the truth? For Rosalie there could be no doubt that Max Marchais was his father. But of course no one knew all the details. What had really happened back then? Max seemed not to know that he had a son, and Ruth, the only person Robert could have asked, was unfortunately dead.

But Paul Sherman, whom Robert regarded as his father, was also, like Ruth, dead. If Paul had still been alive it might perhaps have been better to leave things as they were, because in that case the truth might have been a destructive force, doing more harm than good. But as things were, a young man who no longer had any parents would find his father. And an old man who thought he had no children would find his son.

And so she had provided Robert with the truth—together with a small breakfast.

Robert was astounded. "What nonsense—there's no way that can be true. *Paul* is my father." He had shaken his head vehemently. But the more he listened to Rosalie the more thoughtful he became.

"There's no denying the resemblance between you," she ended. "If Max were younger and didn't have a beard, I would probably have noticed it earlier." That made her think of the way she'd met the two men, and she smiled. "I'd say you even have the same tendency to knock postcard stands over."

"But Max said nothing had happened," he protested helplessly.

Rosalie sat down on the bed beside him. "You didn't listen carefully enough, *mon amour.* He said that *everything* and nothing happened. Perhaps it was ultimately more than just a couple of kisses. Perhaps they did have a night together after all—a magical night where they flew over Paris together." She was thinking of the story.

"And then?"

Rosalie tugged at her lower lip, and considered the situation.

"Hmm. What happens then? Ruth travels to New York, where her fiancé Paul is waiting longingly for her, and they spend the night together. They get married. Ruth is pregnant and everyone is delighted, and perhaps in the beginning she herself thought it was Paul's child—but then she notices certain resemblances."

"Like the blue eyes, for example."

Rosalie nodded. "Absolutely right. Or the birthmark. Or a lot of other things. All the others see what they want to see. But it's too late. The child is already there and Paul is overjoyed to have a son. Ruth doesn't want to risk her marriage. She loves her new life. And it's a good life, a fulfilled life. And so she says nothing. Until the very end. She couldn't reckon on Marchais ever publishing the story, or that you would discover the connections."

Robert seemed uncertain. "So you think she knew the whole time?" he finally asked.

Rosalie nodded. "It was a secret she couldn't share with anyone. Not with Max. Not with you. Out of consideration for your father. For all of you."

Robert sat there for a while without saying anything, his head buried in his hands.

"I have to speak to Marchais," he said finally, looking at her earnestly. "I'm afraid your suspicions may be right."

She put her arm around him. "I think you should go to the bois de Boulogne alone this afternoon and talk things over with Max. I assume he knew as little about the truth as you did. But together you may be able to get a little closer to it."

Robert nodded. Then he seemed to think of something. He pressed his lips together before saying haltingly, "There's something else. Back then, it must have been about six months after my father died, we came to Paris together, Mom and I. I'd just turned twelve and I still clearly remember the way my mother suddenly seemed both happy and agitated. She was so excited. As if something really special might happen in this city. But nothing happened." He shook his head thoughtfully. "At least, nothing I knew about. And at the end of our trip she seemed so sad. That made me very anxious as a child at the time."

Robert shrugged his shoulders and stared out of the window without really looking at anything. "Why did she come to Paris with me after my father died? Did she want to return to the scene of her old love? Did she intend to get in touch with Max? Did things go wrong for some reason?" He sighed helplessly. "So many questions. Will I ever get an answer to any of them?"

"I'm sure you'll sort things out. Give Max my love," said Rosalie, as they stopped outside the famous Brasserie Lipp on the boulevard Saint-Germain early that afternoon. She had accompanied Robert, who was by now feeling a bit uneasy, the short stretch to the taxi stand. From there he'd have to make his own way alone. In the café with the white umbrellas not far from the high cast-iron gates that led into the parc de Bagatelle there would be a conversation between the two men that would be no business of hers.

She hoped that Robert wouldn't lose his nerve and that Max would be able to deal with the truth. And she was sure that the two men had a lot to say to each other.

There were a couple of taxis outside the Brasserie Lipp with its orange awning, and on the terrace all the tables were full. Hand in hand they walked to the taxi at the front of the line.

"When I came to Paris I thought my biggest problem would be deciding whether to take the job at the university," said Robert as he opened the taxi door. "And now all of a sudden my whole life is being rewritten."

"No, it's not like that at all, Robert." Rosalie took him in her arms once more and looked straight into his eyes. "The things that have already been will always be with you. It's just that something new is being added. Paul was a wonderful father to you, and you will always be his son. But to find your biological father now that both your parents are dead is a gift that life is handing you."

He frowned and looked at her with an expression of comic desperation. "You would have been enough of a gift for me."

She smiled. "That may be so. But I still believe that nothing happens without a reason. And Max Marchais isn't exactly someone you need to be ashamed of. He's a famous writer, he's pleasant, he has good taste, he loves literature—he really appreciates me. . . ."

She saw Robert curling his lip.

"He's French," he said, getting into the taxi.

"Hey! What's so wrong with being French?" she shouted after him as the car set off and Robert waved to her with a wry smile. She put her hands on her hips. "You're half French yourself, my dear, and don't you forget it!"

WHEN ROSALIE TOOK HER blue notebook out from under the bed that evening, she was very, very tired. She looked at the dog basket beside her bed where William Morris was sleeping. He had an enormous bandage around his middle. "My poor little doggie," she said softly, stroking his head. Before putting out the light, she wrote:

The worst moment of the day:

William Morris was run over by a car this afternoon. When I saw his little body lying twisted and bleeding in the road, I thought at first that he was dead. I took him straight to the veterinary hospital. Thank God it was only external damage. They gave him two injections and we have to go back again tomorrow for a checkup. It was such a fright.

The best moment of the day:

Father and son have found each other!

Robert has just called. He was still very emotional about their talk in the parc de Bagatelle. Max showed him the spot under the old tree near the Grotto of the Four Winds where he was with Ruth that day.

Apparently Max already knew when we left yesterday evening. A feeling of affinity. And then there was that date on the photo . . . My suspicion was also correct. Ruth spent the last night with him. And almost exactly nine months later, Robert was born. And yet for all those years Max had no idea that he had a son. He never saw Ruth again—not even at the time when Robert was in Paris with his mother.

By that time Max was already married to Marguerite. Did Ruth travel to Paris on that occasion to look for Max and then see him with his wife? Perhaps in a café? Perhaps she found out somehow that he was married? That would at least explain why she was so depressed when they left.

How could she ever have forgotten Max, since she had his son in front of her every day, a boy who was so wonderful that she showered him with love? Perhaps she guessed and hoped that he would combine the best qualities of Paul, Max, and herself.

Robert says they talked a lot, he and Max. About Ruth and everything else.

He's spending the night in Le Vésinet.

Thirty

....

Looking back with the nostalgia of a woman in love, Rosalie had thought that she would never experience such great happiness as she had that night when she first lay in the arms of the professor of literature from New York. She would never forget that night, not least because the lack of an entry in her little blue notebook would always remind her of it.

Robert had whispered the tenderest words in her ear, lover's oaths both invented and borrowed interwove magically in that very personal midsummer night's dream, and Rosalie was almost a little jealous of this precious, unique moment which she would be as little able to keep hold of and prolong as any other moment in her life. And as her feelings flew higher than they had ever done before, she allowed herself the bittersweet and somewhat sentimental thought that their feet would have to touch the ground again sometime—but only to tread a path into the future together.

But she was certainly not prepared for such a crash landing.

She'd thought of everything—except that her relationship with Robert would come to a swift and sudden end.

COMPLETELY UNSUSPECTING, SHE HAD been returning from the vet with William Morris that afternoon when she saw the red-haired woman in the slim, dark-green skirt and white blouse who was walking up and down outside her store in elegant leather pumps. From a distance she had thought it was the Italian woman—Gabriella Spinelli. But as she came closer she saw that it was a stranger. A strikingly beautiful woman.

She carefully put down the bag that contained the softly whimpering William Morris. "*Bonjour madame,* are you looking for me? I'm afraid the store is closed today." The slim woman with the red curls smiled.

"I've already noticed that," she said in rather clumsy French, which didn't quite fit in with her perfect appearance. "I don't want to buy anything, anyway. I just want to talk to the owner of this postcard store."

"Oh!" said Rosalie in some surprise. "Well then, you're in luck. That's me. Rosalie Laurent. What do you want to talk about?"

"I don't really want to discuss it on the street," said the stranger with a strange smile, her gaze resting on a passerby who was looking at her in fascination. "Can I come in for a moment?"

She had an unmistakably American accent, and Rosalie wondered if it was a matter of business. Was this woman with her chin-length curls perhaps a publisher looking for a new illustrator?

"Yes . . . of course . . . come in." In spite of the smile she looked kind of intimidating, thought Rosalie. More like you imagined a tax investigator to be. She unlocked the store and invited the American in.

"Please sit down." Rosalie opened the bag and put William Morris carefully into his basket. "What did you want to talk about?"

The American glanced at William Morris in some confusion, and looked briefly around the store before looking back at Rosalie. Was she just imagining it, or could she glimpse a trace of hostility in her green eyes?

"No thanks, I'd rather stand." She deliberately looked Rosalie over from head to toe. "It's about Robert Sherman," she said.

"About Robert?" repeated Rosalie, not understanding at all. "What about Robert?" A bad feeling took hold of her. "I spoke to him on the telephone yesterday. Has something happened?"

"Yeah, I'd like to know that, too," replied the redhead with a cold smile. "Because I spoke to Robert on the phone over the weekend—and I have to say it was a very strange call. Dear old Robert seemed to me to be quite confused."

"Dear old Robert"? Was this woman an acquaintance of Robert's? Rosalie looked at her in bewilderment. "Well, yes . . . ," she said. "A lot of things happened, you know—"

"I don't want to be impolite, but may I ask what your relationship to Robert is?" the woman interrupted sharply.

"Pardon?" Rosalie could feel herself getting hot. "What do you mean? Robert Sherman is my boyfriend. And who are you, please?"

"Listen, that's what I wanted to have a little chat with you about. Because there's a little problem here." She fixed her eyes on Rosalie. "Robert Sherman is *my* boyfriend—or rather my fiancé." She gave a thin-lipped smile. "I'm Rachel, by the way."

"Rachel?" The name meant nothing to her. Was this woman crazy? Or was there a conspiracy of red-haired women who were all after Robert Sherman? Rosalie shook her head energetically. "There must be some misunderstanding—Robert doesn't have a girlfriend called Rachel."

"Oh . . . doesn't he?" Rachel raised her eyebrows and her voice took on a very unpleasant tone. "I'm afraid the misunderstanding is all yours, mademoiselle."

"No . . ." Rosalie contradicted her, but then suddenly turned pale. She had of course heard the name Rachel once—when she'd been standing outside the terrace door at Max Marchais's villa and Robert's cell phone kept on ringing.

"Oh, that was just . . . Rachel. Someone I know." In her mind's eye she saw him again, sheepishly putting his cell phone back in his pocket.

"But . . . Robert said you were just an acquaintance . . . you sent him the manuscript . . . now I remember," she said in confusion.

"An acquaintance?!" Rachel laughed curtly. "Well, he certainly hasn't told you the whole truth." She held her right hand under Rosalie's nose. "Do you know what this is?" she asked triumphantly. A diamond was glittering on her finger. "Robert is my fiancé, we've been living together for three years in a little apartment in SoHo. But when we marry this fall and Robert takes over at Sherman and Sons, we'll probably look for something bigger."

She pulled her hand back and looked at her perfectly manicured fingernails. "Fortunately he's come back to his senses—a guest professorship at the Sorbonne, really! I told him straight away that it was a crazy idea, but after his mother's death he was understandably a bit out of it." She sighed.

"And then all the excitement about that manuscript." Rosalie felt as if the old stone floor was rocking beneath her feet. This woman knew too much to be just an acquaintance. Was it possible that Robert had lied to her so badly? She could see him again as he leaned back in bed after that unbelievable night, smiling at her as if she were the only woman in the world. "That can't be true," she said in a dull voice, leaning on the counter for support.

"And yet it is," replied Rachel cheerfully. "I've come to Paris to fetch Robert. Didn't he tell you that? On Thursday we're flying back to New York."

"He said he loved me." Rosalie felt as if the pain was tearing the floor out from beneath her feet.

Rachel looked at her pityingly. "I should really be mad at you, but I can see that you had no clue at all. Don't take it too much to heart, you're not to blame." She shook her head, and a keener observer than Rosalie, who was totally floored by this experience, might well have noticed how false her smile was as she now said, "It's always the same with Robert. He's like a little boy—he just can't resist a pretty face. That's why I'll be very glad when he gives up working at the university. All those young students." She clicked her tongue and looked with the utmost satisfaction at the young woman behind the counter, who was staring at the floor, blinded by tears.

"So, no hard feelings," she said, shaking her red curls and turning to go. "I think we understand one another. I'm sure I don't need to ask you to keep your hands off my future husband?"

Without waiting for an answer she turned and left the store.

Thirty-one

....

They had certainly been the three most exciting days of his life, thought Robert Sherman, as he walked on air through the Latin Quarter. An hour before he had been with Professeur Lepage to sign the contract for his guest professorship. The day before he had sat for hours with Max on a bench in the rosarium of the parc de Bagatelle and come to the astonished realization that it looked as if he now had a father again. And the day before—he shut his eyes for a moment and experienced once again that incredible sense of happiness that filled him whenever he thought of his night with Rosalie—the day before, he had found the woman of his dreams.

The ludicrous ultimatum that Rachel had presented to him in New York had almost run out. He remembered their edgy conversation when he called her back after the break-in and told her excitedly about the manuscript that Rosalie had found totally by chance in a box on top of Marchais's wardrobe. "Gosh, it sounds like a novel by Lucinda Riley," Rachel had said with a sigh, and then laughed—although the laugh had not sounded particularly friendly. "Perhaps you two should open a detective agency. Listening to you, I get the impression that you're hanging around with that postcard seller day and night."

"What nonsense. Rosalie's just helping me, that's all," he had said—and at that point in time it had still been the truth. "She's very nice. You'd like her."

"I'm not so sure about that." Rachel had ended the conversation rather snappily, but when she called him again on Friday evening she had been very friendly and understanding. She had kept on asking questions, and so he'd finally told her about his planned visit to Max Marchais and also briefly mentioned that he'd spoken to the dean at the university.

"And?" she had asked.

"We need to talk about that calmly when we have more time." He hadn't wanted to get into an argument with her, not at that moment, not before the other important matter was cleared up. So he'd given her evasive answers and ended the call by saying that he'd be in touch with her again on the weekend. "I'll call you when I get back from Le Vésinet," he had said, and only now did he remember that he still owed Rachel that call. Because it was precisely that weekend when all those events had coincided; his whole life felt like a whirlwind had hit it and he'd tumbled from one excitement to the next. But as he sat at breakfast with Max in the morning and gazed out over the garden he had suddenly become very calm. The decision was made: he would stay in Paris, perhaps forever.

He intended, as soon as he got back to the hotel, to call Rachel and get things straight. Nothing was going to hold him back on his new path through life.

"Oh, Mr. Sherman, you will see, you will like it 'ere with us," the dapper Professeur Lepage had said as he escorted him to the door and delightedly shook his hand. "You already look like an 'appy man."

With a smile, Robert speeded up as he turned from the boulevard Saint-Germain onto the rue du Dragon.

He was a happy man.

He was burning to tell Rosalie everything and could hardly wait to take her in his arms.

Strangely, nobody came to the door. The store was shut as it was every Monday. Robert peered through the store window in the hope of seeing Rosalie inside, but she wasn't there. He rang the doorbell of the apartment several times, also in vain. He looked at his watch. It was six thirty and he'd called her that morning to say that he would drop in on her in the early evening.

Was she still in the veterinary clinic? Had her little dog's condition perhaps worsened?

Robert stood indecisively for a while looking at the pattern on the turquoise gift wrap that was hanging in the window like a cloud in the sky. Then he called Rosalie on her cell phone. But no one answered that either. He left a short message to say that he was now going back to the hotel and then directed his steps toward the rue Jacob.

The receptionist in the Hôtel des Marronniers gave him an amused smile. "You have a visitor, Monsieur Sherman. Your friend said she'd like to wait for you in your room. I hope it was all right for me to allow her to go up." She smiled conspiratorially as she handed him the second key over the dark wooden counter.

Robert nodded, a bit surprised, but then his heart began to beat a little faster in joyful anticipation. Rosalie had obviously already picked up his message and rushed to the hotel. Impatiently, he pressed the button in the elevator which, after a short, worrying buzzing noise, clattered into motion.

That's all I need—to get stuck in here now, thought Robert cheerfully. But the elevator got to the fourth floor without any incident.

He ran his fingers quickly through his hair and tugged open the door in happy anticipation. He saw the silhouette of a woman standing in the sunlight beside the window.

"You're here already!" he said tenderly. "My God, how I've missed you!"

"Hello, Robert!"

The woman at the window turned slowly round, and Robert felt his train jumping the track. An apparition! It had to be an apparition!

"You've missed me? I'm glad about that: when we last talked on the phone I didn't get the impression that my absence meant so much to you." Her green eyes glittered as she took a step toward him to embrace him.

"Rachel!" he blurted. "What are you doing here? This is . . . well, this is a surprise."

Thoughts rushed zigzag through his head like hares fleeing a hunter.

She gave him a kiss—in his thunderstruck state he just let it happen—and he thought he saw a malicious smile pass fleetingly across her face. "So, I hope it's a pleasant surprise, Robert," she purred, stroking his hair. "You really need a haircut, my dear."

"Yes . . . no . . . I mean . . . ," he stuttered. "I thought we were going to talk on the phone, to discuss . . . everything."

"Exactly," she said. "But then you didn't call and so I thought it would make more sense for me to come over to . . . talk." Her smile was now unmistakably ironic. "Although this room is really frightfully small—how did you manage to put up with it the whole time?"

"Oh, you know . . . time has just flown," he stammered. "Sure, the room isn't particularly big, but the courtyard is pretty. And anyway, I haven't spent a lot of time in the room."

"Really?" She raised her eyebrows. "Oh, yes, of course"—she smacked her forehead with the palm of her hand—"you were *so dreadfully busy*." She glided over to the bed, leaned against the headboard, and crossed her long legs seductively.

The telephone beside the bed began to ring, but Robert didn't move from the spot.

"Well, darling, aren't you going to answer it? Don't let me disturb you. Just act as if I wasn't here." She smiled at him like a snake with a rabbit.

He stared at her as if spellbound. Rachel had gotten on a plane and just flown over. That was quite something! A sunbeam fell into the room and her red curls glowed like fire. She smiled at him without saying anything, and Robert had the definite feeling that her intentions were far from positive. He wondered what she'd slipped to the receptionist to persuade her to allow her to come up to his room. The ringing stopped.

"Rachel, what is this? What are you doing here?" he asked.

"I've come to take my somewhat confused professor of literature home," she said with an indulgent smile. "It seems to me, Robert, that you are a bit muddled."

"What?" Robert was speechless. "Take me home?"

"Well, your four weeks are up on Thursday, my love, and I thought we could spend a few days together in Paris before flying home. You could show me around a bit, and I really want to go shopping in the rue de Rivoli. They say they have really great purses there."

Robert shook his head hesitantly. He might as well tell her here and now. "I'm afraid that's not going to happen, Rachel."

"What's not going to happen?" she replied like a pistol shot.

"Anything, Rachel. I'm going to stay in Paris. I was going to call you today. We need to talk."

"About the guest professorship?" She looked at him slyly.

"Rachel, it's not just the job. Since yesterday I've known that I have a father who lives in Paris."

"Aaaah!" she exclaimed. "Now there's a father in Paris as well. How extremely practical!"

"There's no need to be sarcastic, Rachel. I've only known since yesterday myself." He took a deep breath. "And since yesterday I've known that I've met the only woman for me here in Paris."

"Really?! That was quick!" Strangely enough, she didn't seem at all surprised.

"If it's the right woman, it's always quick," he said slowly. "I'm sorry, Rachel."

Rachel sat up and stared at him with unconcealed rage. "If you mean the girl from the postcard store, you can just forget it." She laughed scornfully. "Because you're definitely on her shit list." She said it with indescribable elegance.

"What do you mean, Rachel?" Robert felt his heart sinking.

"Exactly what I say." Her voice rose in a shrill crescendo. "What do you think, Robert? Did you really believe I'd allow my future to be screwed up by a little postcard seller? What do you think you're doing with that child? She doesn't even have a proper hairdo with that stupid braid of hers. Please, Robert, you cannot be serious. Did you drink too much red wine?"

Robert turned white with rage. "What have you done, Rachel? You didn't . . . oh, God, you did. . . ." He took a threatening step toward her, ending up directly beside the French bed.

"Of course I went to see her." Rachel fell back calmly and laughed softly. "Well, what can I say—the girl wasn't exactly pleased to discover you'd lied to her. Then I explained to her that we're not just *acquaintances*. . . ."

"You know exactly the terms I came to Paris under, Rachel! It was you who gave me the damn ultimatum. It was *you* who was going to leave me."

Rachel waved dismissively. "All water under the bridge. I was very worked up at the time. Sometimes you change your mind. Anyway," she continued unimpressed, "I told her what was what and then waved my engagement ring under her nose. The mademoiselle with the braid turned rather pale—I almost felt a little sorry for her . . ."

"You bitch!" He would have liked to wring her neck. "You know very well that that's not an engagement ring." Robert still clearly remembered the visit to Tiffany's when Rachel absolutely insisted on the white-gold ring with the little diamond for her birthday.

"Whatever." Rachel looked at the ring on her finger with some satisfaction. "She was quite impressed, I have to say. Especially when I said we're getting married in the fall."

"You said what?"

Thirty-two

....

Half an hour later Robert was back outside the little store in the rue du Dragon ringing up a storm on the doorbell. He drummed on the door in desperation. He could see that there was a light on in the first floor, but Rosalie wouldn't come to the door. She had shut herself up in her oyster shell, and he couldn't even blame her for it after Lady Macbeth had so successfully spread her poison. He'd ushered a stunned Rachel almost physically out of his room.

"You'll regret this, you moron," she hissed. "That girl will bore you more quickly than you can recite Hamlet's monologue and then you'll come crawling back."

"You'll wait a long time for that," he said between clenched teeth. "Not to say forever and a day. And now beat it!"

She leaned on the door frame of his room. "And where do you imagine I'm going to sleep tonight?"

"As far as I'm concerned, you can sleep under the bridges. But don't scare the *clochards* too much!"

Then he'd pulled the door shut tight and run to the rue du Dragon.

"Rosalie! Rosalie! I know you're up there. Open up Rosalie," he shouted many times.

Eventually the main door of the building opened and an elderly little man with crafty eyes had come out on the street. "What do you think you're doing, monsieur? This is not a fairground. If you don't stop this hullaballoo, I'll call the police." He looked at Robert, who was staggering about. "What's wrong with you, are you drunk?"

"I've got to see Rosalie Laurent!" was all he could say.

"Are you an American?" The old man stared at him suspiciously.

"Please!" begged Robert. "Can you let me in? I know she's in her apartment."

"But, monsieur!" He shrugged his shoulders. "Calm down! Mademoiselle Laurent is not at home, otherwise she'd come to the door."

The old man was hopelessly dull-witted.

"But she's there—just look! The light!" He pointed upward excitedly.

"Really? What makes you think that? I can't see anything." Robert looked up at the first floor. Behind the window above Luna Luna it was dark.

AFTER HE REALIZED THAT he wasn't going to get anywhere that night he'd returned to his hotel. After all, Rosalie would have to open the store the next day.

But when he arrived outside the store again punctually at

eleven o'clock on Tuesday morning, the CLOSED sign was still on the door. He'd tried to leave her a message, but her phone wasn't even switched on. He tore a page out of his notebook, wrote a desperate little message, and shoved the paper between the bars of the shutters.

From then on he patrolled past Luna Luna every hour and finally—it was two o'clock—he got lucky.

The shutters were up, the store was open, but as he pressed down the latch, ready to fall down on his knees and beg Rosalie's forgiveness for his—really tiny little—lie, and then explain everything to her, he found, instead of his beautiful quarreler, a totally unfamiliar woman who looked at him with unconcerned friendliness.

"Isn't Mademoiselle Laurent here?" he asked breathlessly. The woman shook her head, and he remembered that she was Rosalie's assistant, whom he'd already briefly seen. Unfortunately he couldn't remember her name.

"When will Mademoiselle Laurent be back?" he probed.

"No idea," she replied indifferently. "She probably won't be back at all today."

"Do you know if she got my message?" He pointed to the door.

"What message?" She looked at him blankly with her good-natured round eyes.

It was enough to drive you to despair. Robert spun round with a groan, and then thrust his telephone number at the sales assistant.

"Listen, it's *important*," he implored. "I *have* to talk to Mademoiselle Laurent, you understand? Call me immediately if she comes back to the store again. And I mean *immediately*!"

She nodded and casually wished him a good day.

Two and a half hours and four *petits noirs* later he was still sitting in the little café in the rue du Dragon watching the entrance to Luna Luna a couple of yards away on the opposite side of the street. By now it was half past four. The waiter came out and asked him if he wanted anything else.

He certainly did, but the way things looked he was unlikely to get it. He decided to move immediately from one drug to the next and ordered a glass of red wine. And then another. And then he had the idea of calling Max Marchais. Happily, the telephone was picked up immediately, and Robert almost laughed with relief.

"It's me, Robert. Do you have any idea where Rosalie could be? I need to speak to her urgently." He took a deep breath. "There's been a dreadful misunderstanding, an intrigue of truly Shakespearean proportions, and now Rosalie seems to have vanished from the face of the earth."

Max said nothing for a moment, and Robert could sense his hesitancy.

"Is she in Le Vésinet by any chance?" he asked importunately. "Is she at your place?" It was quite possible that in her grief or her anger—by now he was betting on the latter—Rosalie had fled to her old friend the writer.

He heard Max sigh. "My boy, what sort of escapades have you been up to?" his father then said cautiously. "Rosalie isn't here, but she called me yesterday. She was really beside herself. You should really have told her about your fiancée."

"But she is not my fiancée!" Robert yelled down the phone in desperation, knocking his glass over with a wild gesture as he did so. His light-colored pants gratefully sucked in the red liquid. "Shit! Dammit!" he cursed. "Rachel wasn't even my real girlfriend when I came to Paris." He rubbed his pants with his napkin.

"What is she then?"

"A witch, dammit! I was intending to call her and tell her everything and then she was suddenly there in my room smiling at me like Kaa the python."

He tried to paint Max the picture in as few words as possible.

"Of course it was wrong to say she was just someone I knew," he ended. "I admit that now. But at the time I didn't know . . . I mean . . . it all went so fast . . . I just never caught up with things . . ."

"Merde," said Max. "That really was a stupid train of events."

Robert nodded. "But where can she be?" he wondered nervously. "I hope she won't do anything silly."

Max laughed softly. "I can put your fears to rest there, my boy. Rosalie is up in her apartment. She has just called me to say that that deceitful asshole had just been downstairs in the store again."

"She's at home?!" That cow-eyed assistant had cold-bloodedly pulled the wool over his eyes with her innocent smile. He would have liked to storm back into the store, but he forced himself to remain calm.

"Good. What did she say?" he wanted to know.

"Calm down, Robert. All is not yet lost. She said she hates you."

"She hates me? Oh, my God!" He rubbed at the stain on his pants like a madman. "But she can't hate me. I mean, I haven't done anything!" It was worse than he thought. Of course he knew how sensitive she was. How unforgiving. That she weighed every word with the accuracy of an assayer.

"Believe me, my boy, it's a good sign." He heard Max laughing softly. "She hates you because she loves you."

"Aha. An interesting theory. Let's hope it's correct. But I love Rosalie because I love her." He sighed in comic despair. "And what should I do now, Max? What can I do so that she loves me again without hating me?"

"Don't worry, we'll think of something," responded Max. "In fact, I already have an idea. . . ."

Thirty-three

Rosalie was lying in bed railing at the world. After that unpleasant, intimidating red-haired woman had left the store she had
slid stunned to the stone floor and sat there for a while as if she'd
been knocked out. Then she had stood up, locked the door,
and closed the store. She'd tumbled upstairs and thrown herself
sobbing on the bed in her blue silk dress. The fall had been too
great, the pain was boring into her innards. "Keep your hands off
my future husband!" The humiliation had struck home like a
well-aimed dagger thrust.

She remembered Rachel's triumphant smile and thumped her
pillow with a scream. Robert Sherman would soon be flying
back to New York with his lovely bride-to-be. And the damned
swine had not said a single word.

He would presumably have turned up on the last day with
some kind of threadbare excuse, and then she would never have
heard from him again. He'd lied to her, lied about everything,
and she was outraged at how well he'd playacted. But of course,

she thought bitterly, playacting was second nature to him. Rachel had clearly hinted that the oh-so-well-read literature professor was always game for a little adventure. Shakespeare, pah! More like *Shakespeare in Love,* she thought angrily. That's probably why all his lies tripped so easily past his lips.

She thought back to the sweet words that Robert had whispered to her that Saturday night, and held her hands to her ears sobbing loudly. "Oh, hold your tongue, Robert Sherman. Get out of my head! I never want to see you again!" she screamed. Then she stumbled over to her desk and, in a despairing flood of emotion, knocked over all the jars that held the paintbrushes. She felt a little better after that.

She drank three glasses of red wine, smoked eight cigarettes, found she couldn't help thinking about Robert, cried again, hurled out abuse that would have made her mother blanch, and finally got William Morris from his basket.

She carefully laid him beside her on the bedspread. He lifted his head with a faint whimper and looked at her with his brown eyes, showing that steadfast loyalty of which probably only a dog is capable. "Oh, William Morris!" she had said before she finally fell asleep. "It looks like you're the only man in my life who will never leave me."

When Robert Sherman came to the store for the second time the next day, Rosalie was still in bed.

She heard raised voices in the store and crept barefoot to the door. She quietly put one foot on the spiral staircase and leaned forward to risk a careful look.

Robert was standing in the middle of the store with an angry face and was involved in a heated battle of words with Madame Morel, who was blocking his way with folded arms.

"*Non,* monsieur, she's gone away," she was saying. Rosalie cowered on the top step, nodded appreciatively, and bent her head a little farther forward so as not to miss anything.

"What do you mean, she's gone away? What bullshit!" she heard Robert saying loudly. "I know she's there. So stop playing around with me and let me past."

Madame Morel remained standing in front of Robert like a fortress and shook her head regretfully. She was really good at this.

"I'm extremely sorry, Monsieur Sherman, but Mademoiselle Laurent is really not at home. . . ."

Robert looked angrily at the spiral staircase, and Rosalie flinched back.

"There!" he shouted. "I've just seen a foot!"

He pushed Madame Morel aside and stormed up the spiral staircase.

In two bounds Rosalie was back in bed. She had just enough time to pull up the covers and smooth her hopelessly disheveled hair a little before he entered the room. With a certain degree of satisfaction she noticed that he didn't actually look in peak condition either, with his unshaven face and the massive dark stain on his pants. It looked as if his domineering Rachel had given him the tongue-lashing he deserved.

"What do you think you're doing?" she shouted angrily. "Get out!"

She reached for a cushion and hurled it at his head.

"Rosalie!" he cried as he ducked out of the way. "Please! Hear me out!"

She shook her head. "No way!" Then she narrowed her eyes and stared at him crossly. "Well? Haven't you boarded the plane with your fiancée yet?"

"The flight isn't until tomorrow," he replied. "And then there will only be my fiancée on it . . . I mean . . ." He spread his hands in a gesture of innocence. "Rachel is not my fiancée at all." He risked a smile. "Not my fiancée . . . not my girlfriend—"

"But just 'someone you know,'" Rosalie interrupted his stammering words.

He held his head in his hands and groaned. "Okay, okay! I know I shouldn't have said that. I know that everything speaks against me, but believe me, it's all a *misunderstanding*."

She burst out laughing. "I don't believe it! You didn't seriously come out with that bullshit, did you?" She sat up and pointed a finger at him. "Your it-was-all-a-misunderstanding was in my store yesterday and told me all about the way you know each other. Did she show me a ring?" She clasped her forehead in mock confusion. "Yes, she did. Did she say I should keep my hands off her future husband? Yes, she did that, too. Was your it-was-all-a-misunderstanding with you in the hotel yesterday evening?" She thought for a moment, then nodded. "So she was!"

"You came to the Hôtel des Marronniers?"

She shook her head. "No, but I telephoned you there. Gosh, how dumb can you be? Just by chance Carole Dubois, a good friend of mine, was at reception and when I asked for Monsieur Sherman and she tried to put me through and no one answered, she explained to me with a giggle that you were probably very *busy* because your fiancée from America was in your room."

She saw Robert turn pale and nodded knowingly. "So, what do you have to say now, you liar?"

Robert put his hands over his mouth and nose in a gesture of despair and closed his eyes for a moment.

"Rosalie," he said insistently. "Rachel is beautiful and clever and she knows how to create confusion. When I came to Paris, our relationship was already in the balance—because of . . . various things. Then she suddenly popped up here and lay in wait for me at the hotel—"

"And spent the night with you?"

"No she did not! I threw her out. You're welcome to ask your friend Carole about that." He looked at her pleadingly. "I love you."

Rosalie picked hesitantly at the bedcovers.

"Ha! Fine words," she said eventually. "How can I be sure that you really mean it?"

He smiled. "Come on," he said, reaching out his hand. "I'd like to show you something."

ROBERT HAD INSISTED THAT they set out at once. She'd smoothed her crumpled blue silk dress as best she could and had slipped on her ballet slippers. Then they'd walked out of Luna Luna past an astounded Madame Morel.

"Where are we going?" Rosalie asked curiously.

"Wait and see," he said, holding her hand firmly in his as he strode boldly across the boulevard Saint-Germain and hurried down the quiet rue Pré-aux-Clercs, pulling Rosalie after him through the rue de l'Université, the rue Jacob, and the rue de Seine.

"Robert, what is this all about?" Rosalie laughed in bewilderment, wondering where this silent walk was going to end up.

A moment later they had reached the Pont des Arts. They walked out on the wooden planks of the old bridge with its black iron railings. When they'd reached a point about halfway across, Robert came to a sudden halt.

"Which side?" he asked, rummaging in his shoulder bag.

"Which . . . side?" She had no idea what he was talking about.

"Well, would you prefer the side with the view of the Eiffel Tower, or the one with Notre-Dame?" he said impatiently.

Rosalie shrugged her shoulders. "Well . . . hmm . . . the Eiffel Tower?" she asked, wide-eyed.

He nodded curtly and they walked over to the railing together.

"Here," he said, pulling a small package out of his bag. "This is for you." He smiled. "Or rather—for us."

In some confusion she took his gift, which was unskillfully wrapped in some tissue paper and a couple of bits of Scotch tape.

She opened it, and a mixture of joy and expectation caught her throat.

In her hand lay a little golden padlock on which someone had written in thick black felt pen:

Rosalie & Robert. Pour toujours.

"Forever?" She looked at him, her heart missing a beat. "Do you believe in forever?"

Robert nodded. "That's all I believe in." He tenderly stroked a strand of hair from her face. "What a desolate place this world would be if not even a man who's in love believed in it? Doesn't even the greatest realist in his heart of hearts wish for a miracle?"

"Oh yes," whispered Rosalie, the mistress of wishes. She looked over at the Eiffel Tower looming erect and reliable against the evening sky, and smiled, both happy and bemused.

"But how did you know? I mean . . ."

Robert raised his eyebrows. "Soul mates?" he replied.

Rosalie was deeply impressed. Fortunately she would never find out that her American literature professor, who was still carrying an edition of Shakespeare's *Taming of the Shrew* around with him, was not telling the whole truth at that moment. He was lying, but only a teeny-weeny bit. And for love.

After the golden lock had taken its place among the others, Rosalie took a big swing and threw the little key out over the glittering water.

Forever, she thought, and before the key had sunk to the bottom of the Seine where it would lie for all eternity with all the other lovers' vows, Robert had already taken her in his arms.

Rosalie shut her eyes blissfully and the last thing she saw was the incredible sky over Paris, which, with its patches of pink, white, and lavender, assumed the color of a kiss.